When I Get Home

Stephen —
Thank you so much for being a great friend & sounding board — Hope to count on you with both #2!
Always
[signature]

When I Get Home

P J Ranes

Copyright © 2015 P J Ranes
All rights reserved.

ISBN: 150865087X
ISBN 13: 9781508650874
Library of Congress Control Number: 2015918368
CreateSpace Independent Publishing Platform
North Charleston, South Carolina

Dedication

In loving memory of my father Robert Ranes, to my mother Betty with immeasurable love and endless gratitude, to my amazing children and grandchildren who bring me so much joy, and to all of my precious "heirlooms" who make this life worth living.

Preface

I HAVE ALWAYS known I was supposed to write a book. From the time I was a little girl writing stories and poems in crayon, I knew that someday I would write a *real* book.

Being a spiritual person, I had many conversations with God through the years thanking Him for giving me this talent, this ability to string words together. I also shared with Him on a fairly regular basis how frustrated I was that the right story just hadn't come to me yet and asked for His assistance in the inspiration department.

I started writing multiple times only to lose interest when the story didn't flow onto the pages like I knew it should. There were times I sat in front of the computer staring at a blank screen, not knowing how to begin, what story to tell.

That is, until one day in late 2014. It was around the holidays and I was watching something on television. I seem to recall it was a rather innocuous talk show I had on more for background noise than actual viewing pleasure. I wasn't really paying much attention until the guest mentioned how much they would like to go back in time to when they were young, but with the wisdom of their more advanced years. They also talked about their desire to have a conversation with someone they had loved and lost, to heal old wounds, to say goodbye.

In an instant – and I mean immediately – upon hearing them describe that dream the story was in my head. Start to finish. I knew how and where it would begin and how and where it would end. It was the amazing gift I had been waiting for all these years.

I honestly had so much fun writing this story. I love everything about it, and lived it in my head as words spilled onto the page. I laughed on occasion and I cried through many parts as the raw emotions became real through the words. Every time I paused to think of just the right thing to say, just the right nuance, it seemed to pop into my head without hesitation. It truly was a surreal experience at times. And each time it happened, each time the words came into my head effortlessly, I stopped to say… thank you, God.

As with most authors, I have drawn from my experience of certain real and composite characters, places and memories that definitely helped bring this story to life. I hope as you read it you love the gift as much as I enjoyed the experience of writing it.

PART ONE
The Windy City

"Winter came down to our home one night quietly pirouetting in on silvery-toed slippers of snow, and we, we were children once again…."

-Bill Morgan, Jr.

December 23rd was particularly frigid this year. Not that every December in Chicago isn't chilly as blasts of arctic air sweep south for the winter. The icy wind gusts across Lake Michigan, nipping at the wings of migrating geese while beneath them the last stubbornly clinging leaves of autumn spin to the ground.

A certain kind of resignation settles in when heavy gray clouds begin to drape over the city like a widow's shroud as November fades to December, and the bustle of the holiday season begins. Old Man Winter was knocking at the door and would not be denied entry for long.

Penny Raney Tomlin could sense it as she scraped the four inches of fluffy white residue off of her car windows that morning before driving to her job as Chief Editor at the *Chicago City News*. The season of blizzards and snow tires, of closed highways and flight delays was here. "Ugh," she muttered under her breath as she turned on the defroster full blast and pulled away from the curb. "I am just not ready for this."

Her old gray BMW sedan with the faded Bush/Cheney sticker still clinging crookedly to the bumper sputtered and slid down the street as she made her way the few miles to the office. "I need new tires," she murmured, words escaping in a frosty puff of smoke as her breath instantly froze in the air.

While sitting at a stoplight patiently waiting for a green turn arrow, she switched on the radio. Penny loved the old holiday standards and soon was humming along as Perry Como's warm voice filled the air with "It's Beginning to Look a Lot Like Christmas". No argument there, she thought to herself as the wipers battled valiantly to keep the windshield clear of ice.

The light turned green and Penny inched down the street noticing the snow had begun to fall more urgently than when she had left home. "I wonder if Mom will have any trouble picking me up at the airport tonight," she thought to herself. North Dakota usually has every bit as much snow as Chicago by Christmas. Penny made a mental note to call her mother once she got to the office to see if it looked clear at Hector International Airport in Fargo.

For now, she concentrated on following in the exact tire tracks of the car in front of her, assuring she had enough distance to make a quick stop if she needed to. She could tell it was glare ice under the top layer of snow, and tapped the accelerator with extreme caution. One unexpected move by anyone in the line of traffic could cause a chain-reaction accident that certainly would impact her ability to get out of town on time. Penny wasn't taking any chances. Come hell or high water, this year she was going to be home with family for Christmas!

Driving along Michigan Avenue she couldn't help but smile at the animated displays in some of the store windows. They were so sophisticated and intricate compared to when she was a girl, everything now run by computers and timing digitalized. It was so different from years ago, but just as fun to watch.

The Macy's window was decked out like a fantasy candy land with huge red and white canes, oversized gingerbread men and a chocolate fountain spilling a river of the delicious brown liquid into a pool at the bottom of a snowy mountain. Two impish children were stealing the treats and stuffing themselves behind giant brightly lit evergreen trees while a plump elf was chasing two others around the chocolate-filled pond. Penny imagined the wide eyes of kids from all over coming to watch the scene, parents just as delighted by their antics.

When she was a child they would take their annual shopping trip to Fargo before the holidays, since it was by far the largest city in their area. Fargo had major department and specialty stores not available in Lisbon, the small prairie town where their family lived about an hour to the south and west. Penny recalled how magical it was to see all the animated characters in the windows of the stores as they strolled down Broadway. There were elves frantically working away in their toyshop, reindeer hooked to a sleigh, and Santa and Mrs. Claus checking their list. She smiled at the memory of peering through the frosty glass at the lively spectacle.

Listening to the songs of the season filled Penny with a sense of anticipation for the fun she would have this year. It wouldn't be long and she'd be surrounded by family she hadn't seen since the long weekend at her sister's lake home the summer before.

Idling at yet another red light, Penny thought about everything she needed to finalize before she left for the holidays. Finish editing article for Dan Cooper on upscale ballpark stadium food, check. Call Martha Dockery to confirm calendar dates for the *Women in Publishing* conference they were going to attend in San Antonio next month, check. Meet briefly with Carl Wharton to discuss the final changes she had submitted on his "Life's a Beach" winter travel section article, check. Make sure her teapot and coffee cup are empty this time so she didn't come back to a serious science project growing inside them, check.

The aging vehicle sputtered and slipped around the last corner as she spied the entrance to the *City News* parking garage. Grabbing the key card she kept tucked above the visor and swiping it over the security monitor, she waited patiently for the camera to recognize her and the gate arm to rise. Humming along with Bing Crosby as he crooned "I'll Be Home for Christmas," she drove forward. "You aren't the only one, Bing," she cheerily remarked as she slowly made her way to the fourth floor and her reserved spot #480. Penny gathered her belongings and exited the car, struggling to manage everything she was carrying.

Computer bag crammed to capacity and oversized purse in tow, she boarded the elevator packed with a half-dozen coworkers equally bundled against the elements and looking every bit as eager to get started on the day. Most people she knew were knocking off early and heading out in various directions for holiday plans. Penny could feel the excited vibe as they chatted amongst themselves about plans for the long weekend.

Penny had worked at the *Chicago City News* in the Entertainment/Lifestyle division (or ETL as Penny and her coworkers referred to it) for the past eighteen years. She had been Chief Editor for the past dozen years and loved the energetic atmosphere and ever-changing stories that kept her job interesting. Before moving to ETL she worked for twenty years as a Copy Editor and then Copy Manager and eventually Director in a variety of divisions including city government and politics, local news, and even a brief stint in the obituary department.

Although Penny didn't exactly care for the two years she spent editing the life stories of the recent dearly departed, she was frequently entertained by the creativity of loved ones who regularly paid tribute in ways that were often quite humorous.

When I Get Home

One send-off that stuck in her mind was paying homage to an apparently comical centenarian by the name of Olan Detloff. At 106 years old Olan had most likely died of natural causes; however, the obituary declared that he had died under suspicious circumstances shortly after having finally beaten his nursing home roommate at cribbage. The obit went on to relay the name of the horses upon which his winnings were to be bet in the upcoming opener at Hawthorne Racing Course. "Still Lovin' Katie" to win, "Joe's Toes Down" to place, and "Hellava-Ride" to show. Penny opined she would have enjoyed a lively conversation with good old Olan.

The elevator doors eventually parted and everyone scurried off like mice to their respective cubicles in the maze. "Have a good one Penny," said her favorite copy assistant Eleanor as they waited for the people in front of them to clear before exiting last. "Merry Christmas to you and yours," she added brightly as they went in opposite directions. "You too, Ellie," Penny replied as she struggled to keep her bag from slipping off of her shoulder and spilling its contents on the floor.

Penny had been offered jobs at other newspapers and periodicals over the years, but she couldn't bring herself to leave; her heart was with *City News*. She was fortunate to have an amazing staff as colorful as they were talented. Penny had hired Eleanor away from the *Tribstar* in Terre Haute, Indiana, several years ago. Ellie was an astute learner with a bubbly personality that quickly endeared her to the rest of the team. She was always bringing in homemade treats and had easily won the annual 4th of July Best Brownie contest the last three years running.

Ellie was a petite brunette probably only in her late thirties, but appeared much older due to her lack of makeup and a wardrobe more befitting a woman at least two decades older. From the threadbare cardigan sweaters she constantly donned around her shoulders to the round wire-rimmed reading glasses hanging from a chain around her neck, Eleanor was a vision from a bygone era. There is chic vintage and then there is stuck in a rut. Sadly, Ellie's style was decidedly the latter.

Ellie owned at least three cats, pictures of which adorned every open inch of wall space in her cubicle. There was a wall calendar which featured various felines dressed up in human costumes, and an I HEART CATS coffee mug that was sitting atop a coaster in the shape of a cat's head. Her mouse pad was cleverly designed to look as if a cat was ready to pounce on the "mouse." She proudly talked about the antics and accomplishments of her "babies" as eagerly as anyone else would talk about their children.

Any time Eleanor spent more than a few minutes in her office Penny found herself in need of a lint roller and an allergy shot, as inevitably she'd be left sneezing after even brief encounters. Ellie seemed to shed as much fuzz in her wake as the average Tabby, little tufts of nearly invisible gray and white fur cast off with every step.

You couldn't help but love little Ellie, who would do anything for anyone, stay late and come in early if needed to make sure a project was complete and success as a team was achieved. Cat hair and fashion faux pas aside, Penny would eagerly welcome a dozen more just like her to their department.

In the cubicle next to Ellie was L'Shanda Brewer, one of the top editing assistants who had been reporting to Penny almost as long as she had been in ETL. As boisterous as Eleanor was unassuming, L'Shanda was larger than life in more ways than one. A corpulent black woman who often referred to herself as a "BBB" (Big Beautiful Babe) L'Shanda was born and raised in a tarpaper shack in the backwoods of southern Mississippi on little more than "dust sandwiches and okra" as she often put it. Her unique laugh, which sounded a little like a donkey had swallowed a kazoo, could be heard echoing around the newsroom on a regular basis.

Everyone who worked on the fourth floor also knew she was a notorious food pilferer with an appetite as large as her size 13 stilettos. Anyone new to the department quickly learned that leaving a donut unattended while you poured a cup of coffee was an open invitation to the hawkeyed L'Shanda. She particularly delighted in potluck celebrations that regularly were organized by some of the clerical staff. Her initial "well, maybe just a bite" quickly turned into a plate piled as high as Mt. McKinley.

L'Shanda was currently carrying an additional 100 pounds of "maybe just a bite" around on her bulky 5'11" frame, and Penny was concerned lately about how out of breath she would seem after just walking to the copier and back – a total of about a dozen feet. She was inevitably on a new diet just about every Monday, and trying to keep up with what she was and wasn't eating was a never-ending source of entertainment for the office; her excuses for falling off the diet band wagon, equally so.

At one time or another, L'Shanda had been on the grapefruit diet, which consisted of eating a grapefruit several times a day along with plain soda crackers and cottage cheese. That lasted about two days before she declared that eating so much grapefruit was making her hair too frizzy. She had given Weight Watchers a try, but L'Shanda never could accurately calculate the food points and actually ended up gaining five pounds. "I forgot to carry the one."

Then there was Atkins which seemed to suit her fine-tuned palate. That diet mostly consisted of liberal amounts of meat for breakfast followed by meat for lunch and then more meat for dinner. One of her more astute coworkers dropped the bombshell that mincemeat pie probably wasn't considered "meat" as they observed her hunkered over a piece the size of Vermont. There went that diet out the window.

Two weeks before Christmas she announced she was finally on a diet she could live with the rest of her life – the "seefood" diet. "I see food…I eat it!" she laughed heartily as she helped herself to another cookie from the goodies various departments had brought to the lunchroom for sharing. People were already taking bets on what her diet would be come January 1, the annual day when approximately two-thirds of the country made weight loss their New Year's resolution.

Equally as amusing was L'Shanda's unique sense of style, which was a curious mix of rodeo clown meets disco diva. She favored neon colors both in makeup and clothing, and most days sported a streak in her hair that was anything from shocking pink to lime green. By far Penny's favorite, however, was the unusual artwork she generally had airbrushed onto her fingernails, which were usually at least two inches in length. How she ever typed anything with those spikes was anyone's guess.

Penny dropped the bags by her desk, took off her heavy winter coat and hung it on the coat tree next to the window facing the lake. Looking out to see the weather was showing no signs of improvement she mumbled, "Please stop snowing. *PLEASE,*" begging nobody in particular.

Penny filled her teapot with water and plugged it into the wall. She grabbed her favorite mug, which proudly proclaimed her "World's Best Grandma," and pulled a teabag out of her top desk drawer. She sighed, "Last day until holiday vacation; so much to do, so little time!"

"I hear you, girlfriend," echoed a slightly exasperated L'Shanda as she hurried by, arms overloaded with manila file folders. "Lord have mercy, never enough hours in a day!" she exclaimed fleeing quickly down the hall, clip clopping away in bright green heels disappearing into the copy room.

Penny sat back for a moment, letting the cup of freshly poured tea warm her still chilly hands. World's Greatest Grandma indeed. It didn't feel like it this season. It would be the first year since her grandchildren were born that she wouldn't be seeing them tear open the packages under the tree and squeal with delight at what Santa left for them.

She understood married children have two sides of the family to please. It just seemed so odd to her that both kids would claim plans elsewhere this Christmas. Her oldest, son Jamey and his wife Susie, lived in Columbus, Ohio, and were parents to her seven-year-old grandson (and bestest buddy) Stephen.

Daughter Meredith and husband Jason resided in Michigan and were parents to her two beautiful granddaughters Allison and Emmalyn, who were five years old and eight months old respectively. Usually, there was an "every other year" plan in place and last year both of them spent the holiday with their spouse's family. Nothing she said could change their minds. Both had claimed extenuating circumstances that meant traveling to their in-laws for the holidays this year.

Penny loved her kids and grandkids deeply and seeing their faces light up when they opened her carefully chosen gifts was something she looked forward to every year more than they did. And this would be the first Christmas with baby Emmalyn. She hated to miss her at an age where everything would be a wonder.

Oh well, she accepted the decision and tried to make the best of it. She decided it was a great excuse to get out of town to visit her sister and mother, spend a little time just relaxing without having to be in charge of the celebration. Both children had promised next year for sure, they would have a gathering in Chicago for the holidays.

Penny put on her reading glasses and turned to her computer. She knew there would be a mountain of emails to get through before she could think about leaving the office until next year. After typing in the usual credentials and pressing the enter button, she was greeted with a bright red "ERROR" message indicating the system could not identify her. She repeatedly tried to use what she knew were correct logins and passwords to no avail. Three strikes and another error message popped up.

"Oh great," she said aloud. "Now I'm locked out. I just do *not* need this today!"

"Looks like a job for The Jeweler," came advice from L'Shanda as she walked by, this time balancing a cup of coffee and oversized blueberry muffin on top of her stack of folders. Penny couldn't help but wonder if somewhere in the lunchroom there was a confused coworker scratching their head saying to themselves, "I could have sworn I put that muffin right next to the microwave."

"The Jeweler" was an affectionate nickname that years ago had been bestowed upon their department IT resource, Lesterjewel Gaylord Lipnicki III (because clearly two wasn't enough).

Lesterjewel, "LJ," or "The Jeweler" originally hailed from a small burg on the border of Kentucky and West Virginia by the name of Inez. Inez was tucked deep into a holler not unlike the one Miss Loretta sang about when she was a coal miner's daughter. Lesterjewel told Penny he was born on the same day in 1964 that President Lyndon B. Johnson landed in a helicopter on the grounds of an abandoned miniature golf course to promote his war on poverty.

LJ was one of the lucky ones to escape due to winning a full-ride scholastic scholarship to Loyola University. He was hired by *City News* right out of college and had been there ever since. Lesterjewel was a bit of an odd duck, but in possession of a brilliant mind. He loved to tinker and fix things from the time he could remember. It served him well as the age of computers brought about a kind of technology that suited his introverted personality and insatiable desire to figure things out.

Looks wise, Lesterjewel had always reminded Penny of the 1950s actor and comedian Wally Cox. A diminutive man who struggled to reach five feet tall, he was not only saddled with short stature and quite an unusual moniker, but a rather fierce and unrelenting stutter to boot. Penny figured the only thing worse than that trifecta would have been a cleft palate or a limp, but Lesterjewel was never anything but totally pleasant and good-natured – even when other people were less than gracious (which was often enough).

Lesterjewel wore thick Coke bottle glasses that were always just slightly wonky and the least successful comb-over she'd ever witnessed. The few strands that remained on his head were literally wrapped around it starting from behind one ear and ending up clear over behind the other. Penny followed him down the street one brisk spring day when a breeze caught hold of one end and blew the entire hairspray-stiffened patch off to one side. It was a foot long if it was an inch.

Penny tried to tactfully suggest to him long ago that women actually preferred men who embraced their natural appearance and assured him she thought bald was sexy. "Ra-ra-ra-really?" had been his somewhat surprised response. Evidently he hadn't bought what she was selling because the comb-over remained, plastered to his head like hair wallpaper.

Penny knew Lesterjewel was a little sweet on her so she was particularly patient as he would stammer his way through their conversation when others would try to finish his sentences out of sheer frustration at the time it took to relay the message. The letter P was particularly difficult for him, so just saying her name was often a thirty-second ordeal for poor Lesterjewel. Add a "pardon me" to the sentence and you could take care of a conference call and get a cup of java before he got to the p-p-p-point.

Penny picked up the phone and dialed The Jeweler's extension.

"Th-th-th-th-this is L-L-L-Lesterjewel, h-h-h-how m-m-may I help you?" He was as pleasant as ever.

"Hi Lesterjewel, this is Penny Tomlin in ETL. My computer has decided to give me fits this morning and locked me out. Do you have a few minutes to get me up and running? I really need to get things cleared up before vacation."

"B-b-b-be right there!" he said in an animated tone.

Sure enough, not five minutes later he was in the door of her office, not only still sporting the dreadful comb-over, but a bright green sweatshirt with a picture of a sheep wearing a red and white Santa hat with the greeting "Fleece Navidad" in large letters above it.

The Jeweler was not known for his fashion sense, but by golly he had her system up within two minutes. When he was finished, he got up and Penny returned to her chair in front of the computer. He gave her a sheepish grin as Penny put in her password. A split second later up popped her email. Mission accomplished. "Thank you so much," Penny said warmly and with genuine enthusiasm.

"Th-th-th-there you go!" He stammered shyly, lingering in her doorway for a length of time that quickly bordered upon awkward. She could tell he was trying to come up with what to say next and was searching for just the right words that would come out with the least amount of resistance.

"Was there something else Lesterjewel?" Penny inquired in the nicest possible voice, sensing his angst.

"W-w-w-well, I-I-I w-w-w-was wondering if y-y-you might l-like to g-g-g-grab a hol-l-l-iday d-d-d-d-drink after w-w-work? His gaze immediately fell to his shoes, his face turning a vibrant shade of bright pink. Penny could tell that it took every bit of courage he could muster to extend the invitation.

"What a lovely thought," she replied, "if I wasn't taking off shortly for a holiday with my family you could probably have talked me into it." She could visibly see at once both disappointment and relief in his face as he looked up and nodded in an understanding way. Penny got up from her desk and came around to where Lesterjewel was standing and gave him a big hug. "Merry Christmas!" she exclaimed.

"S-s-same t-t-t-to y-y-you!" he managed, thinking as he returned the friendly embrace, she hadn't exactly said no. In fact, he thought for certain it had been a definite maybe! With a big smile plastered on his face Lesterjewel went on his way as Penny focused on her computer and got down to business in earnest.

She busied herself in the first hour clearing her desk of projects, sipping from the mug now brimming with fragrant lemongrass tea, and absentmindedly munching on slices of apple she had packed in her purse for a snack. She called Martha Dockery and added the conference date on her Outlook calendar. The meeting with Carl had been productive, and she was making good headway on the last article she needed to complete.

As the morning progressed, she could see several inches of new snow continued to blanket the ground with a promise of more to come. Big, fat flakes were falling steadily like white rain in perfect slow motion as Penny gazed out the window, thinking for a moment about what she needed to pack for her trip to spend the holidays with her family.   SWEATERS, she wrote in large letters on the pad next to her phone.

"You know it isn't supposed to let up until after Christmas right, Pen?" Roger Hamilton, one of the other copy editors and legendary office lothario offered as she was daydreaming. "Going to be a crap shoot as to whether I'll make it out of town to visit the folks in Tampa. Been watching online and so far my flight still shows as leaving on time later; crossing my fingers!" He laughed and shrugged as he reached for the pot of coffee to fill his cup, which was shaped in the likeness of Santa's face. "Sure would be nice to hang at the beach on Christmas Day. One word for ya: BABES!"

Roger was an excellent editor, but the kind of guy you hope you never run into as far as dating material. Roger was the type who openly boasted of his weekend conquests, had a cell phone filled with names and numbers of women he supposedly had bedded, and was constantly hitting on any impressionable new intern or female employee to the point Human Resources had been called upon to remind him *City News* had a zero tolerance policy against sexual harassment. Penny knew Roger was all bluster and ego and probably desired a meaningful relationship more than he'd ever admit. In her experience, men like him were more insecure than others who never shared the intimate details of their dating lives.

She had caught him off guard and in a vulnerable moment one day last summer, looking at his phone as if willing it to ring. "Why won't she call me back?" he had asked Penny as she walked by his cubicle. "I really like her and I was hoping she thought we had hit it off, too." Then as if he realized he had momentarily let down his guard added with his usual arrogant bravado, "She doesn't know what she's missing." Sigh, back to being the Roger everyone knew and semi-loved.

Roger's comment about his flight made Penny wonder if her own flight might be in jeopardy if the snow continued at the rate it was going. She went online to Delta.com and searched for her itinerary. Flight 5257 left that evening at 6:30 and would connect through Minneapolis arriving in Fargo at 10:00 pm. Reassured for the moment, the screen read "On Schedule."

If everything remained on time, she'd be there for Christmas at her sister's home on what was now a frozen Minnesota lake just over the North Dakota border by about an hour. Looks like she would be there to help her sister Sandra get the pans of lasagna made and everything ready for the celebration Christmas Eve. It had been many years since Penny had made her way back for the holiday – too long.

Penny had left the Prairie Dog State in the rear view mirror right after she graduated with her degree in journalism from the University of North Dakota at Grand Forks. Talk about the ends of the earth. Winter was not just freezing in Grand Forks. It was winter squared, winter on steroids, winter on the rocks with an antifreeze chaser and road salt around the rim of the glass. Northern North Dakota is so flat you can roll a marble from Minot to Grand Forks and never round a curve or breach a hill. There isn't much to break the harsh wind that races east from Montana. Once it turns dark and cold, living in that part of the world tests even the heartiest of souls.

It is hard to imagine what the first settlers, most of whom were either of Scandinavian or German descent, were thinking when they stopped their wagons or got off the train and decided to make that desolate prairie their home. "Vell, at least nutting vill spoil in da vinter in dese parts!" Talk about an understatement. Snow was measured in feet, not inches; storms in days, not hours. Highways were built with iron gates that could be locked across highway entrances. They actually *closed the highways* when the blizzards invaded mercilessly with harsh winds that blew unrelenting for days on end. Not even the snowplows with their massive blades could manage the burden when Mother Nature unleashed her winter fury with a vengeance in that part of the world.

Still sparsely populated, clearly more left North Dakota than stayed. No doubt they kept heading further west or south after the first winter in a place where it gets dark before 5:00 pm and the snow squalls can last for days.

Having grown up in a small farming community on the banks of the lazy Sheyenne River, Penny was used to copious amounts of snow. As much fun as it was to sled and ice skate, ski and snowmobile, build ice forts and have snowball fights, she used to dream of landing a job in Hawaii or some other warm, exotic place; at least somewhere south of where snowplows often rule the roads from December to April. The endless sunny days, palm trees, and sand between her toes at the beach sounded like heaven to a girl who used to have to walk with jeans underneath her dress so her legs didn't freeze as she trekked the mile or so up the hill to school on frigid winter days.

Every car of her childhood had an electric connection hanging out of the front grill so it could be plugged in at night to keep the engine warm enough to start up after sitting in below zero temperatures. Nights, and even days at a time, the temperature never rose above zero degrees. With the ever-present wind chill factor, the thermometer often lingered at a level that would force even polar bears and penguins to seek shelter.

After one particularly brutal blizzard that lasted for two days, she and her sisters made great fun of taking turns jumping out the second floor window and into the big fluffy snow bank that had formed all the way up the side of their house to the top of the roof. They were covered with snow and ice as they struggled out of their snowsuits and mittens, having tackled the drift and won. Rosy cheeked and weary, they sat down to enjoy hot chocolate with marshmallows in front of the fireplace and play board games like Monopoly or Clue around the dining room table.

Mittens and boots were lined up on the heating registers to dry, snowsuits given a long tumble in the dryer to be ready for the next day. Sometimes they would pull plastic bags that formerly held loaves of bread over their socks before they put their boots on as an extra layer of protection against the wet stuff. It was a ritual performed dozens of times as January turned to February and March to the much anticipated first signs of a spring thaw.

When she was in high school she found an article in the *Fargo Forum* travel section of the Sunday paper. It featured a faraway place in the South Pacific called Bora Bora. Penny was mesmerized by the pictures of small thatched huts on stilts that were actually built over top of the turquoise blue water of the Pacific Ocean. Each one had a glass floor where you could see the fish swimming by. Amazing! She cut out that picture and article and put it in her secret wish box with a small padlock on it that she kept in her closet. It was filled with things she had collected through the years of places she wanted to see, things she wanted to do someday. Bora Bora. Even the name was exotic. She hadn't given up hope of seeing it eventually.

But when Penny was offered the job in Chicago as an intern at the *City News* the summer of her last year in college, she was immediately hooked on the Windy City. With its incredible history and architecture, there were so many fabulous places to visit. She spent the entire summer taking in famous landmarks such as the Shedd

Aquarium, Grant Park, Lincoln Park Zoo, the beautiful historic Chicago Theater and even a baseball game at Wrigley Field.

She spent hours riding the Ferris wheel on Navy Pier, wandering in and out of the little shops, looking at all the tourist trinkets until she had reached the very end of the docks. She would buy a cold drink and gaze at the sun setting until the lighthouses standing watch at the end of the sand bars would flicker on.

Chicago was alive, breathing in and out as the waves lapped along the shore of impressive Lake Michigan. It seemed to be bustling no matter what time of day or night, and there was always something new and interesting to do or see. She was assigned to the Entertainment and Lifestyle division which meant she had the inside scoop on what exhibits, festivals or bands were coming to town; so there were often free tickets to be had which was welcome on her skimpy budget.

Penny was fortunate to find a small efficiency apartment to sublet that was close to the Chicago Riverwalk off of N. Stetson Avenue. She loved the Riverwalk and it became a regular haunt that first summer. She'd stop and pick up coffee and her favorite spinach and cheese-filled croissant at a little hole-in-the-wall bakery, wander down the park to a little bench along the way to munch her sandwich. She enjoyed being alive in the moment in one of the most vibrant cities on earth. Not bad for the little girl from Lisbon.

Penny's view of the city from her tiny abode wasn't exactly breathtaking. Her old and somewhat shabby brownstone apartment building had faded green shutters adorned with empty window boxes that desperately needed a coat of fresh paint, and crumbling brick steps that today surely would have been declared a code violation. It was sandwiched in between two others that were equally in need of some TLC. Her view more often than not was of the neighbor's curtained window across the alley. It didn't really matter; she never spent much time there anyway. When she wasn't working she preferred to explore the city in her free time. It was a wonderful summer. She loved her work and coworkers and made a few friends that she looked forward to seeing again.

Penny was thrilled and jumped at the chance to work part-time editing articles for the *City News* once the summer had ended, and was assured full-time employment was waiting for her after graduation. At least she didn't have to worry about finding a job at a time when she knew a lot of her friends were struggling. It was the late 1970s and gas prices and interest rates were high, opportunities low. Penny felt blessed she had found a home at the *City News*.

Every week during her senior year at UND she received a big brown envelope in the mail filled with articles and stories that various staff members were working on. She'd read and make suggested changes, red marks and circles on the typed white sheets late into the night as she sipped tea and ate peanut butter on crackers by the dim light of her table lamp. Every Monday she would drop the return package off at the post office on her way to school. By then she was sharing a small off-campus apartment with two other girls, thankfully neither of whom minded her working till all hours. When she started reading and editing a piece, Penny became immersed and lost track of time on a regular basis. Sometimes it was a struggle to get to class the next day, especially her 8:00 am Creative Writing class with Mr. Nordke.

Tall, blonde and the picture of Norwegian heritage in his ever-present brightly colored, hand-knit sweaters, Mr. Nordke was tough when it came to grading and relentless in giving plenty of homework. But Penny admired the way he brought every subject, every story to life with his exuberant teaching style, his love of the written word evident. It was he who had often encouraged her to explore a career where she could put what he called her "considerable ability to turn a phrase" to practical use. He generally gave her very high marks on her papers and an A when it was report card time. Penny had often struggled to make good grades in school and was pretty proud of the marks she was able to achieve in college.

She would never forget graduation day as she walked across the stage, diploma in hand. Mr. Nordke was sitting with other faculty in the front row and nodded in her direction, clapping loudly as she walked by as if to say, "Way to go, Penny! You are capable of great things." She thanked him for inspiring her as he chatted with her and her mother briefly after the ceremony, telling him about her new job in Chicago. "I won't let you down," she told him. He smiled, shook her hand and as he walked away she heard him call after her, "I believe you."

In a way, Mr. Nordke reminded Penny of her father, sparkling blue eyes and a laugh like jingle bells. Well, except for the sweaters. Her dad, who was always highly fashionable, wouldn't have been caught dead in a sweater with jumping deer emblazoned across his chest!

She moved for good the week after graduating from UND, packing her old blue Chevrolet with boxes of meager belongings and dreams. She headed east across Minnesota and Wisconsin, filled with excitement and a sense of adventure. Penny never looked back. Forty years later, she still loved the city, still enjoyed her job and although she had a much better apartment these days, she remained in the same general vicinity as that first little place she rented as an intern. She was at least a few years from being able to think about retiring, and Bora Bora was still on her bucket list, but she had seen a lot of the world, been married and divorced, and had two children, now grown and happy with families and children of their own. Life was good.

Both of her kids lived out of state, and with small children in the family she knew traveling with little ones was challenging. Penny understood they had other family obligations that wouldn't include her this year. So she wrapped up all of her packages and sent them off to the kids with happy notes and kisses. There would be presents under the tree for each of them, even if she wouldn't see the faces of her grandchildren light up when they opened them. "Take lots of pictures and make sure you post them to Facebook!" Penny said as she had one final conversation with her daughter Meredith before she left for work that morning. "Have fun and know that I'll be thinking of you with lots of love."

Penny was actually looking forward to going back and spending Christmas with her mom Betsy and Sandra, Sandra's husband Todd, their daughter Justine and husband Tom, with the added bonus of their two adorable grandsons Oliver and Miles. Sandra was older by two years and had recently retired as a full professor of music at a small state college in North Dakota. Penny was envious Sandra had long days to do with what she pleased and was anxious to catch up with everyone's news. It would be nice to have some time just to relax after what had been a pretty hectic year. She had visions of leisurely conversations over a glass of wine by the fire, talking late into the night, exchanging funny stories about the grandchildren and feeling grateful to be there.

They would no doubt call their other two siblings while she was there, younger sister Cara and still younger brother Ricky. Cara worked in the emergency room of a hospital in Bismarck and had been married for almost 40 years to Judd, one of the funniest guys Penny had ever met and a world-class musician who still picked up weekend gigs around town. Judd could play anything from guitar to fiddle to banjo and early on had made his living on the road opening for some of the biggest country acts going. He definitely added an entertainment factor Penny would certainly miss this gathering.

Rick had been in Arizona for many years working in the oil and gas industry and was married to Renee. Ricky, as they always called him, had two boys in high school, Daniel and Rodney. Rick and Renee spent a great deal of time keeping up with their sports activities. Daniel was a fabulous pitcher and was on more than one traveling baseball team while Rodney preferred soccer. Both of her other siblings would be spending the holiday with their kids and grandkids but they usually talked over Christmas break. Time marches on, families expand, and it becomes more difficult to gather en masse, especially in the winter, where weather can be a major factor and play the spoiler.

By 10:00 a.m. Penny was worried about the amount of snow still piling up. There had to be at least another six inches on the ground and the wind was fierce and more insistent than when she had left for work just a few hours ago. The look on her face must have been one of obvious concern because as her assistant Kathy walked by she tapped on Penny's desk and said with a warning tone, "I just heard some flights have been cancelled. Maybe you should go ahead and take off in case you have to make other plans. I have a feeling the airport is going to be packed and the lines at the gates could be long. It is days like this when I'm happy my family doesn't have that far to come from Ft. Wayne!"

"Not a bad idea, Kathy. Thanks for mentioning it, I think you're right." Penny started organizing her desk, putting things in neat piles, pens in the drawer, "to do" list updated. "I guess work will be here when I get back," Penny said as her computer screensaver came on and she slid her chair back for the last time in 2014. She wouldn't be back until after New Year's Eve was a memory.

She snapped off the desk lamp and put her laptop in the bag she kept under her desk. "Have a great holiday, Kathy!" Penny said with enthusiasm as she reached for her coat and tucked her purse under her arm. "I hope Santa is good to you!" Kathy looked up from her desk and smiled, giving a wave as Penny walked toward the elevators. "Safe travels," she added as Penny slipped out of sight around the corner.

On days like this Penny was thankful the *City News* had a nice, heated parking garage under the building. At least she wouldn't be shoveling or digging her car out of a snow bank. But still, it was treacherous as she made her way up the parking ramp and out into what was now a very nasty day. Traffic crept at a snail's pace between the stoplights and her tires slipped along with questionable traction.

She switched on the radio just in time to hear the DJ on WLS give the latest weather update. Snow, snow…and more snow expected, with winds topping 20 miles an hour and gusts to 35. Not good. Accidents were everywhere around the Loop, and as she crawled in snarled traffic the few miles to her apartment, the fear was growing. "I can't be stuck here alone on Christmas," she sighed as she turned the last corner and could barely make out her apartment building braced against the elements, "I just CAN'T." She literally slid into in her parking spot behind the building and shuffled quickly through the snow to the warmth of her apartment.

302 Doddridge Street had been home for the last fifteen years ever since she divorced the man she had met and fell in love with the first year she had lived in Chicago. It was a spacious two-bedroom, two-bathroom apartment with vaulted ceilings, exposed brick and hardwood floors. Penny fell in love with it the moment she saw it, with its amazing views of the Chicago skyline and fabulous architectural details like the big, open living room/kitchen

and the wall of windows that faced the street. There was so much natural light, but also lots of trees in the older neighborhood to lend their shade in the summer.

She particularly liked that her home was large enough to accommodate one of her most extravagant belongings – a baby grand piano she bought from a friend who was moving to Europe and couldn't take it along. Penny had grown up in a very musical family, where singing around the piano was almost a daily occurrence and being in the band and choir were the extracurricular activities she looked forward to every year as school would start again in the fall. She took private voice lessons and competed in vocal and instrumental contests, even being chosen by a national organization to tour Europe with a choir and orchestra made up of high school kids from all over the country.

Penny was never a great pianist, not like Sandra, who had her doctorate in music and who was incredibly talented. Sandra was gifted in a seemingly effortless way and Penny envied her natural ability. Sandra didn't seem to mind practicing and never struggled with the "theory" part of learning music. Not like Penny who would rather stick a needle in her eye than learn chord progressions. No, Penny lacked the discipline to learn the art of playing the piano. She hated to practice and REALLY didn't like her old spinster piano teacher. Penny thought she was mean and dreaded going up the steps to the big white house every week to her lessons. She much preferred making up her own songs and playing by ear.

Sometimes when she was supposed to be practicing her lessons, she would play music that just came into her head instead. And nobody was the wiser. In fact, sometimes her mother would comment as she worked in the kitchen around the corner from the piano, "that was lovely, Penny. See what a little practice will do?" Penny would just smile knowingly. Now Penny could sit and play to her heart's content on the beautiful piano that sat in front of the windows in the living room overlooking the street below.

She had so many fond memories of singing carols and holiday tunes with her two sisters by the light of the big Christmas tree while their mother was making dinner in the kitchen, their father reading by the fireplace. Sandra was alto, Cara was second soprano and Penny took the highest soprano part. Their voices blending in perfect harmony as the words to "White Christmas" and "Silver Bells" filled the house.

Sandra, Cara and Penny also regularly performed in a trio as the Raney Sisters, tapped to entertain at many local events, church and school concerts. Penny missed those days. She was looking forward to singing around the piano with Sandra and Sandra's daughter Justine this Christmas. Now…if she could just get there!

As she was rushing around the house packing her last-minute toiletries, the heavy cardigan sweater she was wearing brushed against a family picture that was hanging in the main hallway. It was the one photograph Penny kept on display that included her ex-husband Mark. It dropped to the floor like a rock, glass shattering into a thousand little slivers. "Oh great," she sighed as she picked up the frame and brushed what glass she could from the arrangement of smiling faces. "I have NO time for this!" She stared for a long moment at the picture of the once-happy family. She was so young and beautiful, and Mark dashingly handsome as they stood arms around each other hugging the kids. That was a long time ago.

Penny Jane Raney met Mark Tomlin one sultry evening at the 4th of July party hosted by one of her coworkers, Barb Lugert. Mark was tall, dark and handsome and beyond charming as he took a swig of beer, reached for her hand and with a low sweeping bow planted a sweet kiss on the top of it. "Prince Charming, at your service," he cooed eyebrow raised, tongue firmly implanted in cheek when Barb introduced them. Penny grinned broadly and their eyes locked in a gaze that lingered. Talk about fireworks!

As the night wore on they danced and mingled before finally gravitating to a corner of the room where it was more quiet and private. They talked effortlessly about work, family, favorite this and that. They had a great deal in common including a love of music, and the chemistry was certainly evident. She distinctly remembered how badly she wanted him to reach out and kiss her. They inched ever closer together throughout the evening, hands barely brushing against each other as they laughed and talked. The air was charged with the electricity of their amazing and clearly mutual attraction.

Penny thought he was brilliant and so eloquent in his ability to sound intelligent no matter the subject. She made him laugh until there were tears running down his cheeks and he declared her the wittiest girl he had ever met.

They left the party holding hands, strolling along the shore talking until the fireworks above the city faded to a starlit sky. They found a bench in a little gazebo and with arms wrapped around each other sat in comfortable silence, taking in the sunrise as it broke in pink and yellow hues over the lake. When Mark suggested they get some coffee they set off down the boardwalk to find a cafe that was open.

They stopped on a corner where a flock of pigeons was intently picking at popcorn someone had spilled on the ground. Mark took her face in his hands. "I think I'm going to love you forever, just giving you fair warning." He was so sweetly sincere, all misty eyed and genuine. For the first time ever, she was speechless. He took her in his arms and kissed her passionately. The kind of kiss they write movies around and you remember forever. Her feet may not have been touching the ground as she eagerly returned his affection, everything inside of her filled with hope about where this might lead.

After a year of inseparable courting Mark got down on one knee at the top of the Sears Tower one humid summer evening. The sky was a spectacle of stars and her heart was beating out of her chest as she heard the words every girl wants to hear…"Will you be my wife?" That moment was bittersweet and filled with every possible emotion.

She remembered crying uncontrollably. Mark thought she was just happy he had popped the question, but it was so much more than that. It was overwhelming to think about getting married. MARRIED; and to the man of her dreams no less. Loving, sexy, funny, driven to make sure he was successful enough to provide for them as they began their life journey together. The other people around them applauded and cheered. Penny and Mark had embraced and then responded enthusiastically by throwing their arms into the air and joining in, whooping it up as if the long-suffering Chicago Cubs had just won the World Series.

Later as they had talked about plans, Penny insisted there would be no big church wedding. She couldn't bear the thought of walking down the aisle alone, or with someone other than her father by her side. Tragically, he had been killed in a car accident the winter of her sophomore year in college, and the pain of that time though now a few years distant, still could bring her to tears.

An empty spot in their family's life was created that day; a void so vast it would never be filled. It changed their entire family all dramatically and forever in an instant. The color was gone in the world and for a long time everything was a shade of gray, everyone trying to move on and pretending that life was returning to normal, whatever that would be.

Penny could remember the disinfectant smell of the hospital room, the sad look on her aunt's face as she walked into the little chapel down the hall where they had all been told to gather, her head bowed, shaking. He was gone. She couldn't believe he was never walking out of that hospital. Honestly, even when she could tell the situation was grave, it never occurred to her that he wasn't going to live. A long hospital stay maybe, but it just wasn't possible he would die. Not her strong, athletic father who was never an ounce overweight and was active until the last day of his life.

But it was over, all hope lost. They were left alone in the quiet little hospital chapel, alone to let it sink in. The next thing Penny remembered was the sobbing and wailing. It took her a moment to realize it was her own despair and that of a dozen others, her mother, Sandra, Cara, Rick, a few friends who had driven to the hospital in Fargo where they had taken her father by ambulance after the small, rural hospital in Lisbon knew they didn't have the technology or surgeons to help him.

There was no life flight helicopter back then, no 911. Just volunteers doing the best they could under unfortunate circumstances. Sadly the delay in getting the appropriate treatment gave him no chance of recovery, the damage was too significant, the outcome inevitable.

Somehow leaning on each other, they made it through the next few days and weeks in a kind of numb disbelief. Her father was constantly on the road for work so Penny pretended he was just on another business trip until the inevitable "firsts" came along; the first birthday without him, Thanksgiving and then Christmas.

Father's Day remained a difficult day for Penny even after almost 40 years. She consciously avoided stores that sold cards during that time. The pain of the realization she would never get to buy another card chosen especially for him never seemed to get any easier.

There was not a week that went by when something didn't remind Penny of her dad, when something great or awful would happen and she didn't want to reach out to talk to him about it. In the week or two before he died her parents had been on a trip to Mexico on a well-deserved vacation. Penny remembered saying to herself, "When I get home the next time, I'm going to have a conversation with Dad. I want to start over, to develop a relationship with him as a grown woman, and most of all to make him proud of me." Sadly, there would never be that chance. He was killed before a word was spoken; she never had the chance to say goodbye. There were so many words unsaid.

Penny had desperately wanted to know him as an adult, and not the rebellious, often sullen and difficult child she knew she had been through much of her growing up years. Mostly she wanted to be able to tell him how sorry she was if she ever disappointed him, if she caused him to worry. She wanted to be sure he understood that if she had known there would never be a chance to make it up to him, she would have been a better girl. She wore the years of regret like a blanket around her soul, equally protective and yet smothering a light she knew he would want to shine. What she wouldn't give for just one last hour with him; one precious conversation.

When she would go for walks along the lake and see butterflies she told herself he was following her, letting her know he was there and watching over her. She talked to him sometimes, and pictured him in heaven doing things he always loved to do when he was alive, surrounded by other long-passed relatives and even pets that had gone before. It helped to believe he was in a better place waiting for her and the rest of the family to be reunited. Almost forty years later that time could be as powerful as yesterday if she allowed herself to think about it. And going home for Christmas she knew she would feel in those quiet moments, and even in the moments of celebration…something was missing, always missing.

Her father, Rob Raney, was a handsome man. He was charismatic and charming, loved by everyone who knew him – the original life of the party; outgoing and gregarious, a born salesman. When she was very small, her father sold cars at the dealership on Main Street, featuring the latest models of sleek, shiny Chevrolets and Buicks. Raney Motors was owned by his father (and Penny's Grandfather) Phillip, and Phillip's brother, Uncle Barney. Penny's grandfather Phil died from complications of a stroke before Penny was even born. For years afterward, Uncle Barney carried on the family business and was a memorable figure in Penny's mind.

She remembered as a little girl how her father would come home from work and she and her sisters would run and climb all over him as he got down on all fours. Her brother was much younger, so it was just the three girls for the first eight years of her life. Since Penny and her father were the first ones up in the morning, she would sometimes be treated to early morning breakfasts at the Jet Café outside of town, and sometimes she would get to go to the dealership with him. The smell of the new cars and the sounds of the mechanics working in the repair shop were burned into her memory. She hadn't been back to Lisbon in decades. She wasn't even sure the car dealership was there anymore.

There were so many happy memories of the little gray Cape Cod house with the dormer windows on Weber Street. Years of birthday parties celebrated with all the neighborhood kids, cousins coming to visit, great holiday celebrations with grandmothers in attendance, and picnics in the back yard on the 4th of July. There were snow forts in the winter and lemonade stands out front in the summer, in the shadow and safety of the home where they all gathered at the end of every day, grateful to be there and to have each other.

There were lots of fun hiding places on every floor of the house, little nooks and crannies, closets and storage spaces perfect for rainy day games of hide and seek. Half of the basement was a recreation room where Penny and her sisters played house and dolls for hours, or put on "shows" with singing or acting out short plays. Occasionally their father might set up his old electric train set for them to enjoy taking turns directing the locomotive around the tracks and through the "town" they had fashioned out of building blocks. Ricky had plenty of room to set up his Hot Wheels car races and G. I. Joe battles.

When they got into junior high and high school, it became the after-school hangout place to spin records and drink soda with friends, or host a "boy-girl" party on a Saturday night with dancing and refreshments. One portion of the large room was set off to one side and flanked by two walls, which served as her father's office when he was home. There was a desk set into the space with two stuffed pheasants in flight hanging above it, trophies of a successful hunt.

The other half of the basement, which was separated by the staircase, was the laundry/furnace room where a makeshift shower had been installed. It also held a long wooden work bench where her father would spend countless hours tinkering with this and that in need of repair and where he made his own shot gun shells, carved gun stocks, and meticulously cleaned and carefully stored his weapons out of the reach of curious children. To this day Penny could easily close her eyes and recall the unique smell, a mixture of furnace oil and gun powder.

In the corner near the workbench sat a big oil-burning furnace. The furnace heated water into steam that gurgled and sputtered through the pipes warming the house. As a little girl Penny remembered being scared by the strange sounds as she was trying to fall asleep in the dark. "It's just the water in the pipes, Penny," her father would whisper as he came to tuck them in. "It is nothing to be afraid of."

She and her sisters originally all shared the same bedroom on one side of the second floor. Three twin beds all lined up in a row, white chenille bedspreads against pale pink walls. As they got older and needed more space, the other half of the upstairs was finished and became Sandra's room. At the same time, a divider wall was put between the larger room they had previously shared so both Penny and Cara now had their own rooms, even though the "wall" didn't go all the way down to the floor or up to the ceiling.

There was a gap of a foot or so at the top because the ceiling was vaulted and no way to erect an actual complete barrier. There was another gap of a couple of inches at the bottom of the wall; she supposed to make it easier to clean the carpet. At least it gave them a smidge more privacy and the illusion of their own rooms.

A small white door with louvered panels separated the two spaces, but they still had to share the one closet that was now situated in what was Penny's room. She remembered more than a few battles over knocking on the door versus barging in unannounced to get at the closet. Oh, the fights the feuding siblings would have through the years! It truly must have driven her mother a little nutty.

Penny had to be content with just having a say in the redecoration process. From the many carpet samples her mother had brought home she had chosen a modern (for that day and age) shag carpeting in a variegated dark blue-green color with matching wallpaper, happy bright green and blue flowers on a white background. They hung fresh white curtains with a ruffled valance at the window behind her bed.

They bought a small wooden desk at the furniture store and painted it a glossy white, placing it across from the bed along the wall next to the closet door. Penny had covered it with matching blue and green vinyl flowers. For her birthday one year she had received a small clock radio with a bright green dial that sat on top of the desk along with a Pepsi bottle that had the neck stretched a foot long. Inside the Pepsi bottle was a plastic flower on a wire stem with bright orange and yellow petals. Those bottles and flowers had been all the rage in her high school years. A bulletin board covered with pictures and mementos hung behind the desk.

A couple of years after the renovation was complete, one of her pet rabbits "Bunna Bunna," gnawed relentlessly at the edges of the paper all along the bottom of the wall and for all she knew the tiny little teeth marks were still there. As she recalled, her mother had been less than pleased with that turn of events.

It seemed Penny was forever hoarding at least one small creature or two. Additional roommates at one time or another were an Abyssinian Guinea Pig named Waldo and a litter of gerbils that was a surprise given the fact she had been told the first two were the same gender. Penny could never resist something small and furry and cuddly.

When Sandra moved into the other room, they also remodeled the bathroom and for the next several years endured regular skirmishes over counter space and shower time. Putting dibs on the harvest gold phone that hung in the hallway just outside the bathroom door was always a source of consternation. It was in the days well before mobile communication with family plans so three teenage girls and one telephone set the stage for some heated struggles over the receiver to say the least. The cord stretched all the way into each of the bedrooms and a shut door with the phone cord inside was an invitation for a battle.

Ricky's bedroom was on the first floor next to the master bedroom where their parents slept. Penny was always a little jealous that Ricky had his very own space, with his very own closet, and a real door that closed and locked. Being in such close quarters upstairs for a good bit of her formative years was one of the reasons Penny supposed as an adult she had such an intense need for privacy and appreciation for peace and quiet. She was grateful she had all she needed in her comfy place on Doddridge Street.

As a girl, she had often dreamed that one day she might be married under the big weeping willow in the back yard on Weber Street, surrounded by the flowering hedges of lilac that bloomed with such amazing floral fragrance every spring. It would have been a perfectly picturesque setting to exchange vows among the lily of the valley and fanciful varieties of tulips that were scattered throughout the rock garden along the back of the house.

The beautiful wedding Penny had imagined would sadly, never be. A few months after her father's death, their mother arrived at the unavoidable and agonizing conclusion that she couldn't remain in a place that held so many memories of better times. Once Cara had graduated from high school that May, the house on Weber Street was sold to a nice family who promised to take very good care of it. After the papers were signed, her mother and Ricky moved away from Lisbon. Since the three girls were now grown and gone off to college, she and Ricky moved to Fargo to be nearer a number of friends who recently had relocated due to business. Being near familiar faces would be a comfort to them both during that time of painful transition.

Penny recalled walking through the empty rooms one last time, standing silently looking around each one as if to allow all of the memories of the years she had spent there to indelibly imprint her being.

One time many years later when she was back for a class reunion, Penny actually went to the door and asked the owners if they might not let her walk through the house. To her astonishment, they welcomed her inside and for the next hour or so, she meandered through the place that meant so much to her growing up. It seemed much smaller than she had envisioned it. She was surprised to see so much of the interior and décor, down to the blue and green flowered wallpaper in her old bedroom was exactly as it had been the day the moving van pulled away. Her only disappointment was seeing that the lilac hedges and the big willow tree in the back yard were gone, long since removed by previous owners through the years.

So with no possible option to have the wedding of her dreams standing under the stately willow tree in her back yard on Weber Street, Penny and Mark were married at a suburban Chicago courthouse on her birthday in August, in a simple ceremony witnessed only by two close friends. It was followed by a brief honeymoon at the only place they could afford as newlyweds, the Bide-a-wee Resort on beautiful Lake Delton in the Wisconsin Dells. Not exactly a dream trip to Paris, but they had fun for a few days hiking and swimming, lying on the sun-soaked shore, drinking cheap beer and eating hard boiled eggs for breakfast and then sandwiches they bought at a little mom and pop grocery store within walking distance of the resort. It was the best of times.

They were married for twenty-three years and had two wonderful children. Beautiful porcelain-skinned, raven-haired Meredith was born two years after they married, and quiet, happy tow-headed Jamey came along just 13 months later. Life was good while the kids were young; there were ballgames and dance recitals, slumber parties and high school plays, lots of happy years before things fell apart. Mark hit the road as a salesman for a large, national company and was gone five days a week most of the time, leaving Penny to deal with the kids, the house and her own job.

She could feel the distance growing between them, even before he came home from a trip one Friday afternoon, handed her a glass of wine and asked for the divorce. He was unemotionally matter of fact about it and Penny wasn't shocked. That might have been the saddest thing of all.

They had just been going through the motions for a few years. He rarely even called her anymore when he was gone all week. There was no argument, no hateful exchange of blaming the other; no begging for another chance, no saving what was beyond salvage. The entire divorce process took less than three months start to finish. It wasn't acrimonious, just a realization that passing in the hallways had been all they were doing since the kids had grown and gone. They just decided to make it official by formally going their separate ways.

Penny had grown comfortable doing her own thing in his absence, so when he left for good she sadly had barely noticed. Mark hadn't physically touched her in the months preceding their divorce, and what she had long suspected (but willfully ignored) proved to be true. She found out for certain there was another woman involved, as he announced shortly after things were final, that he was engaged.

Mark's bride Trudy was a tall, leggy blonde 20 years his junior with a toothpaste commercial smile, the mother of two small boys. Soon after they married they sent out a sickening sweet postcard announcing they were adding the "ours" to yours and mine. Penny's response had been an eye roll and a "have fun with that" as she crumpled it up and threw it in the trash. And so the Tomlins joined the ever-growing ranks of families juggling stepparents and siblings. Thank God they didn't have little ones to manage swapping weekends and headaches.

Under normal circumstances she supposed she would have been bitter or taken it personally; he was, after all, marrying someone barely older than his own daughter. When Penny found out, it didn't really even bother her. "Oh well," she told her friend Mavis. "Who doesn't want a trophy wife in their mid-life crisis? Have at it, Mark. We said 'I do,' too. Right up until we didn't." They laughed out loud over a glass of champagne at Penny and Mark's favorite restaurant. It was a week before she found out Mark had eloped and spent two weeks traveling Europe with Trudy – the trip they had always talked about taking together someday when the kids were grown and gone. She had to admit, that one stung a little – no a lot.

Avoiding mutual friends became her mission during Mark and Trudy's giddy, "aren't we such a cute couple" phase. Hearing tales about her former husband affectionately kissing his fetching bride at the top of the Eiffel Tower, strolling hand in hand along the canals of Venice or sunbathing on the island of Santorini was more than she could take.

All the while Penny was the sounding board for the kids in the midst of the inevitable struggle to accept the change, over how much time to spend with each parent at the holidays, and bruised feelings about Dad's "new" life and family taking over time that used to be dedicated to them.

Even though Penny's kids were older they were still surprised and a little hurt by the news. Still, in time they had all managed to forge a civil relationship amongst themselves and at this point in her life, Penny rarely thought about the past with Mark. Her adult children had their own relationship with their father, Penny no longer was brokering arrangements, and for that she was grateful. She was too busy with her weekly book club, visits to the gym trying to stave off the effects of Father Time, and occasionally meeting friends for a night out for dinner or the theater to worry about what Mark was up to. Every time she thought about him changing a smelly diaper, though, she did admit to smiling a little.

There was no lack of work to keep her busy. When the *City News* had to trim staff in the recent economic downturn she felt fortunate to have survived with her job intact, but was doing the work of two people these days. By Friday she was exhausted most of the time, and her perfect weekend was having nothing on the calendar and nobody with expectations that needed her. She cherished her alone time, and liked nothing better than curling up by the fireplace with a glass of wine and a great book or movie on a Saturday night. Far removed from her early years as a divorcee' when not having plans on a Saturday night meant you were being passed over.

And she still had Bora Bora. She vowed to someday send aging Mark and perky Trudy a postcard of herself standing on that sugar-white beach overlooking a crystal turquoise ocean, huts on stilts in the background and a string of flowers around her neck. Wouldn't it be fun to rub it in by adding a strikingly distinguished looking gentleman to the image? She closed her eyes and pictured suntanned arms intertwined, tropical drinks raised in a happy toast, lovebirds wearing matching ear-to-ear grins. Who said it couldn't happen? Mavis told her frequently to get out and strut her stuff, she was still a looker at any age, and a great catch by most standards. Maybe she should.

Penny dated sometimes. There was currently nobody special, but she had plenty of opportunities. Men still found her attractive even though she carried twenty-five extra menopausal pounds around stubbornly clinging to her hips, belly and thighs. There were more wrinkles around her eyes than she cared to confess, but overall she was still pretty put together for her age.

Honestly, Penny's apparent lack of desire was probably the biggest stumbling block on the dating path. It was less work to spend her free time doing exactly what she wanted to do without regard for anyone else's agenda or feelings than get all dressed up only to sit across the table from a date that left her unimpressed and wondering, "Why did I bother?" Mavis asked her once when they were talking about that very subject whether Penny thought her lack of enthusiasm for dating was maturity or apathy. Good question, for which Penny hadn't been able to come up with a definitive answer.

Looking in the mirror some days it was hard not to see the beautiful athletic girl who used to be staring back at her. How is it possible to still feel 35 inside and yet see the soft, round middle-aged woman she had become in the mirror? She admitted to Kathy not too long ago that it would be nice to find someone special with whom to spend her golden years, but if it never happened she suspected her life would be full and happy nonetheless. And she genuinely meant it.

Life hadn't always been easy in the last fifteen years. There were times when she longed to have someone to lean on, to have her back, to hear the words, "Don't worry about it Honey, I'll take care of it." A hug would be nice when she walked in the door, and it could get lonely eating alone watching Oprah reruns or some lame movie on television night after night. Still, she wasn't unhappy. She could come and go as she liked, and regularly turned down plans because, well, she could.

For a while she had a little dog named Donut, a small mixed breed that looked like a cross between Toto and a floor mop. She inherited Donut from one of the other tenants in the building who was moving to a place that wouldn't allow pets. Donut was always a friendly pup, greeting everyone in the building as they would walk in and out. He was well behaved and cute as a bug, and would show off his newest trick for a doggie treat. Penny couldn't stand the thought of Donut shivering in some cage at the animal shelter, or meeting an even worse fate that so many of those poor animals do. When she saw the flyer in the building entrance asking for anyone willing to take him in, she agreed in a heartbeat.

They were fast friends from the moment he trotted through her door. Donut was a faithful companion, another presence in the room to talk to when she got home after a long day. He was always happy to see her, always excited to go for a walk and couldn't wait to curl up beside her on the couch every evening to share her meal. He was the quintessential lap dog and Penny admittedly spoiled him beyond all reason. The house quickly became filled with stuffed toys, rubber balls, and plenty of his favorite goodies and snacks.

He had a special bed beside hers and slept with a stuffed bear she called Boo Boo. She hadn't moved the bed and Boo Boo even though Donut had been gone for almost three years now. Penny couldn't bear to part with them and every once in a while would talk to Donut like he was still there; sometimes out of habit, sometimes just because.

Donut lived to be in the neighborhood of about fifteen years old best as the veterinarian who consoled her as she held him for the last time could tell. One day he couldn't get up as she went to feed him his breakfast. He just lay in his little bed and whined when she tried to coax him outside.

She had seen it coming in the weeks before he died. There was a look in his eye, a tired sadness she tried to ignore. Gray in the face and moving slower every day, cloudy eyed and mostly deaf, poor little Donut smelled atrocious if not bathed regularly. She knew he dreaded the bathtub, but in his waning days didn't even fight that anymore. There was an air of resignation about him.

He hated company and would scurry away and hide under her bed if he sensed someone else in the apartment. She would have to carry him up and down the building steps and he couldn't even walk all the way around the block anymore. "Come on Buddy," she would try to encourage, "let's go for a walk," words that in years gone by would have sent him scampering for the hallway where his leash hung on a peg by the door. He would hop up and down, barking his excited little "woof-woof," urging her to put a move on it as she grabbed her jacket and clipped the leash to his collar.

In the week before he passed away, most of the time he just looked up with those sad, brown eyes as if to say, "You go on without me," and she would let him be, curled up in his little bed with Boo Boo under his chin. That day, his last, she knew he wasn't going to get up. It was time.

She held him tightly as the vet gave Donut the shot relaxing him into eternal sweet dreams. Penny cried softly into his fur when at last his breathing grew from shallow to non-existent. It was the right thing to do, and he passed away quietly in the arms of someone who loved him more than he knew. Penny cried long, anguished sobs every day for a week after she walked out of the veterinarian's office without her Donut. The emptiness felt too familiar, the stillness in the apartment was deafening.

Sometimes she still talked to Donut; felt him under her feet on days when he would have been such a comfort. As much as she missed him, she was relieved that she wouldn't have to find a place for him while she was gone over the holidays. He always hated being in a kennel and she felt so guilty leaving him with strangers. At least she wouldn't have to put up with his indignant way of punishing her when at last she would come to retrieve him. He would ignore her for at least a day, even refusing her offers of his favorite treat. Yes indeed, Donut could hold a grudge.

Finally with everything packed she checked her computer one more time to make sure her flight was still showed departing as scheduled. "Oh no!" she gasped as she read the words she was hoping not to see. "CANCELLED" was written in the space next to her flight in bold red letters. She quickly called the airline but was told in an automated message that all flights were being cancelled for the remainder of the evening and possibly all day tomorrow as the storm wasn't supposed to let up for at least another day. Numerous attempts to get through to a live person were met with a constant busy signal. Brokenhearted, she called Kathy who was still back at the office.

"Cancelled. My flight is cancelled," her disappointment evident as Kathy commiserated with her plight. "Ten years since I've seen my family at Christmas and the airport is shut down! I want to cry." There was a long moment of silence on the other end of the phone.

"Hey, wait a minute...doesn't Amtrak go to Fargo?" Kathy brightly suggested as the idea came to her. "I was thinking my old college roommate went out that way a few years back to visit relatives. I'm positive she took the train."

"I never thought of that," Penny paused racing over to her computer and quickly typing the word "Amtrak" into her search engine. "The train!" Penny had seen many times the big snowdrift busting engines clearing the tracks through town during the worst of Chicago's lake-effect storms. "Surely a train could get through the weather, right?" Penny said as she waited for the results to flash onto her screen. "You're a genius, Kathy. I have to run. I think this could work."

"Yeah, well, remember what a genius I am come annual review time." Kathy chuckled as she hung up the phone, then added a hasty, "Merry Christmas!"

Sure enough, there was a train leaving in two hours. It went through Milwaukee and Minneapolis, and would put her in Fargo by 6:00 am the next morning. That would be plenty of time to get to the lake before Sandra had finished her first cup of coffee. Just then her cell phone buzzed. The cab was downstairs. She grabbed her suitcase, threw her laptop in her bag and locked the door behind her, looking up to Heaven as she ran for the elevator. "Lord, if this works, it will be a Christmas miracle! Not as good as THE Christmas miracle, but darn close!" Penny hurried off the elevator on the first floor and spotted the yellow cab at the curb. She could feel the layer of ice under her feet as she walked out the door and hoped they could make it on time.

She leapt across a small drift into the toasty cab and buckled herself in for the ride as the driver put her bags in the trunk. As soon as he was ready to pull away, she exclaimed in an excited voice, "Change of plans, driver. Take me to Union Station!"

With a nod and a grunt of acknowledgement the driver pulled into the street and they were off to catch a train to Fargo. Maybe her holiday plans weren't ruined after all. On the way she booked her ticket online and called her mom and Sandra to let them know the weather was throwing a bit of a wrench into the plan but she was on her way. She was coming home.

It took almost an hour to go the few miles, but soon Penny could see the massive building and its huge Corinthian pillars gracing the limestone façade. She was going to make it!

An imposing building, Union Station sits on the west side of the Chicago River between West Adam Street and West Jackson Boulevard, just outside the Chicago Loop. That first summer as an intern Penny took a walking tour on one of her weekends off. It was a gorgeous building with gleaming marble floors, terracotta walls, and brass lights around the perimeter of the main hall. Considered one of the greatest indoor spaces in the entire country, most of the station is buried beneath streets and skyscrapers. The station was originally built in 1881, designed by the famed architect Daniel Burnham.

The Great Hall, with its soaring five-story interior boasted a 218-foot-long, barrel-vaulted skylight, which was blacked out in WWII so as not to be a target in case of enemy attack. The Great Hall was magnificent and was regularly used for special social events.

Penny was fortunate enough to attend the wedding reception of one of her coworkers a few years ago in the Great Hall. What a stunning setting in the evening, all lit up with candles, soft colored lights and music resonating around the room. She never imagined herself taking a train trip as she enjoyed the evening sharing in and celebrating the new couple's happiness. But here she was, on an adventure of her own.

The tour guide talked about the fact that more than 100,000 passengers travel through the turnstiles daily and over 6,000 of those passengers arrive and depart from the third busiest station on the Amtrak line every 24 hours. Passenger 6,001 was nearing the station, and would soon join the numerous travelers bound for holiday celebrations at the many stops along the way.

Penny paid the cabbie and dashed as quickly as possible up the steps and into the terminal. It was bustling with thousands of holiday travelers rushing to make their trains and connections. There was a brass quartet playing "Jolly Old St. Nicholas" as she looked around for gate information. Festive greenery and red bows, holly branches, garland and various Christmas scenes adorned the little shop windows as she made her way along the main hall to where the various concourses emerged.

Penny quickly fell in line searching the departure and arrival screens and found a kiosk to print her ticket. Ticket in hand, she checked to make sure she was heading in the right direction. Her hands were completely bulging with her luggage, purse and computer bag, so she tucked her ticket between her teeth and took off walking briskly down the corridor.

She would be traveling on the Empire Builder line that went all the way from Chicago through Milwaukee, Minneapolis, and on across the country following major portions of the Lewis and Clark trail. If you were going all the way to Spokane or Seattle, you'd roll through the majestic wilderness of Montana and enjoy spectacular views of Glacier National Park before ending up on the Pacific coast. This trip, Penny was going to be fortunate just to make it all the way to Fargo.

Penny found her train number on the schedule and saw she needed to go to the South Concourse and Gate C. Realizing she only had 30 minutes before departure, she hurried among the other passengers. Penny had to bob and weave around a woman walking with two small children and an over-packed stroller. The girl, who looked to be about five, was crying and pulling in the opposite direction while her mother trudged onward. Oh, the joys of parenthood!

Next obstacle was an elderly man in a dapper plaid fedora trailing a miniature fluff-ball of a dog dressed in a garishly bright holiday coat. The little sweater was adorned with bells that tinkled every time he took a step. As she made her way around them, she felt a momentary twinge of sadness. The little guy looked a lot like Donut. Looking back over her shoulder Penny flashed a smile and offered a pleasant "Merry Christmas," as she passed them and turned left onto the South Concourse.

Down the stairs and another seemingly endless city block later, she arrived at Gate C. Hurried passengers were boarding the train from each of several entrances. The porter at the first one she entered glanced at her ticket then said with a cheery smile, "Ma'am, you're in the sleeping car two down from here." Just as she was thanking him a nice young man in a perfectly tailored blue uniform and a brass tag announcing his name as JAMES, asked if she would like some help with her luggage. "You're a godsend!" Penny managed as he relieved her of the over-packed parcels.

James took her suitcase and computer bag then turned and walked briskly toward the open entrance to what would be her car.

Since she was traveling overnight, she had reserved one of the sleeping compartments. Penny was one of those people who needed to be reclined with a pillow under her head to get any sleep at all and she felt the additional money was worth the extra comfort. When she woke up, she would be in Fargo and her mother would be there to pick her up at the station. Just a few more hours!

Once inside the narrow hallway, James showed her where the restroom was and pointed to the door of her room. "You're right here in #121," he said, sliding the keycard though the lock and pushing open the narrow door. He must have sensed she was feeling stressed and a little overwhelmed and added, "They always serve drink specials for happy hour in the bar car." He winked as he set her bags on the floor of her compartment and handed her a map of the train. "Right there it is," he smiled as he took a pen and drew a line from her car through the next two in front of her to where she could have one of those happy hour drinks.

"You're a lifesaver, James. And psychic!" sighed Penny as she smiled and handed him a nice tip. He quickly vanished down the hall to help another passenger and Penny closed the door behind him. For the first time all day, Penny was able to take a deep breath, plop down in the little chair by the window and absorb the atmosphere of that historic station. She could see warm hellos as loved ones embraced on the platforms with each new arrival, and the sad sting of last goodbyes as others were left behind. It was a microcosm of everyday life, the coming and going, the joyous looking forward to, and the inevitable anguish of letting go.

Her space was tight but cozy and warm in a nostalgic 1950s way, with wallpaper covered in tiny, faded dusty pink roses. There was a small metal sink in the corner next to an even smaller closet space with a single shelf above it. The entire compartment smelled a little musty, as if someone had forgotten a wet towel under the bed and it had grown a bit moldy. Penny tried to open the window, thinking a few minutes of fresh air before they got underway would help immensely. No luck, the lock wouldn't budge. It must have iced over on the outside due to all the snow, she wagered.

Not to worry, she was always a prepared traveler. She usually packed a remedy for just about any occasion. Penny found her suitcase and from the zippered compartment on the outside of the bag pulled out a small bottle of lavender scented linen spray. "This ought to do the trick," she said as she liberally sprayed the bed covers, the pillow, the upholstered chair next to the small table situated just under the window. "There," she said with satisfaction as she took a deep breath. "That is way better." She tucked the spray back into her bag and took a seat by the window to relax for a moment.

The window looked out at other trains loading and unloading their human cargo. Everyone was rushing more urgently now as the loudspeaker announced imminent departures.

Penny tucked her computer bag into the small closet, threw her suitcase on the pint-sized foldout bed, and sat in the chair thinking for a moment what it must have been like when people traveled this way all the time. She imagined it was once considered glamorous and extravagant to ride in such a fashion. Now, for her anyway, it was a matter of necessity.

The last of the goodbyes were exchanged outside her window and the porters yelled their final call to passengers. Soon there was a slight jerky motion and Penny felt the unsteady movement as her train began pulling out of the station. Creeping slowly at first, they picked up speed heading through the underground maze. It was dark for some time as they made their way out of the pitch-black labyrinth and into what was left of daylight. She sat in the chair looking out the window, watching the darkness become lighter and lighter, the sleek steel horse going faster and faster until they burst out of the tunnel and the snow churned around the windows like billowing clouds.

It wasn't yet dark as they pushed on through the city, skyscrapers obscured by the blizzard. They were leaving Chicago behind to deal with Mother Nature's wrath. Penny watched as they moved past miles of red tail lights, cars she could tell were stuck in traffic inching through the streets and around the Loop trying desperately to get out of the elements. The storm definitely had the city in its grasp and was showing no signs of mercy. At least she was safe and sound…and getting out.

Once they had been underway for an hour or so, Penny shut off her email, stowed her computer back in the bag and got out the little map of the train James had left with her. "Now, where is that bar car?" She was ready for a nice, relaxing glass of wine and then figured she would turn in early after grabbing a quick bite to eat.

She combed her hair, put on a little fresh lipstick, and then smoothed the wrinkles in her sweater proclaiming that was as good as she'd look today. Penny walked unsteadily down the hallway and through the next two cars grabbing onto the railing to keep from falling over as the train swayed rhythmically down the tracks.

The bar car was brightly lit, very crowded, and there was holiday music playing softly in the background, "Have yourself a merry little Christmas...." Penny hummed along as she searched the car for a place to sit down and order a drink.

The long, half-moon shaped wooden bar was a thing of beauty from a bygone era. The back wall was mirrored glass with intricately etched, beveled edges running the expanse of the bar. Behind the serving area there were shiny brass shelves with narrow rails to keep the honey-colored bottles of alcohol from falling while in motion.

The bartender was dressed in what appeared to be a period costume, perhaps turn of the last century, complete with a waxed handlebar mustache and dapper English-style herringbone cap tilted jauntily at an angle. He wore an emerald green bow tie, a crisp white apron was around his waist and he was hustling back and forth delivering drinks to an enthusiastic crowd, laughing and making conversation as he did so.

She soon realized the bar area itself was packed; so sitting at one of the seats was impossible. It was strictly standing room only. She was way too weary to stand and fight the crowd, so for a second she thought about turning around and relying on room service for a drink and something to eat. But her room was so small, and the desk space could barely hold her laptop much less a tray of food and a drink. She moved a little further into the car and looked around.

There were several booths under the windows that stretched the length of the car. She spotted an empty seat across from an older woman who appeared to be in her eighties, wearing a navy blue crepe dress with a white Peter Pan collar and a strand of large pearls. Her neatly coiffed chignon was tucked up under a small, burgundy pillbox hat and a pair of black gloves was sitting neatly beside her napkin on the table. She was plump in a soft, huggable way, yet stylish and neat as a pin. "She looks friendly," Penny said to herself as she headed that direction.

As Penny approached she saw the woman remove a pair of rather thick glasses from her nose. She dabbed briefly at each eye and then continued with the glasses themselves, wiping each lens with a handkerchief she had pulled from a rather large tapestry handbag that was sitting on the bench seat beside her.

By the time Penny made her way through the crowd, the woman was staring out the window mindlessly fingering the stem of a glass of red wine. A little out of breath from struggling through the crowd standing at the bar Penny managed, "Do you mind if I join you?" while flashing a tentative smile, "this seems to be the only open seat in the room."

Looking startled for a moment, the woman replied, "Oh my yes, please do have a seat. Some company would be so nice." She looked up as she spoke in a somewhat shaky voice, clearing her throat while motioning for Penny to sit across from her. As Penny began to sit down she hesitated a moment. That fragrance! My gosh, she would know it anywhere. The woman was wearing the same perfume that her grandmother Mary had always worn. It was Shalimar. The familiar scent flooded Penny with memories and in that moment, she wished it was her grandmother sitting across from her. She wanted to hug her, to breathe in that wonderful perfume, to feel the welcoming hug, to feel the breath of her.

Born in Kentucky in 1899, Penny's maternal grandmother Mary Rolliver was a woman before her time. She traveled with her family by train to the prairie town of Bozeman, Montana, where she rode in a horse-drawn wagon to a one-room schoolhouse. Penny loved it when Grandma M (or just M sometimes) told stories that Penny thought were really quite something about growing up in such a rustic place.

There was a wood burning stove in the back of the wagon and they would pile blankets on their laps to keep from freezing in the winter. Penny loved to hear stories of "the olden days" and probably asked a lot of questions. M never seemed to mind, she eagerly shared her tales.

Grandma M graduated from high school in Montana, eventually moving back a little further east. She opened a beauty shop in the back of a men's clothing store in a small town in North Dakota by the name of Hebron. She ended up marrying a handsome gentleman who worked across the street in a bank owned by his father.

Henry Truman was a big, burly man who smoked smelly cigars and always came to visit with shiny new pennies to hand out. Sadly, he would die of a heart attack when Penny was a very small girl so she didn't remember much about him. But Grandma Mary lived to be 102 years old and Penny had many wonderful memories of her.

Sometimes M would come to stay when Penny's parents were away on trips or business. She would make the most amazing caramel rolls and homemade chicken and noodles or pot roast with brown potatoes and glazed carrots. Penny loved Grandma Truman fiercely, she suspected in part because M always told Penny she was special. "I could always tell you needed a little extra love," she would say. And that was probably true.

Penny was the middle child of three girls that were born within five years. She supposed she might have gotten a little lost in the shuffle; it couldn't have been easy for her mother with three little ones to attend to. She knew how tough it was when her own were young, and there were only two of them!

Growing up, Penny was always the clown in the family pictures, the funny goofball doing outlandish things to get attention. She was both animated and yet a bit of an introvert, a dichotomy with a creative streak a mile wide who liked to draw and write poetry and stories. She had a vivid imagination and was incredibly sensitive, probably overly so.

Penny knew she worried too much, was a bit of a hypochondriac, and never really felt at peace with herself or around others, the proverbial odd duck out although she didn't know exactly why. She always felt a little nervous and lacked confidence, although in some situations she was fine, like playing music or writing. She knew those were skills where she was at least decently talented. Grandma Mary made her feel special and that it was okay to be a little different.

Penny struggled sometimes in class and looking back on it might have had a mild case of what they now call attention deficit disorder. Her mind would often race with repeated thoughts, words, numbers and phrases and sometimes concepts would jumble together in her head. She still found it difficult to focus on one task at a time even today.

When there was a project due and a tight deadline Penny had to silently talk through each obstacle, willing herself to take it one step at a time. She was still very easily sidetracked or distracted. Thankfully her assistant Kathy was highly organized and often knew exactly when Penny was struggling, offering her expertise and assistance. Kathy was a jewel, and Penny made sure she rewarded Kathy appropriately with bonuses and nice raises whenever she could.

As a child Penny had little confidence when it came to school. Maybe it was the fact she had no brain at all when it came to math. None. Zero. Nada. Zilch. They introduced "new math" when she was in sixth grade and the battle for passing grades in that subject set in for good. She wasn't so sure what was wrong with the "old" math, but the new stuff had her completely baffled.

And forget it when everyone else in high school moved on to Algebra...and even Advanced Algebra. Penny would chew her fingernails to the nub and become overwhelmed with dread just thinking about having to take a math test. Even her kindest teachers would look at her like she was missing a gene when they would show her a problem over and over until she was literally cross-eyed. Yet to her it remained as difficult as trying to decipher ancient hieroglyphics.

Ditto her lack of ability in science, save for maybe geography. The formulas and concepts around physics and chemistry completely eluded her and left her doodling instead of paying attention. It all seemed so far over her head. When it came to literature and history, music and creative writing, however, Penny could definitely hold her own. In fact, she could more than just hold her own. Her English teacher Mrs. Trott would often put positive remarks on her papers, and in side conversations tried to encourage her to gravitate in that direction as she developed a certain writing style by the time she was well into high school.

Penny knew Mrs. Trott was right, that she did have at least a modicum of talent when it came to cobbling words together. Besides, she truly loved words and how they could tell a story or evoke emotion. Didn't winning high marks in vocal competitions speak well of her abilities in that regard as well? To be fair, she wasn't a total loser by any stretch; just lacked poise and self-assurance for some reason.

It might have had something to do with the fact that Sandra was such a shining star. It was tough to measure up to someone for whom outstanding grades and talent seemed to come effortlessly;

at least by Penny's perception. No doubt Sandra had to work hard and put a lot of time into her studies too, but her brain seemed to work in a whole different way than Penny's did. Penny wished she could have the ability, the talent, confidence and friends that Sandra did.

Everyone loved Cara, so sweet and kind, never gave anyone a moment's worry and got along with everyone. Cara was two years behind Penny in school. She was more quiet and studious, also made good grades, and was popular with lots of good friends. Even today Penny would tell anyone who would listen that Cara was one of the nicest, funniest people you'd ever want to meet and if she weren't her sister, she'd want to be Cara's best friend.

And then there was the baby of the family, Ricky. He came along eight years after Penny was born, the only male in her entire generation. She used to joke that the angels sang and the sun shone at night when he came into the world, the much-anticipated heir to the Raney dynasty. But that lofty position too, would have its share of challenges. She couldn't imagine growing up having to be the only boy in the bunch with three sisters already entrenched in their roles. There were plenty of times she drew the short straw as they chose who would be left to babysit him when their parents went out to one social event or another – which was a regular ritual.

Still, Penny loved Ricky as they all did, and spent her fair share of time babying him, feeding and playing with him like he was an overgrown baby doll. And most of the time he went right along with the program; until he got a little older and was following their father around like a shadow.

Penny just seemed to be "that" child, you know, the one no one could ever quite figure out. When she was in college and researching information for a paper she was doing on sibling rivalry for a psychology class, she came across this quote from researcher and

When I Get Home

author Ellen Galinsky that made sense to her. *"In families children tend to take on stock roles, as if there were hats hung up in some secret place, visible only to the children. Each succeeding child selects a hat and takes on that role: the good child, the black sheep, the clown, and so forth."*

She printed it out and for a long time had it pinned to her dorm room bulletin board. Penny had scribbled in red pen on the page, "clownish black sheep hat, second from the left." It was as if finally after all those years a label existed for what she had been feeling.

When she was a child, Penny enjoyed spending time alone wandering in the hills across the railroad tracks from their little gray cape cod with the red door on Weber Street. She loved the outdoors and was always bringing home little critters she would find or the family dogs would manage to raid from a ground nest in the spring. Baby bunnies, birds, even a stray cat or two found their home in the Raney garage or backyard playhouse at one time or another. Much to her mother Betsy's chagrin, it wasn't unusual to find frogs and lizards, even snakes living in a box on the back porch. She was a rescuer, a saver of tiny forlorn souls of the animal world.

When a friend had recently asked her if she'd like to volunteer at one of the local animal rescue shelters with her every other weekend, "Good Lord no," was Penny's adamant reply. "I'd see one sad face in a cage and I'd be overrun with pets at my apartment in no time. I can't stand to see an animal looking lost or alone. I'm happy to donate financially or help in any other way, but if I actually saw their little faces my neighbors would accuse me of stocking an ark somewhere within a month." She laughed. But it was true. She couldn't resist a helpless animal in need.

When she was older she was drawn to music and drama. She especially loved to be in the school plays and used to secretly dream of being in musical theater someday. How exciting to be under the lights of Broadway, showered with applause. Playing some other character always seemed like a way to do more than express herself; she could BE someone else for a little while. She had confidence playing another person, much more than just being Penny.

By the time she was in high school and regularly performing in plays, her dad was traveling all the time having landed a much more lucrative and important position with a manufacturing company. He was gone most of every week and was busy on the weekends. On one of the rare occasions he actually got to see her performance in one of the school productions, Penny was portraying a rather outlandish character that dressed in a wild costume with a turban on her head, not unlike an overly dramatic old Hollywood actress. It was a very fun part to bring to life and Penny did just that…she played it to the hilt!

After the show as they were driving home her dad remarked with a chuckle, "Not sure how much of that performance actually required acting!" Their whole family had laughed and teased her over that one. She supposed it truly wasn't much of a stretch to play the part.

Penny recognized the power of words even as a young child and perhaps that is why she was drawn to writing. They could wound and cut and scar deeply, or they could be healing and nurturing, arousing emotions of all kinds. Never feeling like she fit in, she grew up with few close friends and always felt like a bit of a misfit. Unable to put her own finger on it, maybe Grandma Truman was right. Maybe she did just need a little extra love. She always felt that warm sense of understanding with Grandma M, and in that moment on the train, longed for it again.

When M was at least 100, Penny knew she probably wouldn't be around for many more years. On one visit Penny started asking her all kinds of questions and wrote down the answers so she wouldn't forget. "Tell me about your first car ride, about prohibition, about women getting the right to vote." All of those and so much more happened during her lifetime. Grandma M's face would light up as she talked about memories from years and years ago, telling stories of her childhood, of her courting and marriage. She and Grandpa Henry had spent their month-long honeymoon taking a train all the way across Canada. What an adventure that must have been! And now here was Penny taking a long train ride herself.

When Grandma M was in a nursing home and was close to death, Penny went to visit. She was there by her bed in the nursing home for several hours, the two of them alone in the dim light. Penny held M's hand and put a cool cloth on her head. "That feels so good," were the last words her grandmother would say out loud. Penny talked to her as though they were having one of their normal conversations. She talked about Mark and the kids, of work and friends, of Sandra and Cara and Rick, of plans for the summer. When she left she never really thought that would be the last time she would see her. But it was.

When she got the call the next morning telling her Grandma M was gone, Penny was inconsolable. Mark was at work and she had taken the day off because it was right before the 4th of July. She cried alone all day and into the night, long anguished sobs. Another person she loved and who loved her back was gone. Part of her was afraid nobody would ever love her so unconditionally again; nobody would ever see the good in her like M did, the "special."

The smell of that perfume brought those memories rushing back to the point her eyes filled with tears and it took her a moment to realize she wasn't being polite.

"Oh my goodness, I am sorry. I completely forgot to introduce myself. I'm Penny." She reached out her hand and the woman took it in her own frail hands, which were shaking slightly.

"It is a pleasure to meet you. I'm Madeline. But you can call me M. All of my friends just call me M." The look of surprise on Penny's face must have been evident, for Madeline quickly said, "Are you all right, Dear?"

"Sorry. Yes, I'm fine," she hesitated. "It's just that, well, my grandmother's name was Mary. And everyone called her M, too. You wear her same perfume. It is just such a funny coincidence. I didn't mean to act surprised. It is lovely to make your acquaintance."

"Where are you heading on this stormy night?" Madeline asked, taking a sip of wine.

"I'm just heading home to visit my family for the holidays. Last stop for me is Fargo. And you?" Penny replied.

"We're getting off at the same stop. How funny is that," she took another sip of her wine and smiled across the table. "I wasn't sure we'd even be able to make the trip because of the awful weather. I'm so glad you sat down. I believe we were meant to be travel companions."

Penny tilted her head and with a confused look asked, "We? Are you traveling with someone? I hope I'm not taking their seat."

"Oh no," Madeline said softly and then added solemnly; "I'm taking my husband home to be buried where we both grew up and have family. I have a sister and several cousins in the Mapleton area and Walter has a younger brother Tom, who lives in Moorhead. Tom had planned to pick me up but I'm wondering if the weather might make it impossible for them to venture out to get me. None of them drive much anymore when the weather takes a turn."

She went on, "Walter passed away a few days ago. Heart issues," Madeline said wistfully as she placed her hand over her own. Penny could see her soft gray eyes fill with tears and she reached across the table placing her hand on Madeline's. "We're having a service the day after Christmas. The funeral home was kind enough to make all of the arrangements, so I won't have to worry about a thing once we arrive."

"Madeline, I'm so very sorry for your loss." Penny said quietly. "I hope you had many, many happy years together. I'd enjoy hearing about him if you'd like to share."

Madeline sniffled slightly, dabbing her nose with her handkerchief. She managed what resembled a half smile and her eyes brightened a bit. "Oh, he was a handsome man. Not terribly tall and always a little stout, but he had the most wonderful green eyes and oh my, could he dance. He could jitterbug and lindy hop like nobody's business; even won a contest or two in the day." Bragging a little as she continued, "I'd had a few beaus before Walter, but once I laid eyes on him," she rolled her eyes and laughed, "well, it was love." The look on Madeline's face was one of absolute joy as she went on telling Penny about that cherished memory.

"We met at a dance when Duke Ellington came to perform at the Crystal Ballroom back in 1940 before Walter joined the service. What a place that was. I remember it was on the second floor of the Fargo City Auditorium and had a huge glass ball hanging from the ceiling that reflected the dancehall lights. Oh my, we really thought we were something dancing around that fabulous room under the sparkling lights." She stopped talking and looked down at her glass with a smile on her face. Penny could tell Madeline had been transported for a moment back to the Crystal Ballroom in the arms of her beloved Walter.

"Years later we found out the performance had actually been recorded and Walter surprised me for Christmas one year with the records. I still have them."

"What a treasure," Penny said with honest sincerity. "Isn't it funny how just thinking about a song can take us back to that time and we're there again; even if it is only for a moment?"

Madeline continued, "We were together 63 years. We owned a hardware store bought with money I'd scrimped and saved while he was in the Army during WWII. We unfortunately weren't ever blessed with children, so the store and all of our regular customers were our family. It truly was a wonderful life.

We sold the store a few years ago and bought a little place in Florida by the ocean so Walter could go fishing and we could enjoy the sunshine. Two rocking chairs are sitting on the porch where we would rock and visit every night as the sun went down," her voice trailed off a little and became quieter. "We were in Chicago visiting friends when he fell ill. My only regret is that he went first. I miss him terribly." Madeline stared out the window and took the last sip of her wine.

"I haven't known you long, M, but I think Walter was a lucky man. You were fortunate to have found each other." Penny said as she held onto Madeline's hand.

"Are you married, Penny?" Madeline asked as she folded her napkin and began looking for her purse.

"I've been divorced for several years. But I'm fine. I have a great job and wonderful children and grandchildren, friends. I certainly can't complain." Penny responded.

"You're such a beautiful woman," Madeline said with a touch of sadness in her voice, as if she felt sorry for Penny. "I wouldn't give up on finding that special someone. You never can tell where you'll find the right person. And when you do, never take love for granted,

Penny." Madeline went on, "Sometimes love finds us, sometimes we find love. And the best surprises are always unexpected. Everyone deserves the kind of love I had with Walter. If it comes your way, in whatever way, hold onto it. I'm going to wish that for you." She had the most loving look on her face as she patted Penny's hand.

"Now," Madeline said with a deep sigh, "I'm going to go back to my room and finish reading a book I brought with me. It has been a very long day. Thank you so much for your company. I feel much better than when I sat down."

"The pleasure has been all mine," Penny offered. "I appreciate you letting me share your table…and your memories. You must let us give you a ride to wherever you're going when we get to Fargo. I absolutely insist. Moorhead is right on the way to my sister's lake home. It is the very least I can do for you allowing me to share your table and wonderful conversation." Madeline started to protest, "I won't take no for an answer!" Penny insisted. "I'm in compartment 121. When we near Fargo, please come by and I will arrange for a porter to help with our bags."

"Are you sure it isn't any trouble?" Madeline asked hesitantly, but clearly relieved for the assistance.

"We were meant to be travel companions, remember?" Penny smiled reassuringly. "We're BOTH going to get where we're going, as my grandmother used to say, "if the good Lord's willin', and the creek don't rise!" With that M laughed and reached for her purse. "You win. I will come by 121 and we'll finish our trip together." Madeline took her purse and got up from the table a little unsteadily. Penny reached out and gave her a long hug, taking in the familiar scent of Shalimar, grateful for the cancelled flight that gave her the chance to meet such a lovely lady. The nostalgic scent lingered in the air long after Madeline had made her way out the door and down the hall.

"Next stop, Milwaukee!" a voice over the speaker said loudly. Several people in the bar car finished their beverages and started to make their way for the doors at either end of the car, one stop closer to their destination and anxious relatives waiting to greet them. Penny decided to have one more glass of wine since the first one had tasted so good and gave her a warm glow as she stared out the window into the moonlit sky. Why not, she wasn't getting off at this stop. She still had hours to go.

The snow was madly swirling around the train but she could make out the city lights of Milwaukee in the distance. From a vintage jukebox in the corner a scratchy old 45 record was adding the cheery tune "Up on the Housetop" to the already charged atmosphere. "Ho, ho, ho, who wouldn't go", she hummed along as she sat by the window. By now she was enjoying the jovial ambiance and laughter surrounding her as her fellow passengers chatted about the holidays and toasted to the upcoming year. "Click, click click…down through the chimney with good St. Nick."

Glasses clinked and the hum of happy conversation in the background mixed with the holiday music made Penny glad she was part of it all. She was excited to be one of the lucky people going home to be with family. She wondered if Roger ever made it to Tampa, and whether Kathy's family had arrived from Fort Wayne. She hoped so.

As the train slowed down they wound through downtown Milwaukee. The Milwaukee Station was near the 6th Street Bridge, which was all lit up for the holidays. Even through the snow it was a beautiful evening. As they pulled into the station, Penny watched as throngs of people made their way off the train carrying packages and suitcases, bundled up against the cold weather. In a few more short hours, it would be her turn to make her way through the terminal. No doubt her mother would be losing sleep in anticipation of their long-awaited visit.

The old train depot in downtown Fargo is on 4th Street, a stone's throw from Viking Ship Park along the great Red River of the North. Hopefully the snow would let up as they moved further west and the roads wouldn't be too bad. She didn't want her mother out so early in the morning and could certainly call for a taxi if need be. Maybe Sandra would even drive the hour into Fargo to get them both if the roads were icy. She would find Madeline and make sure she got to her destination as well.

More passengers, more bags boarded the train as Penny ordered the cheese plate to have with her second glass of wine. She was pleasantly surprised when the waiter brought it to her, beautifully presented with fresh grapes and melon, strawberries and orange slices surrounding a generous portion of various hard cheeses and a basket of assorted crackers. It was just what she needed, as she was feeling a little lightheaded from the wine.

Penny munched greedily on the delicious assortment of fresh cheese and fruit, nibbling crackers in between sips of wine as she watched the activity going on outside her window. Her face glowed in the light of the candle that sat on her table and for a moment she caught the eye of a little boy about 5 or 6 years old as he tugged on what appeared to be his frenzied mother's arm. They were rushing to get on the train with way too many packages. He grinned at her and waved as the boy's mother snatched his arm and took off for an open train entrance. Penny waved back but he had already disappeared into the mass of people coming and going.

She was still watching the crowd when she spotted a tall man in a dark coat with a bright red scarf wrapped around his neck. He was wearing dark glasses and had a shock of stark white hair that made her stop and take a second look. For a moment she thought she recognized him. She was sure it couldn't be, but it looked like her old high school sweetheart, Jake Henderson. That gait, that slight swagger as he made his way through the mass of passengers reminded her so much of the dashing quarterback of their high school football team – and the very first love of Penny Raney's life.

Jake Henderson was a star athlete in football, basketball and a 4-year letterman in track as if that weren't enough. He was first string All-State football team three of his four years, and was awarded a full-ride scholarship to Iowa State. At ISU, he set passing records that stood for two decades after he graduated. Penny knew he had gone on to medical school at Stanford and that he was a rather famous surgeon somewhere in the Midwest, although she was unsure of the exact location. To hear that he was extremely successful didn't surprise her at all; he was always driven to be the best. She supposed he was married to some willowy model of a wife, living the classic American dream happily ever after; a big house in the suburbs and elegant cherub-faced children in private school.

Penny had long since lost track of him but who ever forgets their first real love. Neither of them had gone to any of the recent class reunions. Even with the internet making it much easier to stay in touch, she hadn't made much of an effort to reconnect with anyone she had gone to high school with, least of all Jake. Part of her didn't want to know about his sophisticated wife and career filled with accolades. Not that she was embarrassed about where she was in her own life, but Jake Henderson was someone you just don't get over losing. Merely thinking about it brought about feelings of jealousy. She didn't want to know the woman who was spending her life with the man she had considered her soul mate. Thinking about him was still tinged with sadness regardless of the passage of time.

Although it had been years since she had seen Jake, she still thought about him often. She would see a tall, athletic blonde in a crowd and her heart would skip a beat. She fantasized about running into him like a scene out of some inane chick flick. Their eyes would meet across a crowded room, the music would swell, he would rush to her side and they would embrace as if they had never parted. How many times through the years she had wished it were true, they had never parted.

Jake was a year older and a senior when she was a junior. They had chemistry and algebra together – both classes Penny struggled with and he breezed through. Not just a great athlete, but a star student as well, he would help Penny while she toiled with math and science. Jake never even seemed to open a book and yet he had all the answers.

She always made sure to sit by him and he was kind enough to help her with homework during their 6th period library time. Their romance blossomed under the watchful eye of Mrs. Haveling the librarian, who would walk by repeatedly when she saw them together. She looked down at them through her reading glasses, which were perched precariously at the end of her pointy nose and hissed a soft "QUIET!" if they giggled too loudly. And they giggled often.

Jake was almost 6'4" tall, with a lean, muscular build and a full head of white-blonde hair that stood out against his blue eyes and bronze skin in the summer. He had a wicked sense of humor, which attracted her more than anything. "Hey hey, Babydoll, what's shakin'?" he would yell as he walked down the hallway at school or bounded up her front steps to take her out for a date.

Jake greeted her the same exact way every time. Penny wore her long brown hair parted in the middle, which was the style back in the early 1970s. Jake would take his fingers and softly brush her hair away from her face and give her a kiss on the lips. "Hey hey, Babydoll! I missed you," he would whisper in her ear.

The summer before he went away to college was so much fun. They ran with Jake's best friend Bud Chandler and his girlfriend Rita. They went to dances at the Lisbon Park Pavilion and swam at the local pool down in Sandager Park almost every afternoon when Bud and Jake were done working in the fields for one of the local farmers. Most boys found jobs working on farms in the summer – no shortage of work to be done in farm country.

Penny and Rita both worked as carhops at the local drive-in burger joint so they always had tip money to buy the latest records and 8 track tapes, makeup and movie tickets. They would take off on the weekends in Jake's black Ford Mustang and drive over to Detroit Lakes in Minnesota where Bud's family had a lake cabin. They would go water skiing and tubing all afternoon until they were dog dead tired. At night after his parents went to bed they'd sneak Pabst Blue Ribbon beers from the fridge in the garage and stare up at the stars from blankets on the beach. Most of the time they all fell asleep before the bonfire they built flickered out.

It was on one of those magical, warm summer nights when Jake rolled over, brushed her hair away from her face and said, "I love you, Penny," for the first time. She told him she loved him too and he smiled his big toothy grin. They kissed for a long time, and then curled up together on that blanket holding hands until morning. It was so beautiful, so innocent. And of course when you're 17, you think…forever.

Jake's parents John and Myrna owned one of the two drug stores in town. His father was a pharmacist and his mother worked in the front of the store checking out customers at the cash register. They were lovely people and treated her like a daughter, inviting her to the big Lutheran church on the hill for Sunday services and often having her over for dinner afterwards. They made her feel as if she were part of the family, and she loved spending time with them playing cards and making popcorn on Saturday nights.

I think they were every bit as disappointed as she was when Jake broke things off when he went away to college in the fall of her senior year. Penny was completely inconsolable. Heartbroken was more like it. She missed him so terribly, and lay awake at night in jealous fits over all the pretty college girls he was probably flirting with. Every night that went by when the phone wouldn't ring she would cry into her pillow and tell herself maybe he never missed her at all.

She knew why he wanted to end things before he left, even appreciated his reasoning. Penny believed him when he told her she would always be his first love. He said he wanted to be fair to her, knowing there would be more football games, school dances, and prom. He wanted her to enjoy her senior year without guilt if someone else asked her to go, as he wouldn't be home in all likelihood until Christmas what with football and then basketball, plus school and final exams.

Jake would be getting used to his new life away at college and wanted that same freedom. It would be a whole new world for both of them. He assured her no matter what, he would always care for her. She would forever be his Babydoll.

The first few weeks he was away were the hardest. It was before the days of internet and cell phones, when talking and being connected was not as easy as the touch of a button. They wrote letters for a while but it became too painful to just be friends when they had been so much more.

By Christmas break they hadn't spoken or written in weeks and it was awkward when they did run into each other. They made polite conversation about how school was going and wow, wasn't it cold this early in the winter; she wished his basketball team well.

He told her he knew she would ace the next algebra test and give Mrs. Haveling a hug from him, ha-ha. It killed her to have him walk away and drive off with his buddies instead of her by his side. Her pulse would race every time she would see a black Ford Mustang drive down the street thinking it was him coming to pick her up for a fun night on the town. It never would be. All these years later the thought of him made her heart beat a little faster. It was like she was 17 again, the sting of loss and regret as fresh as yesterday. Jake Henderson was the type of guy you never stopped missing, and could never truly replace.

Sitting on the train looking out through the foggy window she could have sworn she saw Jake towering above everyone below, but she knew it had to be just her imagination. It was Christmas, the season of miracles, but even she knew that would be asking just a little too much.

"Aaaallll aboard!" They were getting ready to pull out of the station again. She heard the clanging of bells and felt the now familiar jerking motion as they slowly crept forward. Soon Milwaukee would be behind them, Minneapolis in front of them and the long night of winding west through the Wisconsin countryside had begun.

Penny took the last sip of wine from her glass, swallowed the remaining grapes on the plate in front of her and asked for the check. It was time to go get a little more work done before she turned in for the night. It seemed like it should be very late, but it got dark so early these days, it really was just after 6:30.

She paid for her drinks and food and got up to make her way back to her sleeping compartment. The train was going faster now, and it was rocking back and forth much more than she had remembered as they left Chicago. She had to hold on tight to the railings that ran along the wall to keep from losing her balance.

When I Get Home

"Man, that wind is really blowing," said one of the porters who was carrying a small tray of food down the hall as he passed by her. "Hang on Ma'am." She did just that and finally made it back to her room, slid the key in the door of compartment 121 and kicked her shoes off.

The tiny space was cozy and warm, and the rhythmic movement of the train soon would make her drowsy. She certainly hoped she could get to sleep in the tiny bed that was no wider than a child's crib and barely any longer. As she was looking for a place to put her bag, she realized it was too big to keep on the bed, and it wouldn't fit in the miniature closet above the sink. Penny noticed the top berth was fastened to the wall on either end by a strap that looked like it just snapped into place.

She thought if she could get that top berth down it would make a good storage spot for her bag and give her a little more room in case she needed to use the restroom in the middle of the night. The last thing she needed was to trip over her own bag and break an ankle or something. No, she wanted to arrive in one piece.

Sure enough, with one try she was easily able to get the snap holding up the right side of the bed undone. "Wow, this bed is heavy," she thought as she moved to unhook the left side.

The snap on the left was much more stubborn, like it hadn't been unsnapped in ages and was partially rusted together. She pulled and pulled but couldn't get it to budge. "Oh great," she muttered to herself as she tried one last time to get it loose, "there goes that ingenious plan."

Her assistant Kathy always made fun of the myriad of unusual items that inevitably seemed to find a home in her purse. Always one to carry tools for every need when traveling, she shuffled through her big brown Coach bag to see if there was anything she could use to help pry that snap loose. She was now on a mission, and that darn snap was NOT going to get the best of her.

The light wasn't the best, and she was having trouble seeing into the bottom of her sizable bag when her fingers finally closed around an old metal letter opener that she had thrown in at the last minute when leaving the office. She had taken some mail with her to read on the train and as an afterthought tossed in the opener.

"Eureka!" she grinned as she pulled the tool from her bag and proceeded to wedge its metal point between the snap and its rusted housing. Penny worked at it with determination and all the strength she could muster. Again and again she worked the tip of the letter opener around the crusty brown edge of the snap case. "Come on you stubborn bugger, open up."

Outside her compartment she could hear a porter talking to someone, laughing and apparently providing directions to somewhere in the train. She thought for a moment about asking for assistance, but they sounded like they were having a fun conversation so she kept at it on her own.

She had grown exasperated and was about to give up when without warning the strap itself broke where the two pieces of worn gray leather were fastened together. At that same exact moment, the train took a sudden and rather violent jerk to the left as they rounded a curve in the track.

Almost as if in slow motion, the weighty top berth gave way and slammed down hard right on top of her head. She stumbled forward grabbing the spot where it was now throbbing as she fell. The room was spinning, she was seeing stars and everything was becoming darker, the sounds more and more muffled. The laugher in the hallway now seemed far off in the distance. Had they moved away from her door? She thought she heard the howling wind making a slight moaning sound through what must be a crack in the window. Was that Penny's own voice?

She fell onto the bed and began drifting in and out of consciousness. "I'm so tired," she whispered. All she could think about was going to sleep. Penny managed to curl up under the coverlet on the bed, fumbling for the small square pillow she knew was there and shoved it under her head. "So very tired." She was barely aware of her surroundings, just the ever-present click click, click click, as the train swayed softly side to side down the track. Click click, click click......click click. "I just need to rest."

Penny thought the soft lavender scent and the downy comfort of the pillow cradling her head felt so wonderful. She breathed in deeply and felt calm and snug and safe. A peaceful, warm feeling came over her as she slipped off into a slumber as deep as the snow in January and as dark as the bottom of an empty wishing well. The train rolled down the track and the wind blew hard, and the whole world was quiet under the stars. The hours ticked by as Penny slept.

She had no idea how long she'd been out, but it seemed like it should be well after midnight when she first began to stir. As the fog started to lift from her sluggish brain, she became aware of a familiar sound somewhere in the back of her mind. It was barely audible and faint at first, but as she lay in the shadowy stillness she began to hear it more clearly. Music!

She strained to hear the words that were becoming purer and more distinct. Penny soon realized it was a song she knew by heart. "What Child is this who laid to rest, on Mary's lap is sleeping." There was a piano, and a voice. No, two voices. They were singing beautifully in harmony. "Whom angels greet with anthems sweet." She could make out a rich alto and sweet, lyric soprano as the melody continued into the chorus. "This, this is Christ the King whom shepherds guard and angels sing... "

As her eyes fluttered open, she tried to adapt to the darkness of the room. It slowly dawned on her that she was not moving. Had they stopped again? Minneapolis maybe? There was no swaying of the train; no hushed voices in the hall. It was pitch black and quiet except for the strains of one of her favorite holiday songs somewhere off in another room, maybe down the hall. The bar car? "They must be having a sing-a-long," she said to herself as she tried to get her bearings, gingerly pulling herself up on her elbows to listen more closely.

As her eyes adjusted to the darkness, she could see a dim light coming from across the room, which appeared to be much larger than her little train compartment. Where could she be? It dawned on her as thoughts became more vivid with every passing minute – she wasn't in the small berth in her compartment on the train. But how on earth had she gotten off the train without remembering it?

Penny lay back down for a moment. She touched her face in the blackness, her arm, her leg. She felt the covers. She was breathing, warm, all moving parts accounted for. Still completely confused, Penny was becoming more aware of her surroundings, brain racing. "Where AM I?"

Eyes becoming more accustomed now, she could see the faint outline of flowers on the wall. It was flowered wallpaper in shades of bright green and blue on a white background. Hadn't her wallpaper on the train had small pink roses? Penny could now see that the muted light was coming through louvered slats on a small, white-hinged door that was on the wall in front of her. It was a few feet off the foot and a little to the right of what she could discern was a bed. She could feel it was much bigger than where she was to sleep on the train. She was lying on a real bed! Her heart was beating fast now. This was starting to be a little unnerving. Penny swallowed hard, her throat was achingly dry.

In the shadows she could make out a small white desk against the wall to her right, and made out the soft green glow of something sitting on top of it. To her left close enough to touch was a row of what looked like built-in drawers. As she focused more intently Penny thought she could see white curtains that hung around a narrow window on the wall behind the bed. Through a small crack between the window and the pulled shade she could see a sliver of moonlight and snow on barren tree branches.

"On the first day of Christmas my true love gave to me, a partridge in a pear tree." The voices down the hall continued, "On the second day of Christmas my true love gave to me, two turtle doves and a partridge in a pear tree."

Ever so deliberately Penny sat up and swung her legs over the side of the bed. With her bare feet she could feel soft, shag carpeting. She stood up and the room swirled a little. She walked tentatively forward and braced herself on the wall in front of her, making her way toward the light coming through the door. She knew instinctively she needed to push the door open, not pull it towards herself. "That's funny," she thought as she shuffled, one foot in front of the other, "how would I have known that?"

She moved forward again, realizing there was a bigger room just to her left as she passed through the louvered door. Penny moved several careful steps and found herself in a narrow hallway directly in front of the room where she had just awakened. She stopped in her tracks. Sudden recognition swept over her in waves and she gasped in total disbelief. "Oh...my...God."

Panic was rising from her toes and made her stomach instantly seem as if it was in her throat. Goosebumps the size of haystacks rose on her arms and the hair on the back of her neck bristled. "It can't be." By now she could feel her heart beating so loudly it felt as if it would jump from her chest completely. Her breaths came in short, rapid succession when she could breathe at all. Suddenly, Penny knew where she was.

"On the fifth day of Christmas my true love gave to me, five golden rings!" The sounds came floating up through the stairwell, up through the floorboards, notes that for a moment seemed suspended from the ceiling before they drifted into the hallway and flooded her with recognition. She knew more than just the words. She knew…those voices. Her lip began to quiver and her eyes brimmed with tears.

She wasn't in Chicago. She wasn't on the train. She wasn't in Fargo or at her sister's lake home in Minnesota. She was standing in the bedroom of her old house in Lisbon.

Penny…was home!

PART TWO
Lisbon

After getting her bearings, Penny knew the bathroom she had shared with her two sisters all through their growing up years was directly to her right. She fumbled for the switch around the corner, flipped it up and squinted as light flooded the room. She would recognize that bright orange, yellow and green flowered wallpaper anywhere, remembering when they poured over (and no doubt fought over) the wallpaper sample books their mother had brought home from the local Coast to Coast hardware store on Main Street before choosing the most "mod" one.

They also covered the matching pale yellow cabinets with stick-on vinyl flowers in matching bright yellow and orange shades, very popular back in the '70s. The vanity in front of her was littered with makeup containers, brushes, brightly colored yarn hair ties and an oversized blow dryer was hanging out of one of the cabinet drawers.

She laughed at the memory of their clutter; three teenage girls in one small bathroom always stepping around each other and fighting for precious territory for their belongings. Looking at the mess around her she wondered how they ever managed to get ready for anything at the same time.

There was a big plate glass mirror that hung over the length of one wall above the sink and vanity. Penny was so busy looking around and remembering every item, she gasped when she finally noticed the image staring back at her. Instead of the plump middle-aged woman with slight jowls and visible crows feet around her eyes, there was young, beautiful Penny; long brown hair parted in the middle, big hazel eyes full of youthful exuberance. She swallowed hard and leaned in closer, turning her head to one side and then to the other. "It can't be," she whispered.

Penny noticed a music program bulletin sitting on the counter in front of her, half hidden under a plastic bag containing various sizes of pink sponge rollers. "Lisbon High School Holiday Concert, Thursday, December 13, 1973 was emblazoned in green and red letters on a white background with a picture of a Christmas tree on the cover. "1973," she said out loud. "It's 1973!" She threw her head back in disbelief and looked at it again slowly shaking her head in utter confusion.

She opened the program and suddenly remembered each and every song they had done that year, including her favorite, "Have Yourself a Merry Little Christmas." Penny Raney was written across from the title as "soloist." Every song listed brought back a memory. "I Wonder as I Wander," with Darlene Renner as lead, "Little Drummer Boy," with a drum solo by Scott Frebis, and performances by the Pop Singers, a smaller group of vocalists made up of some of the better male and female voices in the choir. She and her sisters were members of Pop Singers all through high school and could probably still do some of the dance moves they had learned, hands up, hands down, swinging side to side.

Seeing all the familiar names and songs made her wish she had arrived back in her old bed two weeks ago. How fun it would have been to be up on stage performing for what was always a packed house. Most everyone who could get to the high school was in the audience for concerts and plays; high entertainment for a small town whose only other real options were the movie theater and the bowling alley; high school kids who weren't in band or choir even showed up. The events were always well attended, no matter the weather.

As she was staring at the program, lost in fond memories of concerts in years past, she realized the music downstairs had changed. "I'm Dreaming of a White Christmas..." Penny put the program back on the counter and walked out into the hallway. She found the stairwell to her left and started tiptoeing down the carpeted stairs, hanging onto the railing on the right side of the steps, listening more intently with each step down. She could see the door at the bottom of the stairs was slightly ajar and as she got closer to the bottom, the voices became clearer, the music louder.

Penny took a deep breath as her foot hit the last step. She paused for a moment and then gradually opened the door.

As she opened the door wide, the voices stopped. There at the piano were her two sisters, Sandra and Cara. Penny wanted to cry. They were so young, so wonderfully ageless. Sandra, with her long blonde shag hairdo, sat on the piano bench dressed in a short black skirt and a winter white sweater. Tall, beautiful Cara was wearing a pretty blue velvet dress with a matching rope belt draped off to the side. She was standing to the right of Sandra. They both stopped and turned around at the same exact time. They stared at her for a long moment. Penny couldn't move. She just stood there, wondering if they could really see her. What they would say?

Overwhelmed with emotion, she just wanted to run and hug them. "It's me! Penny!" she instinctively blurted out, expecting they would rush to embrace her.

"Geeze Goofball, 'bout time you got up," Sandra said with a slight tone of irritation. "Rip Van Winkle took a shorter nap than you. We should probably go over what you're singing later. Do you want to practice?" Sandra raised her eyebrows and gave her a questioning look. When Penny didn't respond she spoke again, this time a little louder. "Earth to Penny, come in Penny. Do you want to practice?" Sandra said, this time with more insistence.

For a moment Penny was more confused than ever. But of course, if she was back in 1973 and her two sisters just thought she'd woken up from a long afternoon nap, it made perfect sense they wouldn't be terribly surprised to see her.

"Um, ah, sorry. Practice what?" Penny managed, moving closer. As she walked toward her sisters, she stopped for a moment to marvel at the tree standing in the corner across from the piano. She could smell the scent of fresh pine and took in the sweet fragrance of it. The busy green branches were lit from bottom to top with big, old-fashioned bulbs; its shining star almost touched the ceiling. It was draped in silver tinsel and decorated with ornaments and bulbs that made her say out loud in an excited tone, "I remember that. Oh gosh, I remember THAT one!" She reached out and touched an ornament that was a tiny manger scene surrounded by silver glass. "It's so beautiful."

"Yeahhhhh," Cara said hands on hips looking slightly annoyed, "same tree different year, Pen. What is up with you anyway? Not like the tree hasn't been there for a month." Rolling her eyes she continued, "You're doing the solo on 'O Holy Night' tonight at church during the candlelight service, remember? You probably should run through it unless you think you know all the words. You sure didn't yesterday." Cara handed her a sheet of paper that had the words to the carol on it.

"Ready Penny?" Sandra turned back to the piano.

Penny took the paper from Cara's hand and walked to her place on the other side of Sandra, a place she had stood a thousand times and from where she had sung a thousand songs. Sandra began to play the introduction to what in her mind was the most meaningful and lovely of all Christmas carols. All Penny could do was smile; the grin spreading across her face was wide and genuine. She was at the piano with her sisters, in her old house! At that moment she didn't care how and she certainly knew there was no logical explanation as to why, but it was a feeling that was real and nothing less than amazing. Cara gave her a sideways glance and said, "Seriously Penny, are you ok?"

She had never been better. After taking in a deep breath, Penny opened her mouth hoping a 17-year-old voice would fill the room instead of her raspy middle-aged effort only used in the privacy of her own home these days. She sang along with the music…"O holy night, the stars are brightly shining…"

As the words came out, strong and perfectly in tune, Penny smiled inside. She closed her eyes and was transported back to the vivid scene remembered from a Christmas Eve long ago.

Back in the moment, they ran through the song twice more. With each note Penny marveled at how effortless her breathing, how deeply she felt the notes resonating from her diaphragm; how clear and rich her voice sounded. It was so easy to take it for granted when she was young. Like everything in a 17-year-old's mind, wouldn't it last forever?

As they finished up the last verse, around the corner came Ricky, arms full of G.I. Joe action figures, hair wet from his Christmas Eve shower. "Hey, Mom said one of you guys has to set the table," he called as he dropped to his knees, scattering the soldiers. He began rifling through the festively wrapped packages that completely filled the area around the big tree. As Ricky searched through every one, he methodically placed the ones with his name in a particular spot. "Wow," he exclaimed, well satisfied with his project. "I have ten presents under here, SCORE!"

Penny looked at her sisters, still unable to comprehend that she was really here, in 1973, singing like they used to. "You better not open any of those yet, you have to wait until after dinner," chided Cara. A disappointed Ricky put the present he had been actively shaking and turning over in his hands back under the tree. "Aw, okay," he said and instead moved on to check each of the stockings hanging along the mantel over the fireplace.

"I'll set the table if you two see what else Mom needs help with," Sandra said as she pushed herself away from the piano and walked around the corner toward the dining room.

"Mom!" Penny gasped out loud as if it had just dawned on her that in 1973, she and her siblings weren't the only ones likely to be home on a Christmas Eve.

Penny turned around until she was directly facing her younger sister. This whole experience was so unbelievable; she needed to tell them all she was BACK. Suddenly Penny couldn't wait to get everyone around the dinner table. They would be so shocked to hear about where they would all be in forty years, all of the inventions that were to come. Her mind raced with excitement. This would be one Christmas nobody would forget.

She reached out and touched Cara's arm. In her mind she said to Cara, "I can't believe I'm here with all of you, back in 1973. This is just crazy!" To her surprise, the words that actually came out of her mouth were, "I'll see if Mom needs any help with getting the salad or garlic bread ready. Cara, make sure Ricky doesn't tear the stockings down. Nothing is going to be in them until tomorrow morning anyway."

Penny was startled. The words she knew she had formulated in her brain to explain why she had acted so confused came out completely different than what she had intended. As Cara started to walk away towards Ricky, Penny tried again. "Forget just landing on the moon. We're going to have people living in space on an international space station. Computers are going to allow us to actually see each other as we have conversations. Every single person will have a personal cell phone on them at all times and don't even get me started on this thing called the Internet." Penny watched for any recognition of shock and awe on Cara's face.

But there was no sign of amazement as a simple, "Thanks, just keep him out of trouble until dinner," came out of Penny's mouth as Cara casually strolled away to make sure the stockings were safe.

It became clear to Penny as she stood in the midst of this surreal setting that she would never be able to tell her family the incredible events that were to unfold in the years to come. They would never know of her fantastic story, her absurdly improbable journey back to her childhood. Every time she tried to speak about her adventure, to share details of the extraordinary experience she was having, it was more apparent than ever she was having this unique experience totally and utterly…alone.

While Cara busied herself talking with Ricky, Penny stood there gathering her thoughts. As she did so, she recognized a most tantalizing smell was permeating her senses. LASAGNA! Every Christmas Eve their family, though not remotely Italian in heritage, always served lasagna for dinner before opening gifts. Now, the perception of her surroundings included not only the familiar people of her world in 1973, but also included the delicious food as well. It was all becoming a little too much for Penny to grasp.

As she breathed deeply, taking in the mouth-watering aroma of what she knew was baking away in the oven, she heard a familiar voice coming from the kitchen. "Would one of you girls come put the salad together, please?" She knew immediately it was her mother, Betsy. Penny also understood by now that she would not see the elderly, silver-haired version of her mother when she walked into the kitchen, and she wasn't at all sure how to prepare herself for that encounter.

Penny looked forward with anticipation to seeing the younger figure of her mother but the thought was a little overwhelming as well. Even though in an instant the time had melted away, Penny still carried within her all of the memories…good and bad…of the past forty years. When they met face to face across time, she and she alone would have the benefit of perspective, of hindsight. The realization was deeply bitter sweet.

Walking down the hallway toward the kitchen, she wished more than ever she could have conversations that reversed unkind or harsh words exchanged in moments of heated teenage fury, to undo bad choices. She wanted to reach out and hug her mom with the arms of a woman who understands as a mother herself what a difficult job it must have been to manage a house filled with rambunctious kids. Instead, her mother would still see before her the stubborn, willful child she remained in the 1973 present. Her mother's present.

Not sure she would ever be prepared for what would happen next, Penny walked into the kitchen where her mother stood working intently over the kitchen sink. "There you are," her mother said as she busied herself rinsing vegetables and without looking up, reached into the cupboard for a bowl. "The lettuce is in the fridge and I just washed some cucumbers and tomatoes."

Penny looked around the kitchen, smiling at the memory of how times had changed. Everything in her Chicago apartment was stainless steel and granite, walls painted in muted earth tones. She had forgotten how much 1973 really loved avocado green. Her eyes scanning around the room, she remembered the mess they lived in a few years before while it was being remodeled into what was then a pretty state-of-the art kitchen.

Sleek Formica countertops in a pale lemon yellow were installed that included a feature for a counter-top blender. The blender itself and the knobs to control the blender attachment fit right into the countertop. Groovy! That was a very cool and modern convenience back then.

Along with the major kitchen remodel that replaced flooring as well as added those "chic" avocado green appliances, was the addition of a large family room, walk-in closet and screened-in porch off the back of the house. It was much needed space for their family of growing kids.

The small galley-style kitchen once looked out into the back yard through one small window above the sink. After the remodel the wall came down and it was open through to the family room. A long bar was built on the opposite side of the now half-wall where they would sit on stools and do homework or have a quick dinner when they were on the run to some event or other at school.

"I'm back, Mom, I'm really 58 years old and I've been living in Chicago for the past forty years, and you won't believe what the world is like in 2014." Penny desperately wanted to yell out loud. The words formed succinctly and clearly in her head, but a banal "Ok, I'll get working on the salad," was all she heard when she spoke.

She stood there a moment, wanting to cry and to scream and to somehow make sense of what could never, ever make sense. There was so much she wanted to share, to explain. Penny wanted to gather her family and hug each one of them until it hurt, to tell them how much she loved them and how much she appreciated everything they have meant to her. The whole experience was overwhelming to say the least, but as the minutes ticked by in the space where past and present collided, it became intensely more distressing to realize only she knew in the not-too-distant future, they desperately would need each other more than ever.

How many times had she jokingly wished how fabulous it would be to be able to go back and have her young body with the benefit of years of experience and maturity of a grown woman? How many times had she heard others wish for the same super power? Forget Superman and his otherworldly strength. Who cares about Aquaman and his ability to hold his breath indefinitely underwater or Iron Man and his ability to fly at sonic speed?

No, given the opportunity most people would surely opt for the physical beauty and unparalleled energy of their youth combined with the knowledge and perspective of their adult selves. How many heartaches and costly errors could we avoid? How much more appreciative would we be of the opportunities presented and blessings squandered in our delusion that the grass is always greener and possibilities are unlimited?

The ability to go back and relive the past with her mature adult mind at first had felt like the most amazing gift, but with each passing minute it began to feel more like an insufferable burden. She understood she couldn't go back to change the past or sadly, intervene in events the future held. The weight of what Penny knew was to come knowing she was merely doomed to relive it made her want to run back up the stairs, crawl into her bed and pray for a reverse miracle, the antidote which would take her back to the train, back to comfort of 302 Doddridge Street.

As much as she had initially been excited to relive a time in her history, she quickly became frustrated at not being able to express meaningful sentiments and information that could make a difference. It was a miserable feeling. This was insane, the whole concept of being where she was in the year she found herself. How cruel to stop the spell so short of perfection. Penny could effortlessly articulate in her mind exactly what she wanted to say, but the only words she could actually speak out loud were things relevant that day, Christmas Eve 1973, and only how her 17-year-old self would express them.

Just then her mother spoke again reminding Penny to get moving on the salad preparation. As Penny turned to open the refrigerator and pull out the lettuce, her mother turned around, smiled and said, "Well, did you have a nice rest? I was beginning to wonder about you. Not like you to sleep so long, especially not at Christmas!" Her mother was right about that.

Ever since she could remember Penny never slept a wink on Christmas Eve, lying awake a shivering bundle of nerves, beyond excited to see what would be left under the tree. Santa was coming! In her mind she didn't understand how anyone could sleep. Christmas was always such a highly anticipated time of year in general, but for Penny it was truly enthralling.

Shortly after Thanksgiving every year, Penny would walk in their home after school to find her mother had decorated the entire place in holiday merriment. There were fresh greens placed along the mantel over the fireplace where four Christmas stockings were hung in a row. Something festive adorned the piano and the coffee table. A garland of more fresh greenery held in place by bright red felt bows hung around the double doors that led out to the screened-in porch.

The dining room table was covered in a crisp, white tablecloth. It held a centerpiece of yet more winter foliage, small pinecones and sparkly pillar candles covered with gold or silver glitter. The whole house smelled of fresh pine. Seeing their home all ready for Christmas made it that much harder to wait for the holiday to arrive.

Of all the decorations set out every season, there was one display in particular Penny spent a lot of time arranging and rearranging. On the top of the small bookshelf to the right of the fireplace sat a vintage ceramic crèche. There was baby Jesus in the manger, Mary and Joseph and the three Wise Men with their camels, cattle and sheep. So well adored and played with, more than one of their delicate china legs had to be meticulously glued back on over the years.

Her family attended the small Presbyterian church a block off of Main Street behind the Piggly Wiggly grocery store. She grew up singing in the choir from the time she was old enough to sing "Jesus Loves Me." Penny knew the story of the Christmas angel announcing the birth of Jesus who could be found in a manger wrapped in swaddling clothes. What an amazing story! Seeing the miniature figurines, placing them around the petite wooden structure that served as the stable brought the most significant part of the Christmas celebration to life.

One of the other highlights of the season, going to pick out the tree at one of the gas station parking lots downtown, was a fun family affair. Penny's favorite was the Scotch pine with its long, soft needles; the big, bushy variety that took up an entire corner of their living room. The grown ups would string the lights and put the star on top, but she and her siblings made a big event out of adorning the tree with its bulbs and tinsel. Sometimes they would sit around the dining room table with needle and thread, stringing together row after row of popcorn and cranberries to add a homemade touch to the tree. And inevitably, every year they declared THIS tree was surely the most beautiful they'd ever had.

Outside, her dad would decorate the giant evergreen tree by the garage with large multi-colored lights, and smaller strands along the bushes that lined the front of the house under the big picture window. Her mother routinely dressed the front door like a big red package, bow and all.

The holidays were party season in Lisbon, and frequently her parents would dress themselves in Saturday night finery and head out to attend a gathering or a dance at the Take Out Inn just south of town. Penny liked it when the party was at their own house, because she got to help put together the food before the guests arrived.

While she was in the kitchen arranging slices of cheese and meat on the tray or little cocktail wieners in delicious sauce in the fondue pot, she would sneak her share for certain. Yum! Pretty paper plates and napkins, bowls of fancy nuts and chips with various dips were set out. Sometimes she and her siblings got to take a few down to the basement, where they typically were sent with a babysitter to be out from underfoot. The chatter and laughter, music and high spirits went well into the wee hours most of the time. Penny thought to herself as a child sneaking up the steps to peek at where all the noise was coming from, that adults sure get to have a lot of fun – and someday, it would be her turn.

Her mother was a prolific baker during that time of year, starting after Thanksgiving to fill the ancient white chest freezer in the basement with cookie tins filled to the brim with all of her favorite goodies: snow on the mountain, crunchy molasses ginger, Mexican wedding cakes, chocolate and vanilla pinwheel rounds, and her father's favorite (and pretty much the only ones Penny couldn't abide) fruitcake cookies. But her all-time favorite, the ones she looked forward to more than all the others, were the rolled sugar cut outs baked until they were a crisp light golden brown.

When it was time to decorate the sugar cookies, her mother laid out all the different colored icing bowls along with the various toppings like green and red crystal sugar, tiny silver beads, red cinnamon candies, chocolate sprinkles and multi-colored nonpareils. She and her siblings would spend hours icing every Santa, bell, Christmas tree, angel, wreath and reindeer. The variety of shapes and colors made a beautiful addition to the dessert table and to set out for guests who might stop by (which plenty of people did that time of year). And of course, Santa would be left a plate next to a glass of milk.

Penny freely admitted she was the absolute worst offender when it came to raiding the freezer and those cookie tins before Christmas. Many times her mother would scold, "There won't be any left to set out for Santa if you keep sneaking those cookies!" The memory of the sweet melt-in-your-mouth treats made Penny want to sneak down to the basement right that very moment and steal a few of those scrumptious delights. But there was salad to be made.

Lettuce in hand, Penny walked over to the counter where her mother was still busy putting a large cloth napkin covered with poinsettias into a breadbasket. As Penny suspected, there stood a much younger Betsy wearing a holiday apron over her crimson dress, busy putting together one of her legendary meals. Her mom was a great cook, so wonderful food was something Penny remembered distinctly.

Penny realized as she watched her move gracefully around the kitchen, she couldn't believe she had forgotten how beautiful her mother truly was. Betsy had big brown eyes, and soft waves of thick brunette hair that fell just below the chin and delicately framed her face. Her complexion wasn't nearly as fair as Penny's, but it was lovely and smooth with just the right hint of makeup and lipstick to show off her somewhat delicate features. She wore earrings that were small clusters of pearls and a matching pearl necklace, clearly dressed for the evening's celebration.

Penny smiled as she went about tearing the lettuce into pieces and adding the chopped cucumbers and tomatoes her mother had already prepared. There was a bottle of Italian salad dressing on the counter and Penny gave it a shake before pouring it over the salad and tossing it with the silver tongs sitting next to the bowl. Grabbing the box of croutons, she put a generous handful over the top of the vegetables and stood back satisfied it would pass muster.

"Mom," Penny hesitated, by now not at all sure what would actually come out of her mouth as she spoke. "You look really pretty tonight." Her mom turned around looking a little startled. For a moment Penny thought maybe she would be the one person able to see right through her, the one person who could understand what was really going on. Did she see her middle-aged daughter before her?

Penny soon realized there was no special recognition, only a slight look of surprise. Blushing slightly with the compliment that must have seemed odd coming from typically her contrary teenage daughter, Betsy replied, "Why thank you, Penny. What a nice thing to say." She paused slightly before adding, "I hope your father thinks so. He went out to chop some kindling in order to start the fire in the fireplace and plug in all the outside lights. I would think he'd be getting cold right about now. I'll bet he could use a hot toddy."

At the mention of her father, Penny dropped the silver salad tongs to the floor. Her heart began to pound and she felt the blood rushing out of her face. How could she not remember her father would be home? It was Christmas 1973, three years *before* he died. The enormity of knowing in a few minutes her father would walk through the door, someone she hadn't seen or hugged or touched in nearly forty years was overpowering. She was trembling on the inside, invisible tears welling up in her eyes, emotion flooding her with an inescapable feeling of dread mixed with elation and just enough terror to make her go weak in the knees.

"Goodness, Penny," said her mother as she leaned down to retrieve the tongs, rinsing them in the soapy water in the sink. "It looks like you aren't quite awake yet." But if she hadn't been wide awake before, the notion of seeing her father walk through the door any minute certainly erased any remaining sleepiness from her consciousness.

Seeing her siblings and her mother again was surreal but in a way that Penny felt she was handling pretty well, all things considered. Seeing her father again having been in the hospital when he passed away, after sitting numbly through his funeral, after struggling with the rest of her family to come to grips with the tragic reality of his passing was simply too much to comprehend. "Oh God, please let me wake up, please let me wake up. This has to be a dream." Penny pleaded again and again in words nobody would hear with whatever forces might save her from what was about to come.

Just as Penny was regaining her composure, taking deep breaths and holding on firmly to the counter in front of her, there was a noise at the back door. She gripped the wall and peeked cautiously around the corner, trembling hand almost knocking the trim-line phone off of its perch on the wall.

There in the back entryway by the walk-in closet, feet stomping on the rug to remove the clinging snow, stood her father. His face was red from being out in the cold, his arms loaded with sticks of splintered wood for the fireplace. Scurrying around him in a sudden flash of brown and white fur and flying snow was Jiggers, the family dog. "Oh my gosh," laughed Penny. She had completely forgotten about Jiggers, their lovable Brittany spaniel pup. "Come here girl," Penny called eager to give good old Jigs a big hug.

Jiggers dashed up the step and around the living room, raced down the hall and through the kitchen, down around the dining room table and began jumping all over Penny in an excited greeting that said, "I missed you!" Just her luck the only one in the room who would recognize her as long lost was the only one who could never say a word about it.

Penny gave Jiggers a good scratch behind the ears, and in return received a showering of warm, wet doggie kisses. When she looked up again, there was the handsome figure of her father still wiping his black cowboy boots on the back entry rug. She was flooded with mixed emotions as she continued to watch the striking man in the tan cowboy hat. He was every bit as handsome as she recalled, athletic and fit with slightly graying hair and hazel eyes. Transfixed by the image, Penny was unable to catch her breath much less stand up. For what seemed like a long moment she held onto Jiggers tightly for support as the excited pup continued to lick her face.

Without seeming to detect she was there, he walked up the step into the living room, and with beads of melted snow still clinging to his brown woolen coat, began loading the armful of kindling wood into the fireplace. Ricky and Cara had since moved back to inspecting presents under the tree and barely even noticed that their father was working in close proximity.

Penny watched as he went about methodically arranging the sticks of wood, tucking pieces of crumpled newspaper underneath and in between the logs. After striking a match and setting his handiwork ablaze, he opened the flue and observed the dark, billowing smoke start to snake its way up the chimney. The fire quickly crackled to life and after a few minutes he closed the screen and stood back making sure the logs themselves were aflame.

Satisfied the room would soon be filled with the warm glow from the hearth, he walked back to the closet, took off his coat and hat and moving back toward the kitchen finally spotted Penny, who by this time had let go of Jiggers and was standing there silently.

"Something smells great," he declared rubbing his cold hands together still not acknowledging she was standing there. "Hey Betsy, how about a little cocktail before dinner?" he called cheerily. "That table looks beautiful," he complimented Sandra, who was still busily putting the silverware at each place setting.

Penny watched in amazement as Sandra barely looked up from her duties. "Sandra, look up. Dad is here!" Penny was shaking inside, but nobody – not Sandra, Cara, Ricky or her mother paid much attention to what she realized was simply another routine preparation for dinner in the Raney household.

Penny gulped hard and stood observing as he stepped into the family room and flipped on the big console TV in the corner. David Brinkley was asking the audience to stay tuned for a special Christmas episode of Rowan and Martin's Laugh-In. With his usual "Good luck...and good night," the broadcast closed out and a commercial showing a youthful Shelley Hack bounding merrily down the street charming a series of attractive men flashed on the screen as Mel Torme crooned in the background, "There's a fragrance that's here today and they call it, CHARLIE! A different fragrance that thinks your way, and they call it, CHARLIE! Kinda young kinda now, CHARLIE, kinda free, kinda wow, CHARLIE..."

She wanted so badly to run over to him, throw her arms around his neck and weep with gratitude just for a glimpse of him again. In her head she was telling him over and over how much she had missed seeing him, how much they had all missed him, how this was so unbelievable. But she stood alone at the top of the step like a stone statue, paralyzed and unable to move an inch. "I'm here Dad. Please stop. Can't you see it's me? "Penny's brain formulated the words as he moved closer. "Oh God please let this be real. Don't let me wake up. Not yet." He was close enough to touch.

"Hi Dad," the barely audible words sputtered out when she finally spoke as he appeared in the doorway of the kitchen. Penny could hear the clinking of ice behind her. He grabbed the drink her mother had just poured from a crystal decanter. Hi Dad. HI DAD? Really? Is that all she could say? Penny couldn't believe just two words out of the cacophony ringing in her head were all that managed to come out of her mouth, which by now was as dry as the Sahara.

He didn't say anything, but picked her up and gave her a warm bear hug with a kiss on the cheek offering her a hasty, "Merry Christmas!" Penny felt his strong arms around her. "Please don't let go," she thought to herself as she closed her eyes and breathed in the scent of him, a mixture of freshly cut wood and Dentyne gum. She held him tightly in a grasp that was desperate and yet grateful. "Please, don't ever let go."

As quickly as he had scooped her up, he had set her down and was now twirling her mother playfully across the kitchen floor as if they were dancing alone, just the two of them in the room. They glided across the linoleum to some imaginary tune all the while her mom feigning a protest, "Oh Rob, not now, I've got dinner in the oven!" Penny could only watch, awestruck, confused, elated. How many times she had watched a similar scene between her parents, and how many times had she nonchalantly ignored it with a teenage eye roll and silent "whatever." Now she realized it had spoken volumes and had been imprinted in her memory as role models of what love looked and felt like between two people who cared deeply for each other.

Drink in hand, her father patted Betsy friskily on the backside and with a wink in her direction, walked around the corner. Penny started to follow but her mother handed her a basket of warm garlic bread as she passed the stove. "Time to start getting things on the table," she said. "Dinner before presents, and we don't want to be late for church." Penny complied and took the bread to the dining room, Cara following closely behind with the salad.

Sandra had done a wonderful job with the table, and was carefully placing wine glasses by everyone's plate, the finishing touch. Christmas Eve dinner was the one night when each of the older girls got to have their own pint-sized bottle of Mogen David wine. Barely more alcohol than grape juice, it still made them feel very grown up. Penny set the bread next to the salad and walked over to shut off the TV, which now featured the gleaming white smile of someone clearly thrilled with their Pepsodent purchase.

Her mother appeared with the steaming pan of lasagna and set it down as they all gathered around the table, Father at one end, Mother at the other and the four children, two on either side all dressed in their Christmas best. When everyone was seated, napkins in lap and candles lit, the kids began a prayer they recited whenever they were all assembled together as a family.

"Thanks be to God," Sandra started, the other three including Penny joining in, "for blessings that surround us, given us to share. Remember those in need around us, show them Thy care. Amen." Heads still bowed Ricky added an enthusiastic "AMEN and Merry Christmas, HO HO HO!" Everyone laughed at his antics.

Penny looked with amazement and sheer love at the people who were sitting around her at the beautifully decorated table, candles flickering, eagerly anticipating the delicious meal about to be served. How she wished her siblings could comprehend what was happening, to feel the overwhelming sense of belonging to something so incredibly special and everlasting Penny cherished in this moment. Penny wished they could experience her look back from the future and marvel in thankfulness at all the fun memories they would create together; knowing with certainty as each new marriage, each new branch and limb was added to the family tree, every new baby welcomed into their close-knit bunch, the circle of love would only continue to grow.

Penny sighed deeply inside and took comfort in the thought that years from now they all would understand what she knew right now; that nothing matters in the grand scheme of things save for the people you love, and the people who love you back.

Before the meal got underway in earnest, her father raised his glass. They all instinctively stopped and did the same with theirs. Penny knew what was coming, and her soul ached to tell her father how through the years it would be something that would undeniably link their kin together, past and present. Just seven ordinary words would bind them all in extraordinary tradition and devotion to each other with the simple phrase he was about to utter. But tonight, nobody would understand the significance they would have in the coming years ahead. Nobody but Penny.

It was the toast that still echoed every time they gathered as a family at every important event. They would raise their glasses and eyes toward Heaven at every holiday, every wedding, family reunion and special occasion where they came together as if to invoke the spirit and constant, eternal presence she felt so strongly as she held her glass aloft.

"May we never have it any worse," her father spoke the words almost reverently, at once both celebrating and earnestly giving thanks in general for how good they had it compared to so many others. It was meant to be a reminder not to take what they had for granted, to remain grateful, and to treasure each other and all that they had been given. "May we never have it any worse!" everyone chimed in around the table, glasses clinked together in a sort of prayer acknowledging that this moment, *this very moment*, was appreciated and cherished.

Penny dabbed her napkin at the non-existent tears she was sure were streaking down her cheeks and watched the faces of her family as they lowered their glasses and busily set about passing the dishes around to have a portion of the steaming pasta piled onto their plate. "I want an end piece!" added Cara as the conversation turned to school and the various activities each of the kids was involved in.

Penny was hoping nobody would realize she was relatively silent through the meal. Not because she didn't have plenty to say, but because she wasn't at all sure WHAT she had been up to prior to dinner that day. Her most recent memory, after all, was a train ride through a snowstorm – in 2014. Although her bizarre tale certainly would make for interesting dinner conversation, she knew it didn't matter what she wanted to say. Penny most likely wouldn't be able to verbalize it anyway.

The rest of the meal was spent savoring the amazing lasagna and listening to everyone else talk about their day, adding a short comment here and there so as not to raise suspicion there was an imposter in the room. Well, sort of. Ricky was tearing through what was on his plate in record time, having announced the first one done gets to play Santa and start the gift opening afterwards. For a second Penny thought she should probably be a little more eager to down her food as well seeing as how back in 1973 she would have been every bit as anxious as Ricky to tear into the packages that were piled in stacks under the tree. Right now though, her stomach was too filled with butterflies to consume much of the delicious lasagna.

Once everyone had finished the main course and plates cleared, her mother returned with a holiday platter filled to over flowing with all of the cookies and baked goodies she relished as a child. As the serving dish went by, Penny grabbed two frosted sugar cookies, one Santa and one ornately decorated wreath with a red cinnamon candy for the center of the bow. Although they looked like Ricky probably was the artist with globs of green frosting cascading over the edge, she munched greedily on the crunchy delights, enjoying every bite until there was nothing but a few crumbs left behind.

"Hey everybody, time to open presents!" Ricky was urging from the living room. Chairs were pushed back in place and the last sips of wine were consumed. They all moved to the living room, all the while Penny trying desperately to recall what she might have asked for as well as what she would have given to each member of her family for Christmas.

As she sat on the edge of the piano bench watching Ricky busy himself passing out a gift to each person in the family, Penny remembered how much she used to love going shopping downtown when Main Street was transformed into a winter wonderland with all the stores and light posts enhanced with holiday decorations.

Every Friday evening the stores and Farmers Union Bank would stay open late to allow those who worked during the day an opportunity to get their shopping done. The old-fashioned light posts that lined Main Street had silver garland roped around them all the way up to where the light hung, and from there swung a lighted holiday decoration in the shape of a candle, a star, or the image of Santa. Each store had cheerful seasonal displays inviting shoppers to linger, and beckoning them to enter and check out the merchandise.

Strains of Christmas music could be heard up and down the snow-covered street as customers wandered in and out of the stores, loaded down with their purchases. Penny particularly loved Dahl's Jewelers, which not only sold lovely jewelry that sparkled and shined from the glass cases, but also carried a variety of gift items. She would save her allowance or babysitting money when she was younger (and her drive-in money when she got to high school) for weeks in order to be able to choose just the right gift for each one in her family.

When she was in grade school she and the rest of the kids in town would line up along the street the Saturday before Christmas to see Santa ride in on the town's shiny red fire engine. They would follow him down to the building at the north end of town where they stored the school buses, and one by one sat on Santa's lap whispering with hopeful anticipation their list of toys into his ear and assuring him they had definitely been "nice" that year.

After they were done sharing their list of wishes, Santa would give each of them a small brown paper bag filled with assorted Christmas candy and they'd walk a few blocks to the historic Scenic Theater for free movies. Tom and Jerry and Disney cartoons were followed by the hilarious antics of The Three Stooges or Ma and Pa Kettle. The theater was noisy and raucous, every seat filled with a child who by then was overcome with excitement and too much sugar.

Penny wondered as Ricky continued to hand out presents what exactly she had purchased for everyone this year. As Ricky set a present in her lap, he announced, "That one is to you from Mom and Dad." She looked down at the gaily wrapped gift, a tiny snowman complete with scarf and plastic carrot for a nose dangled from the fastidiously tied red ribbon.

When I Get Home

Penny always loved the way her mother took extra care to make the presents pretty. It wasn't enough to put an ordinary peel n' stick bow on the package (the way Penny routinely did these days). No, her mother meticulously saved Christmas cards from years past along with little ornaments and holiday trinkets that elevated the packages from common to special and even elegant. Penny shook the box and discovered it shifted slightly from side to side when moved back and forth. "I wonder what it is?" she said out loud.

Penny patiently waited her turn as she watched her mother open a lovely paisley scarf and Cara unwrapped a record album with a picture of Judy Collins in the midst of a field of wild yellow daisies on the front. "Both Sides Now" is one of my favorite songs!" Cara exclaimed genuinely thrilled with the gift. Sandra was next to open her box, revealing a collection of "Slicker" lip gloss by Yeardley. "Thanks so much, I love their stuff!" Penny realized Sandra was looking at her. Eyeing the package of frosted lipsticks, Penny suddenly remembered picking it out among all the makeup options behind the counter at Rexall Drug Store. She had been torn between the lipstick and a case of 20 different shades of eye shadow in all the hot colors of the day. "Slicker over, slicker under...slicker alone" the words to the old Yeardley television commercial suddenly popped into her head. "You're very welcome," she answered back with a smile. Ricky had opened a big box that revealed a neon orange Hot Wheels racetrack and was already on to the next delivery.

It was Penny's turn. She removed the perfectly tied bow and put it carefully beside her along with the little snowman so it could be used again next year. She ran her thumb along the back seam and loosened the tape that was holding the paper together. Neatly wrapped in tissue paper was a beautiful bright blue turtleneck sweater and matching yarn hair ties. Penny held it up for everyone to see, remembering the day they were in Fargo and she spotted it hanging on a rack at the Vanity 3 store in the West Acres Mall. Her mother must have somehow snuck behind her back and bought it when she wasn't looking.

All eyes were on her father as he took a present from what was now a fairly sizable stack of presents in front of him and unwrapped it. Penny recognized immediately that it was something she had chosen for him all those years ago. Looking over his wire-rimmed reading glasses, he smiled across the room at her as he admired the book she had given him. It was all about native North Dakota wildlife. Since he was an avid hunter and outdoorsman as well as a voracious reader, she thought it was something he'd truly enjoy. It was filled with lots of pictures taken in various parts of the state, and as the clerk rang up her purchase she recalled feeling fairly confident he would like it.

She walked over to where he was sitting in the moss green velvet chair to the left of the fireplace and gave him a long hug. "I hope you like it, Dad," was all she could manage as she felt his warm embrace in return. Even though inside she was an emotional hot mess, she knew he wouldn't be able to detect anything but what he was supposed to see.

For the first time since waking a few hours ago, Penny allowed herself to look right at him. What she saw was a genuine expression of approval on his face. He really seemed to like it! She lingered for a moment just taking in the sight of him, the happy look in his eyes, letting the sound of his rich baritone voice wash over her and burn into her mind. In the many years since his death the memory of his voice had faded, the ring of his laughter, distant. What an incredible gift to have the chance to hear it again. She was crying inside, unbelievably joyful tears.

After composing herself, she returned to where she had been sitting and they continued their family tradition of taking turns until the last gift was opened and the living room was a colorful sea of crumpled holiday paper. Penny received many lovely gifts including what was then a very new invention – a Polaroid instant camera. It seemed so oversized and bulky in her hands, the film cartridges the size of an 8 track tape. It was impossible not to be amazed at how far technology had come since then. She went around the room snapping pictures of her siblings and parents opening their gifts, pulling the prints from the bottom and setting them on the dining room hutch to dry. Penny made sure to take one of her father holding the gift she had given him.

What she wouldn't give for her smartphone or iPad so she could instantly and permanently save this incredible experience to relive someday. Her journey back in time would sure make some kind of post on Facebook! The thought gave her pause, and while waiting for the pictures to develop Penny wondered whether she was truly going to be starting her life over again.

Was this really that magical second chance everyone dreams about? The bigger question was could she even handle being 17 again with the power to undo choices and decisions that had, after all, contributed to her becoming the person she was in 2014? Hers hadn't been a perfect life by any stretch of the imagination, but Penny wasn't *unhappy* with how she had evolved as a mature 58-year-old woman.

Penny had loved and been loved, had suffered broken hearts and bruised ego, endured the pain of losing loved ones, dealt with financial hardships that probably would have defeated other less resilient souls. But she'd also known the feeling of pride and accomplishment in overcoming unfortunate circumstances, and deftly handled challenges in both career and relationships. Hadn't she, regardless of what life had thrown her way, dealt with it head on and risen above the obstacles?

Her history was more than just the sum total of her life experiences, it was *who* she was, who she had become as a result. She couldn't help but think that had any one of those events or encounters turned out differently, she would have, too. She was the embodiment of fifty-eight years of showing up to live each day of her life the best way she knew how, given what came her way that day, and the next, and the next. All things considered, she felt immensely fortunate to be where she was, to have the job she had, to be blessed with the family and friends that meant more to her than any single achievement ever could.

Everyone has baggage, those unavoidable life-altering experiences – the good, the bad and the downright ugly – that shape us into the person we are. Would she be the same person today if she hadn't lost her father so young? Surely if she had been severely neglected and abused as a child that would have changed her, right? What if she had lost her job, become homeless or the victim of violent crime? How could those experiences *not* have a significant impact on how a person turns out along the way?

Would she have made different choices if she could marry someone other than who she did, if she hadn't had children, and a million other "what ifs" that began streaming into her consciousness. What to change? What to undo? Where to tweak, to make adjustments, to realign the sails and set off in a different direction? Suddenly, the very thought of that monumental responsibility was even more overwhelming than pondering the alternative of just being Penny Tomlin in 2014.

"Let's get all the paper cleaned up," her mother said as she took her glass of wine and her father's hand. "It is going to be time to leave for church here in a bit."

The "whoosh" of something rapidly combusting in the fireplace brought Penny back into the festivities at hand. Ricky had thrown a big handful of discarded wrapping paper into what was by then a roaring fire. Sandra and Cara were busy stuffing a large plastic garbage bag with the rest. Her mother and father had moved off to the family room, and she could hear soft conversation and occasional laughter coming from that direction.

Just then the sound of the telephone ringing pierced the air and immediately Sandra ran over to pick up the receiver. "It's for you," she said gesturing in Penny's direction. "It's Jake. He probably wants to know what time to come and get you for church," Sandra added as she laid the phone down on the kitchen counter, grabbing a cookie off of the tray sitting nearby.

Jake! How could Penny have forgotten Jake Henderson? In the fall and winter of 1973 they were sweethearts, and she was very much in love with him. The thought of seeing his young, incredibly dashing figure at their door sent her heart into uncontrollable flutters. "Well, he's not going to wait forever, ya know." Sandra rolled her eyes as she walked past and headed upstairs to get ready for church.

Penny sucked in a deep breath and gingerly picked up the phone. "Hello?" she managed, barely able to get the words out without choking. Her throat completely parched again, she reached over to take a quick gulp of water from a glass that had yet to make it into the dishwasher. "Jake, is that you?"

"Of course it's me," he laughed heartily, "you were expecting Santa Claus?" The silence from her end of the phone as she tried desperately to formulate something in her mind must have been longer than she thought, because Jake continued, "Pen...are you there?"

"Yes, I'm here, sorry. I was just taking a drink of something when you called." Again, Penny stalled, trying to figure out what she should say next, what she *could* say next that would make any sense at all to Jake. She already knew that nothing suggesting she was anyone other than Penny Raney in 1973 would escape, even by accident. Remembering that Sandra had indicated Jake was coming to pick her up for church she fumbled, "Um, er, are you coming to get me for church?" Penny held her breath, hoping that was the reason he was calling, and he would understand everything she was barely able to verbalize.

"You bet, Babe. I figure I'll swing by in half an hour." Then in more hushed tones, "We can take the sloooow route. If you know what I mean." Penny laughed with the recollection of what he was talking about. He used to make excuses to pick her up earlier than where they had to be so they could drive up and down Main Street for a while, waving and honking at their friends.

Sometimes they would swing by the drive-up window at the little ice cream store for a snack. The Creamery served the best burgers and fountain vanilla or cherry colas in town. Jake always ordered one large drink, one straw…and they'd share the tasty beverage as she snuggled next to him in the front seat of the Mustang. Inevitably as the time grew closer to arrive at their destination, he'd stop along a side street or some other out-of-the-way place like behind the car wash or Lover's Lane down by the park and they'd kiss and tease each other until the very last second before they would show up late.

"I'll be ready," Penny blushed; now more excited than ever to be her youthful self. She hung up the phone and hurried up the steps taking two at a time – a feat 2014 Penny would have never been able to accomplish. She felt exhilarated, filled with adolescent expectation for what was only a few minutes away. Jake Henderson, first true love, was going to be there soon!

She headed straight for her bedroom, opened the closet door and without hesitating knew exactly what she would wear.

When I Get Home

Hanging on one hanger in the middle of her closet as if she had put it together and placed it there especially for this occasion, was a brown corduroy vest, ivory sweater with bell sleeves, and a short skirt made of supple velvet in a patchwork of muted autumn colors.

Directly below the outfit was a pair of dark brown suede boots with fringe going down one side. "Oooooh," she squealed inside, "I remember these." She picked them up admiring the downy soft leather. How could she forget how incredibly stylish she had felt the day she first wore those boots to school. She had stopped in her tracks when she spotted them in the window of Herbst department store one Saturday before Thanksgiving when they had been shopping in Fargo.

Her mother wasn't at all on board thinking them far too extravagant, but Penny nonetheless spent a full drive-in paycheck on those boots. She just HAD to have them. All of her girlfriends were jealous, as she received tons of comments the entire next day. Nobody else in school had anything even close to those fabulous kicks. Jake had twirled her around in the hallway and with a whistle announced, "Look at you, Hot Stuff! Those boots were *definitely* made for walking!"

Penny hurriedly changed out of the dress she had been wearing into her favorite clothes and headed for the bathroom where Cara and Sandra were in the midst of getting ready. Like it was something she did every day, Penny took a spot along the mirrored countertop in the bathroom. Sandra was busy applying a brash shade of frosted chartreuse eye shadow that made Penny giggle inside. "Gotta love the '70s," she thought to herself. Cara was brushing her teeth with one hand and struggling to get a new pair of pantyhose out of a silver egg-shaped package with the other.

Penny looked again at her image in the mirror. In 2014 it took more time than she liked to admit to get her makeup just so, to apply the "age defying" foundation which promised to suspend time with regular use, to fill in her thinning eyebrows with the right amount of light brown pencil. With every advancing year it was getting harder to replicate the natural look every woman strives for; no, these days an errant over application could easily leave her looking more Joan Rivers than a young and popular Joan Baez.

She moved her face closer to the 1973 version of her reflection, still astonished by the flawless smoothness of her fair skin. There were a few faint freckles sprinkled over her nose, but she could tell there was no heavy foundation, no powder or even blush on her cheeks. In her state eau' natural, Penny decided she had at one time, been a very pretty girl.

Looking around the countertop she spied a pale gray shade of matte eye shadow that was much more in line with the palette she would use forty years into the future. She leaned in and lightly dabbed some of the color across her eyelid, smudging carefully with her fingertip until it was perfect. Next, she located the long tube of mascara, carefully brushing each of her long lashes with just the right amount to make them stand out, but cautious not to cake or leave her looking like a raccoon. Opting for a pastel pink blush, she applied it sparingly, barely gliding the applicator over her silky skin.

Penny was going for coquettish ingénue, purposely understating her makeup so as to avoid any potential reference to Barnum and Bailey. Besides, Jake liked her with or without makeup, often remarking at how beautiful she was without all that "junk" on her face. After adding just a hint of rose-tinted lip gloss, she ran a brush through her long hair and stood back admiring the fashionable young girl who was smiling back at her. "Good enough," Penny declared, and back down the stairs she bounded just in time to hear the doorbell ring.

When I Get Home

Smoothing her clothing and taking one last quick peek in the hallway mirror, Penny nervously opened the front door. "Hey hey, Babydoll!" chimed the familiar voice. There stood all 6'4" of one strikingly fine Jake Henderson, his stark blonde hair visible under a florescent orange stocking cap and sporting his black leather letterman's jacket, his name in script on one sleeve and proudly proclaiming his status as a 1973 All Star on the other.

It was a good thing he bounded across the threshold and scooped her into his arms before she could catch her breath, because Penny went a little weak in the knees at the sight of him. My God he was gorgeous! How she could have ever recovered after losing a hunk like that was anybody's guess.

Jake bent over and placed a tender kiss right on her lips, looking straight into her eyes. She giggled like the 17-year-old girl she was and thought to herself, "Oh my, this is going to be a fantastic evening." Then, realizing she wasn't a grown up with every option for indulging her selfish pleasure available, added, "Behave Penny girl...get a grip and control yourself!"

Even though Jake had never been anything but a perfect gentleman with her at all times (well, mostly anyway), never had the word "restraint" been so difficult and problematic as she stood drinking in his movie star looks and chiseled physique.

"Hey Mr. and Mrs. Raney," he called over her shoulder giving a polite nod as he spotted Penny's mother and father in the kitchen. "Don't worry, I'll make sure we get to the church in plenty of time," then playfully poked Penny's arm adding, "This one's the star of the show tonight. I'm carrying precious cargo." Penny blushed.

"Don't you forget that, young man," her dad cautioned in a tone of mock consternation. "We'll see you at church."

Penny opened the closet to the right of the front door and looked for what she knew had to be hanging there. Sure enough, she spotted her navy blue wool maxi-coat and grabbed it off the hanger. She put her arms into the sleeves as Jake held it behind her, and fastened two of the gold polished buttons all the way. "Baby it's cold outside," he crooned taking over the task of securing the remaining buttons until she was snug all the way to her neck.

From the box of hats and gloves on the shelf she plucked her old red knit cloche hat with the crocheted flower on the side and a pair of black gloves. She was ready to head out into the chilly evening with the love of her life holding her hand. Maybe this wasn't a dream after all she thought to herself, because right now it sure felt real and blissfully genuine.

"Ready Freddy?" teased Jake giving her another quick peck on the cheek. "More than you could ever know!" was Penny's honest reply, delivered with a grin that was ear to ear. As they raced each other toward the car Jake reached into the drift by the front steps and threw an undersized snowball in her direction. She ducked and screeching with laughter wagged a gloved finger in his direction, "So THAT's the way it's going to be tonight, huh?"

While Jake opened the car door for her, Penny looked up at the twinkling stars overhead noticing the dazzling firmament was unobscured by a single cloud. The winter sky was shimmering like a blanket of precious gems in the calm, crisp night air. Each star seemed to shine more brightly than the last as she surveyed the wondrous universe above her. Each breath was visible as it escaped into the air, proof that she was alive, here and now in this magnificent time and place.

Penny stood there for a second trying desperately to commit to memory how incredibly special and perfect her life was at that moment. Smiling irrepressibly, she threw open her arms, tilted her head back and stuck her tongue out, eager to taste the tiny flakes of ice that had begun to gently fall. The entire scene was reminiscent of a Norman Rockwell postcard, standing there in the dim light of the flashing Christmas lights, snow falling. Pausing for a moment, she silently thanked whoever had to be watching over her for this priceless opportunity, this miracle.

"Hey Babydoll, get in here. It's freezing outside!" urged Jake as he dusted the remaining snow off of the windshield and came around to help tuck her coat into the front seat. The Mustang was just as she remembered it. Jake revved the engine and backed carefully out of the slippery driveway easing south on to Weber Street.

Penny smiled as she caught a pleasant whiff of his "Brut" cologne. She reached out to touch the polished gold medal dangling from the rear view mirror – a prize she'd watched him win during that past September's regional track championship meet in Bismarck. His latest victory took place on an unseasonably warm day and they had celebrated his new state record by going skinny-dipping out at Johnson's lake afterwards.

It was just the two of them shivering in the moonlight, hair dripping, sharing passionate kisses…and very nearly more than, she realized much later, they would have been emotionally ready to handle. The distant lights of a passing car had interrupted their ardent interlude, but the closeness of that evening forever bonded them in a way both of them knew was significant. Until their relationship began to dwindle as the following fall approached, there was no question that Penny Raney and Jake Henderson were a serious item.

Penny sighed deeply, biting her lower lip as she silently relived the tenderness of that evening all over again. She was overcome with the desire to experience those warm, tingly feelings she knew would undoubtedly overtake her at the touch of his hand on her bare skin. They drove without saying anything for what seemed like a long time. For now it would have to be enough just to be together, to be Penny and Jake in love. It was the best present she could ever ask for.

Jake reached for her hand, which she willingly gave to him, nuzzling a little closer as the Mustang carried them down the slick, icy street. She decided it was probably not a bad idea that the big console where he stored his 8 track tapes was between them. Penny confessed if it weren't for that obstacle, Jake would probably be wearing her like a coat. She couldn't get near enough, couldn't touch him enough. Rolling the reality of her current situation over and over in her mind, Penny wondered if reuniting with Jake was a supernaturally predestined opportunity for the most amazing "do over" in the history of do overs.

Of all the lost relationships Penny had lamented in her life, she had often remarked through the years that never knowing what might have been with Jake was at the top of the list. Maybe he would have tried harder to keep in touch if she hadn't acted like a spoiled child when he tried to talk with her about the reality of a long-distance relationship when he went off to college. Perhaps if she had been more mature, more supportive, made more of an effort to write and call or hitch a ride with friends to visit on the weekends, they wouldn't have drifted apart.

No, she had to behave in such a manner that he probably dreaded having to put up with her constant pouting when they did connect, and quickly grew weary of the awkward silences during phone calls when both of them were hurting, neither of them knowing what to say. If this truly was her opportunity to change what the future held for them, she would *not* blow it this time. *Not this time.*

"You look awesome tonight, by the way," Jake finally broke the silence in the car. "I hope you don't have to be home right away after church," he winked, "I have a surprise for you."

Just then Penny recalled exactly what she had given Jake for Christmas in 1973. And she knew exactly where she had hidden it. Reaching deep into the pocket of her coat, she felt the small square box she had placed there earlier that day. Penny had chosen his gift with great care and was growing more excited with every minute to be able to give it to him. She had wrapped the package and placed it at the bottom of her pocket, but she couldn't recall exactly how or where their gift exchange had happened that evening. Some things are better when you don't know what is coming, she supposed, which made her all the more anxious to see what this very unique Christmas Eve would hold for them both.

"I have something for you, too, but you can't have it until after church. And you have to sit quietly and not fidget the WHOLE TIME." She laughed, and purposely bumped his arm abruptly causing the car to swerve a little. "Hey now, settle down there, Missy," he joked. "We need to get you there in one piece. And I promise not to take my eyes off of the prettiest girl in the choir." He looked at her, beaming in a mischievous way that immediately captivated her heart and made her stomach do flips.

Penny couldn't believe that across the continuum of time and tide she was still so in love with that boy. Sitting there next to him, basking in the sight and smell of him, chatting about nothing in particular like they were never apart was at the same time exhilarating and incredibly troubling.

Could she, as instantly as she had awoken to find herself in his presence again, fall back asleep only to wake in the downy comfort of her big feather bed on Doddridge Street in Chicago? Back in 2014? The thought of losing Jake again seemed too cruel a hoax when the prospect of reimagining their future together so clearly felt within her grasp. More troubling still, was there even a remote possibility of waking years in the future as a decrepit, elderly woman living out her final days alone in the corner of some dismal nursing home?

Penny shuddered slightly and tried to shake those thoughts out of her head returning to the comfort of feeling Jake's arm resting on her knee as they pulled into the church parking lot. The lot was filled with vehicles and there were cars starting to park up and down the streets around the little stone church. Even if they didn't attend services on other Sundays throughout the year, most anyone in town who was Presbyterian or the least bit spiritual showed up for the candlelight service on Christmas Eve.

Penny knew the church would be packed and urged Jake to go toward the front and save some seats in the middle for her mom and dad. Cara and Sandra were already in the choir rehearsal room putting on their burgundy robes with the big white collars and taking turns straightening each other's bows. "About time you got here," Sandra chided as Penny went to the closet and hung up her coat, retrieving her own robe. "I put your music folder over there on the chair."

Penny put on her robe, expertly manipulating the bow tie in the mirror and grabbed her music folder just as Mrs. Hammond, the choir director was lining them up for the processional down the center of the church. She opened her folder to the first hymn and cleared her throat as the organist played the opening strains to "Angels We have Heard on High" and they began walking two by two down the aisle.

Their voices joined with those of the congregation as the energetic chorus of "Gloria in excelsis deo," echoed filling the room with its reverent, yet excited message of the birth of the Christ Child in Bethlehem.

As in years past, the little sanctuary was packed to the point they had to open up the sliding doors at the back of the worship area and put folding chairs behind the last row of pews to accommodate the holiday crowd. Candles were glowing from every part of the small chapel along the aisle, up to the altar and on either side of the pulpit. The flickering light made the tall stained glass windows that flanked each side of the nave even more beautiful.

The choir proceeded down the main aisle, through the door to the left of the pulpit and up the few steps to the choir loft directly behind where the minister, Reverend Spector, was standing. Penny was situated in the middle of the first row, positioned there so she was front and center for her upcoming solo.

The first hymn came to a close, and Reverend Spector opened with a prayer welcoming the worshipers and giving thanks for the great gift they had come together to celebrate – the birth of Jesus. Sneaking a glance up as he spoke, Penny caught a glimpse of Jake sitting with her mother and father in the third row. Jake looked up at the very same time, winking at her. Penny quickly bowed her head again, grinning even as she could feel herself blushing slightly. Oh, those pesky butterflies!

The minister motioned for everyone to be seated as one of the deacons came forward to give the reading of the first scripture starting at Luke 2:1. "In those days Caesar Augustus issued a decree that a census should be taken of the entire Roman world. This was the first census that took place while Quirinius was governor of Syria. And everyone went to their own town to register."

He talked on about how Joseph and Mary went up from the town of Nazareth in Galilee to Judea, to Bethlehem the town of David (because he belonged to the house and line of David). All the while, Penny's gaze was focused on her father, the handsome man with the graying temples sitting next to her mother, listening intently to the story being shared, absent mindedly rolling the program in his hands. He didn't notice Penny staring, still in complete disbelief that he was right there in front of her. She was fighting back tears thinking about all the things she somehow knew she had to find a way to say to him.

Only a week ago she had been having dinner with her friend Dora at Au Cheval on Randolph Street. She had recently attended the funeral of Dora's mother, who had passed away from a sudden heart attack the month before. Dora was still in deep mourning and mentioned to Penny over a glass of their favorite Pinot Noir how badly she wished she could have had the chance to say goodbye, to tell her mother how much she loved her and would be lost without her. "Losing someone is difficult enough, but gone without warning is such a gut punch," Dora said as she tried to maintain her composure. "You don't have time to make things right."

Penny knew those feelings all too well and they talked about how amazing it would be to have one last conversation with the people they loved who had passed away. Being here in this time and place just *had* to be God answering the prayer that she had offered up over and over again. "Please, let me have one more day, one more hour, even one more minute to thoughtfully express what I need to say."

Years of sadness and regret, thousands of silent petitions whispered into Heaven yearning for reassurance her dad was listening would be wiped away if only she could say the words herself; if only she could have the sure knowledge he heard, he understood, he forgave. "I'll never ask for anything ever again," she promised, "if you just let him hear me." Sitting in church on the eve of God's greatest gift to the world seemed a pretty good place to give it one more try, one more hushed request in her own head asking one last time.

The deacon finished his recital with, "The shepherds returned, glorifying and praising God for all the things they had heard and seen, which were just as they had been told. Here ends the first reading of the gospel according to Luke."

Sandra was sitting to her left and gave her a quick elbow nudge whispering, "You're next." With that, Penny stood up, took a deep breath and smiled at the audience. The organist, Mrs. Montello, looked at Penny and nodded. The organ began to play the slow 1-3-5 chord progression of the introduction as Penny tried hard not to be nervous. Even though this certainly wasn't her first solo, not even almost the first time she had sung alone in front of an audience, it suddenly felt like the most important. She was used to performing in front of crowds and never seemed particularly unnerved about it, but that night the first person she spied in the audience sitting front and center beaming up at her from the third row back, was her father.

"O Holy Night, the stars are brightly shining, it is the night of our dear Savior's birth." Penny began tentatively, her voice becoming more clear and powerful with each word, her confidence soaring as she followed the notes that now seemed to come to her effortlessly. "Long lay the world, in sin and error pining, 'til He appeared and the soul felt its worth." Her father looked so dashing in his dark suit and tie, a smile on his face as he watched his middle daughter take command of the performance, slowly building each stanza, each line until she was singing from her toes. The music urged her on as it told the story, "Fall on your knees…O hear the angel voices." Jake sat riveted, completely still and appearing to pay rapt attention.

Penny could see her father's head was bobbing slightly along with each note and she thought she saw a look of great pride in his eyes as she sang. "O night divine, O night when Christ was born," then more urgently as she built to the final high C, with a grand crescendo, "O night, O holy night" drawing out the last word, pausing slightly, organ and voice together more pianissimo for the reverent closing, "O night...divine."

She stood motionless while the organ played the remaining notes of the song, holding her breath in relief as the final chord reverberated around the room. No mistakes, no wrong notes, all the right words, big smiles and robust applause from the congregation. Penny Jane Raney had nailed it.

There were more readings and a brief sermon to follow. The whole audience chuckled and took pictures as the adorable Cherub Choir made up of preschool children sang, "Away in the Manger." Fidgeting and snickering all the while, they made it through three slightly off-key verses easily providing the evening's most enjoyable (not to mention comical) presentation.

The service ended as it always did, with the singing of "Silent Night." Small white candles were passed from row to row. A volunteer holding a large candle in the aisle would light the candle of the first person in the pew. Each subsequent person down the row lit their neighbor's luminary until the room was glowing with their radiance, while everyone softly sang, "sleep in heavenly peace... sleep in heavenly peace." It would forever be Penny's favorite memory of the Christmas Eve observance, a symbol of Christ's light in the world and in each heart.

After the song ended, Reverend Spector opened his arms wide and dismissed the crowd with "And now may the Lord bless you and keep you; may the Lord make his face to shine upon you and be gracious unto you. May the grace of God and the fellowship of the Holy Spirit be with you now and forevermore. Amen." As the congregation answered with a chorus of "AMEN!" the organ jubilantly burst into a rousing rendition of "Joy to the World."

The choir formed into a line once again and quickly filed out, leading the procession back down the center aisle followed closely by the rest of the congregants. Everyone was greeting each other with pats on the back, handshakes, warm hugs and "Merry Christmas!" as their Christmas Eve 1973 commemoration was history – again.

Penny and the rest of the choir returned to the choir room and began taking off their robes while chatting pleasantly among themselves. Penny hung her robe on the designated hanger and turned around to find a grinning Jake standing behind her. "You were awesome, Babe," he said leaning over to grab her hand. "I could listen to you sing all night." The tender expression on his face earnestly conveyed that he meant every word.

Caught a little off guard by his sincere show of affection, Penny quickly responded, "Oh yeah, well then you'd NEVER get your present!" She laughed reaching for her coat, "Come on, let's get out of here."

Hand in hand, they bounced down the steps and out into the bitter night air. She spotted her parents and gave them a quick wave and an "I'll be home in a little while" as they headed in opposite directions. Penny was hoping her dad would still be up when she got home so they could talk. Really talk.

They raced down the sidewalk and hopped inside Jake's Mustang. He put the key in the ignition and the engine roared to life. "We're still on church property or I'd give you a kiss," he joked peering at her, one eyebrow raised. Leaning over, he surprised Penny by planting a warm, wet smooch on her lips, whispering in her ear afterwards, "I guess I was just born a sinner." And as he gathered her in his arms and kissed her again, longer this time, so gentle and sweet and full of emotion he added, "Only you can save me." She let herself go limp in his grasp and lost herself in the overwhelming happiness. Jake loved her, too, didn't he?

Their passionate kisses continued as the car idled and the defroster worked on the layer of ice that had formed while they were inside. It felt like they were wrapped in a cocoon and nobody else existed as they shared another, more urgent kiss holding each other tightly. Jake stopped for a moment and turned the radio to their favorite station broadcasting out of Fargo. KQWB was playing the latest Top 40 hits and the genial voice of Jim Croce filled the air.

Immediately recognizing the tune, Penny began softly singing the familiar words to a song she couldn't have chosen more perfectly had she planned it all in advance.

"If I could save time in a bottle, the first thing that I'd like to do, is to save every day 'til eternity passes away, just to spend them with you." She looked at him intently as she sang, and he took both of her hands in his, blowing on them to keep them warm.

"If I could make days last forever, if words could make wishes come true, I'd save every day like a treasure and then, again, I would spend them with you." Jake sat back and tilted his head slightly, nodding for her to continue.

"If I had a box just for wishes, and dreams that had never come true, the box would be empty, except for the memory of how they were answered by you." Jake, who was also in their high school choir and in possession of an excellent singing voice himself, joined in on the final chorus.

Like something out of a sappy Rogers and Hammerstein musical, their voices blended together in unison, "But there never seems to be enough time to do the things you want to do, once you find them. I've looked around enough to know that you're the one I want to go through time with." They held each other's gaze in a moment of intimate understanding as the strumming guitar slowly faded into a commercial for the holiday sale at Herbst Department Store.

Simultaneously, they broke into laughter. "Man, if anyone on the football team had film of that I'd never live it down!" Jake said as he shifted the car into reverse and pulled out of the parking lot, which by now was completely empty.

As they made their way down a deserted Main Street, the store windows were still gleaming and blinking, advertising their dazzling holiday wares. Penny thought about the words to that song. How desperately she wished she could save every vivid moment she had been experiencing the past few hours forever and ever in a bottle so she could drink of the sheer joy of it on demand.

Right now, holding Jake's hand, driving in this picturesque winter wonderland, she couldn't imagine being back in Chicago, a slightly frumpy middle-aged woman, back at her desk at the *City News*. She was becoming comfortable as 17-year-old Penny again, and thought to herself that whatever was next, she could handle it. One thing she knew for sure, she would do everything in her power to keep Jake Henderson in her life. She was not blowing this chance to undo the past.

They drove north up Main Street until they approached the bridge that would lead to the golf course, down a meandering valley road on the outskirts of town. They took a sharp left on 1st Avenue West, driving along the river until they came to Elm Street and Sandager Park.

The park was nestled in the heart of the valley where Lisbon was founded back in 1880. It was built along the Sheyenne River in one of the least elevated parts of town. The river was prone to flooding every spring, and Penny recalled many years when the raging water would almost touch the underside of the two bridges that connected the west and east sides of town. Through the snow Penny could see still see remnants of sandbags piled high along the bank across from the swimming pool, no doubt a leftover from the flooding last year, or in preparation for what would inevitably come with the spring thaw.

Sometimes in the summer, when the river was at its shallowest point of the year having dried up in the oppressive July heat, they would take canoes and glide along lazily with the slow current, coolers packed with ice and soda and sandwiches for a picnic along the way. Most often they would paddle out to the small island that was actually more of a peninsula, a favorite camping and make-out spot for teenage sweethearts.

Penny and Jake frequented "Lovers Lane" on a regular basis before he went away to college. It was where Jake first kissed her, the first time they skinny dipped, and where everyone met on Friday nights after the football game for impromptu cookouts roasting hotdogs and s'mores around a roaring bonfire.

Sandager Park was a place filled with fond memories, and as Jake parked the car she recalled fun times playing on the playground equipment as a child. She had spent nearly every summer afternoon of her youth swimming in the community pool, buying snacks at the Canteen or roller-skating. The big rocks at the edge of the park where they used to sit, soft drinks in hand, were still there, covered with graffiti from one class stunt or another.

When she finally was in high school and old enough to attend, the Lisbon Park Pavilion was where kids gathered on weekends to hear some of the most popular bands of the area perform.

When they were tired of dancing or of the crowd inside the pavilion, they would take a blanket out into the park and lay under the stars, listening to the music.

This Christmas Eve the snowplows had yet to make their way through the park after the latest accumulation. Jake and Penny's two sets of footprints were the only thing visible on the pristine

When I Get Home

white blanket. The moon was almost full, and its luminescence made the snow appear as if it were shimmering.

There were brightly lit displays in every corner of the park, which made it look dreamlike in the moonlight. Bounding up one of the small hills was Santa in his sleigh full of toys, being drawn by all of his reindeer with Rudolph and his shiny red nose in the lead. There were tiny elves playing an imaginary game of hide and seek, hiding behind various evergreen trees, and a row of gigantic presents with bows flashing a merry red and green beneath the words MERRY CHRISTMAS.

A lighted life-sized ceramic manger scene complete with a bed of straw for baby Jesus and three extravagantly adorned wise men stood vigil at the entrance to the park. Jake and Penny walked over to where the cattle stood with wooly lambs curled at their feet, admiring the stately camel with its blanket saddle rimmed in multi-colored jewels and tassels of gold lame'.

Seeing the serene grounds aglow in its seasonal splendor made Penny wax nostalgic for the carefree days of childhood again, with all the traditions and fun activities this time of year inevitably brought with it.

Penny remembered fondly riding all over town, their whole family piled in the big silver Buick Electra 225 (the old deuce and a quarter), to admire the houses dressed in their festive holiday lights. They made it an annual event on a Saturday every December, looking at the lights and then coming home to make Jiffy Pop popcorn on the stove and sip hot chocolate, maybe even nibble from a plate of Christmas cookies. Such a treat! Holiday light tours were one of the most highly anticipated rituals she continued with her own children when they were little and still dazzled by all the fantastic light spectacles.

Looking out over the glimmering landscape made her all the more grateful to be there with Jake, her most significant person in 1973. She reached out and took his gloved hand in hers, squeezing his fingers softly as if to say, "There is no place I would rather be." There truly wasn't.

"Come on, race ya!" shouted Jake as he suddenly tore off and dashed for the large limestone bandstand, a stately landmark in the middle of the park near where the old iron merry-go-round and swing set stood vigil until the children returned with the warm weather.

Jake bounded up the stairs, waiting for her to catch up. The snow was up to her knees and with her long coat it was more of a challenge to make her way up the slight incline. He held out his hand and helped her climb the remaining two steps. While she was still off balance, he grabbed her causing them to tumble into the sizable drift that had formed on the bandstand stage. They giggled and looked at each other, kissed softly and then rolled onto their backs staring up at the wooden beams of the ceiling, taking a moment to catch their breath.

The gazebo was lit all around the bottom and along each of the roof beams with clear, white holiday lights that made it look like twinkling stars were shining above the two young sweethearts. Penny started moving her arms and legs up and down, up and down making a snow angel. Jake did the same, every once in a while tossing a handful of the fluffy white stuff in her direction. The icy cold spray made her shriek with laugher as it melted on her face and tongue. The night air was brisk, but there was no wind and she had a warm glow regardless of the temperature. It was a perfect winter night for leaving behind frosty cherubim imprints under the watchful eye of the man in the moon.

When they were satisfied that no two finer angels had ever been left in a pile of snow, they stood beneath the twinkling lights of the gazebo and kissed again, this time more slowly and gently as if touching their lips together any harder would leave them easily bruised. Penny felt emotions long buried flowing to the surface in a rush of pure joy. And yet this incredible time, this gift of being with Jake was tinged with the ever-present cloud of uncertainty. How long would her amazing experience last? The thought of losing Jake again weighed heavily on her even as he enveloped her deeper in his grasp, the warmth of his body radiating through her.

Jake pulled away and whispered, "I love you, Penny Jane Raney." He brushed the hair from her eyes and kissed the tip of her nose. Their eyes locked and for the first time she saw him. Really *saw* him; through his steely blue eyes, beyond the deep of his wide dark pupils into his spirit. For the first time she knew what it was like to experience the essence of him with the intelligence and maturity of a woman who had loved and survived broken hearts, had learned to trust her instincts, embraced a history that was less than perfect, and was grateful to be who she had grown to become.

Looking at him in the silvery moonlight she could clearly see Jake was more than handsome, funny and smart, an athletically gifted, chiseled frame as he towered above her. He was warm, kind, caring and considerate. He would never have knowingly hurt or deliberately wounded her, nor intentionally caused her torment with his leaving. Penny had blamed him, even cursed him after he left for college, a self-centered brat who couldn't see beyond her own shortsighted needs. His goodbye stung, leaving her anguished and inconsolable for months. Looking at him now, she knew it must have been equally hard for him to be away in a new place.

No, Jake was decent to the core, honest and genuine. As he lovingly returned her gaze, touching her as if she were delicate bone china, she felt ashamed and unworthy of such unabashed affection. In her heart and soul, she knew without question he meant every word. "I love you more," she managed. Pulling him closer, she was overcome with a sudden cloying desperation that even the nearness of him and the assurance of his love couldn't disperse. He held her for the longest time as she choked back tears she prayed he couldn't see. "I don't ever want to let you go again."

"Again?" Jake cocked his head and smiled his big toothy grin. "I'm right here, Babydoll," he said as he moved away from her slightly, taking off his gloves. "I'm not going anywhere. At least not until I give you this." Composing herself quickly she squinted at him with hands on her hips in mock consternation, "What are you up to, Jake Henderson?"

He took something from his pocket and asked her close her eyes and hold out her hand. She removed her own gloves, shoving one into each of her pockets. With eyes squeezed tightly shut and both hands cupped in front of her as if about to receive the sacrament, something warm and metallic dropped into them. "Okay," Jake went on, "go ahead and open them."

Penny opened one eye and then the other, closing her fingers around what Jake had just dropped into her waiting hands.

She gasped slightly and whispered, "Oh Jake, oh Jake, really??" She looked up at him wide eyed. There in the palm of her hand was a large gold ring with a brilliant sapphire blue stone in the middle. Etched into the metal surrounding the stone's setting were the words "Lisbon High School, Class of 1974." It was Jake's class ring. Her heart swelled in her chest and was doing flips as if it were the very first time she had seen it, the very first time it was given to her. How could she have forgotten!

Visions of walking down the school halls after the holiday break, flashing it for all to see flooded into her mind. The precious gift had been much too large for her petite digits so she had carefully wrapped the underside band in pale pink yarn so she could wear it on her ring finger rather than on a chain around her neck like some of the girls. Nope, Penny wanted that bit of jewelry front and center. It was official – she was Jake Henderson's steady girlfriend. They were *definitely* a couple.

Penny couldn't help herself. She had positively flaunted the prize whenever one Dandra Kay Holland was in the vicinity. Dandra Kay was a Barbie Doll of a girl, all lithe and slender with gorgeous long blonde hair and voluptuous curves in all the right places. Most guys in the school flagrantly chased after her and she knew it. Dandra Kay walked down the halls between classes with an exaggerated wiggle in her behind and her nose a mile in the air. She treated Penny (as well as most classmates) as if they were unworthy of sharing her space and absolutely relished the idea that every boy was constantly drooling in her direction. She was a notorious boyfriend poacher, something Penny was keenly on the lookout for at all times.

The whole school knew Dandra Kay had a major league crush on Jake and had been trying to get him to notice her for months. She had practically thrown herself at him after one of the football games that fall, hoping he would ask her to the big homecoming dance.

But Jake had politely excused himself and walked over to Penny who was standing by the bonfire chatting with two of her friends. He asked her right in front of them to be his date for homecoming. How she ever kept from squealing out loud and jumping up and down like half an idiot she'll never know. That was really the beginning of their courtship, but certainly not the end.

Dandra Kay's father was the banker in town and their stately manor was built on a hilltop west of town, its elegant stone façade and circular driveway reminiscent of an old English estate. The grounds of the home boasted the most beautiful flower gardens in the summer, with fragrant roses and hydrangea plants that had blooms the size of softballs. The front gate to the house was guarded on either side by two colossal granite lions, paws in the air and mouths open in a silent roar.

The front lawn, which was approximately the size of a football field, was adorned in the middle by an imported Italian water fountain designed in the shape of two immense back-to-back koi fish spewing an aqua-tinted geyser twenty feet into the air.

As the spoiled only child she was constantly catered to by her doting mother Laura, and everyone knew that "Daddy" Curt would give her anything she wanted – including a brand new BMW for her 16th birthday. Penny had heard on good authority that Dandra Kay's closet was as big as most bedrooms, and she regularly bragged about shopping trips to Saks and Nordstrom's in Minneapolis. She rarely wore the same outfit twice and Penny was convinced her wardrobe of shoes alone rivaled any Hollywood starlet.

The Hollands even had an in-ground pool, which was the only one in town. Dandra Kay would hold lavish pool parties in the summer, complete with a hired DJ and catered BBQ, and to which Penny was never invited. If she hadn't been invited before, she surely wasn't going to be invited now – not after Dandra Kay got a gander at the bauble Penny was presently flashing at every opportunity. No, by next summer she and Jake would have been together a whole year and Penny never did see the inside of the house OR swim in that pool.

Sensing that Penny was slightly intimidated by Dandra Kay, Jake regularly reassured her that girls like Dandra Kay were definitely not his style. Deep inside Penny had to admit that she was secretly delighted knowing her rival for Jake's affection was absolutely green with envy because it was Penny Raney and not her that held the attention of the most amazing guy in the whole school.

"Look inside," he motioned for her to turn the ring over. Penny rotated the gold band until she was looking at the underside of the stone setting. "There," he pointed to something engraved on the inside of the ring. Penny held it up in the moonlight to be able to see it better. "PJR...Always and forever yours," she read slowly. When she had finished reciting the words aloud, Jake pulled her close to him and looked directly into her eyes. "I mean it, Penny. Nobody will ever wear that ring but you. Not ever."

"Thank you SO much, Jake. I am the happiest girl in town. Heck, in the state...the country, the UNIVERSE." He laughed and pulled her close. They sealed the exchange with a kiss that took her breath away. His warm mouth tasted of cool icicles and Juicy Fruit gum and she eagerly returned his ardor, putting her arms around his waist and holding him tightly in the middle of the bandstand. As they parted, flakes of snow began falling gently.

"I have something for you, too," Penny said as she reached down into her pocket and pulled out a small, black box about the size of a deck of cards. She held her breath as he looked at her and then opened it.

Inside was an even smaller sterling silver box in the shape of a heart with a place for a key to fit right in the middle. Beneath the glimmering heart was a long, thin chain at the end of which dangled a tiny silver key no bigger than a paper clip. He lifted the chain up, looking at the key. "Put it in the lock and open it," urged Penny, smiling with anticipation.

Jake took the delicate box in one hand and with the other put the key into the lock and turned it ever so gently. The heart-shaped lid sprang open to reveal something nestled in red velvet. It was a small snapshot of Penny and Jake that had been taken at homecoming. In the diminutive photograph Jake was looking down on Penny as she was standing on an old wooden crate and reaching up to kiss him. They were both laughing because Jake had just remarked he was going to carry that crate with him wherever he went if it meant she would kiss him again.

"I love it, Pen. Honestly I do. It is just you and me. I will remember exactly how happy I am right now every time I look at it." He smiled and kissed her sweetly. "Thank you for the best Christmas present ever." Jake put the chain around his neck and tucked it into his shirt and then the box into a pocket inside his jacket so as not to lose it. He leaned down and picked her up, twirling her around in the snow. "Have I told you lately how much I love you Penny Jane Raney!" he yelled loud enough for the entire neighborhood to have heard. All she could do was giggle and savor every second.

Lights from a passing car interrupted their enchanted Christmas Eve celebration. Jake took off in a dead run towards the playground, where a blinking Frosty the Snowman in his top hat and bright orange carrot nose appeared to be gathering Alvin and his Chipmunks together for a holiday sing-a-long. The Chipmunks were holding lighted sheet music and Frosty held a lighted baton that moved up and down as if he were conducting the whole scenario.

Penny followed Jake over to the swings. He dusted one off, bowing low and gesturing grandly for her to take a seat as if she were royalty mounting her throne. Before he gave her a push he snuck up behind her and nuzzled her ear, giving her soft kisses on the neck. The sensation of his warm lips on her cool neck sent chills down her spine, for all the right reasons.

She tilted back and pointed her toes back and then to the sky pumping her legs as he pushed her higher and higher. In that moment, Penny was a child again, grinning ear to ear, reveling in the weightless feeling of flying through the air. Jake stopped pushing her swing and walked around to stand right in front of her. "Jump!" He urged her, "Come on, bail out!" He stood there, arms wide open daring Penny to let go and trust that he would catch her. He was knee deep in the snow, stocking cap slightly askew, white breath hanging around his face like a dense fog.

"I can't!" Penny shrieked as her pumping legs sent her soaring ever higher. "I'm afraid." Although she was laughing, there was something undeniably scary about letting go, giving in to the urge to abandon logic and embrace something slightly dangerous. It was petrifying to think what would happen if Jake stepped away, even an inch. But wasn't that the way it was with life, with love? At some point you just have to do it, to let go and conquer the fear that's gripping your guts and whispering in your ear "he'll drop you" even as you edge closer and closer to surrender. The allure of the unknown can be intoxicating, the regret of chances taken only to be disillusioned, soul crushing. Even life altering.

Penny could hear her mother's voice as it echoed in the recesses of her mind, "Penny Jane, you're going to break your neck if you fall off that swing!" She had a sudden flashback of lingering over too many glasses of wine with her best friend Lindsey admonishing, "Nothing ventured, nothing gained. If you don't enter, you can't win," as she struggled with the idea of dating again after the divorce. "Make like Nike and JUST DO IT, Penny!" Lindsey had pleaded with her until she finally capitulated and joined an online dating website.

"I'll never let you go, Penny. I promise!" Jake implored, his arms open to receive her. "Ok, just promise not to drop me!" Penny winced and closed her eyes as gravity pulled her back to earth. She thrust her legs heavenward as the swing went up over

Jake's head one last time. Penny yelled, "1…2…3!" She let go at the very top of the arc and sailed through the air as the swing clanked and fell empty behind her.

It took only split seconds, but in those moments between the release and the landing, Penny was convinced there would never be any safer place on earth than in the arms of Jake Henderson. She wasn't just jumping from a swing; she was letting go in an act of pure faith, and receiving a reciprocal expression of assurance in return. Just as he promised, he caught her in mid-air and they both tumbled into the bank behind them laughing so hard they had tears in their eyes. Jake had her comfortably in his grip as their inertia splayed snow in every direction. "See," Jake said puffing up his chest. "I told you I'd catch you."

All Penny could think was yes, he had. Jake had caught her attention, her adoration, her admiration, her always and forever love. She landed on top of him and though still hooting over their grand trick, Penny took his face in her hands and kissed him with an abandon that felt as if her flight had freed her from every moor she'd ever felt holding her back. There was no doubt in her mind; she loved Jake Henderson deep and fiercely.

The two of them lay there for a long time holding hands looking up at the stars, until the gently falling snow had turned their dark coats to white. "I think we better get you home," Jake said breaking the spell. "I don't want your father to come looking for you, especially not on Christmas Eve. I need to stay in good standing, ya know." He got up and pulled Penny out of the snow by her hands, helping to brush the snow off of her coat.

Penny felt her heart sink even though she knew he was right. They were alone here in this fairy-tale winter kingdom, just the two of them leaving their prints in the snow. It made her sad to think the night would be over, and briefly Penny allowed the reality of what was to come temporarily steal the ecstasy she had been experiencing in their solitude.

Together they walked back to his car, chilled to the bone but beaming inside and out. Always the gentleman, Jake unlocked her car door first and made sure her coat was tucked inside before he shut the door. He climbed in the driver's side and revved up the engine. "We better let it warm up a little," he said as the defroster kicked in to clear the frosted over windows. "Gosh, I wonder what we could do until it warms up?" Jake winked at her and they leaned in to share another kiss.

Penny's heart was melting faster than snow falling into a fire as Jake brushed the hair from her eyes and carefully removed the hat from her head, placing it in her lap. As his fingers entwined in her long, brown hair, he pulled her lips gently to his, cupping her head with his hands. "I love the softness of your hair, it always smells so wonderful." He whispered as he breathed in the scent of her, lips touching, warm tongue seeking. "It's my Herbal Essence shampoo," Penny quietly giggled as her mouth found his.

As the car idled quietly in the darkness, they remained locked in each other's arms, desire building more urgently with every kiss. Her heart was racing, and she was sure Jake must be able to hear it as he slipped his hand inside her coat. As he wrapped his hand around her waist, Penny felt the cool of his hands on her warm flesh. Penny could tell Jake wanted her as much as she wanted him, for this night to continue, to be endless.

The stillness was suddenly interrupted with the noisy roar of the engine as Jake's foot accidentally slipped and came down hard on the accelerator pedal. Startled, they quickly regained their composure as Jake hastily released the accelerator. Smoothing his hair back, he fumbled for words as if still very much caught up in the heat of their passionate moment, "Well, I guess that's our sign," he said, regarding Penny through heavy lids as if to say, "You know I didn't want to stop." Face flushed and still breathing rapidly, Penny took his hand in hers as she settled back into the passenger seat. "To be continued," smiled Penny.

Jake shifted the gear to reverse and paused briefly. They looked at each other one last time, co-conspirators in this extraordinary memory of their first Christmas Eve, knowing something incredibly intimate and special had transpired between them. Their evening was something nobody else could ever share, would ever even know about. Well, until Penny showed up in school with Jake's class ring on her finger, anyway. Take THAT Dandra Kay Holland!

Finally resigned to the fact their time together was coming to an end, Jake pulled out into the street, being careful not to go too fast. The snow had continued to fall over the past two hours and the roads were slicker than ever. The evening's festivities drawing to a close, lights were dimming all over town as they made their way down the slippery side roads to Main Street.

As they briefly stopped at the single stop light in town, Jake reached over and pulled her hand to his lips planting a warm smooch on it before setting it back in her lap. She held his hand tightly as they continued the last few blocks to her house.

All the while they were driving in silence, Penny was slowly acclimating herself to the present, to the time and space she had traveled to be home again; and to the prospect of being able to have a conversation with her father. She was hoping she would catch her dad alone, although she wasn't at all sure how to approach him.

He liked to read by the fireplace sometimes until late into the night, probably relishing the quiet as all parents do, with his four boisterous progeny finally in bed. Maybe he wouldn't want to be interrupted, maybe he would brush off her attempt to talk and tell her he was tired and for her to just go on up to bed; scarier still, what if he gave her his undivided attention and listened intently, patiently waiting for her to somehow muddle through her homily? She would have no choice but to offer at least some explanation as to why she was standing there all tongue-tied.

Penny was beginning to feel an underlying current of nervousness running through her as the car turned onto Highway 27, taking them closer to Weber Street. Her house was now just a few blocks away. The beating of her heart was not quickened now by passion, but by fear. What to say and how to say it, what would his reaction be? Could she even come up with the right words to say what was in her heart?

She had already learned in these few short hours that sometimes in *this* present, in *this* 1973, she literally couldn't speak her true thoughts, what her mind and emotions wanted to convey. Would she even be able to coherently form the sentences she had been rolling over and over in her head for the past forty years? Could she adequately express the thoughts she hoped, by some small miracle, were making their way to her father's ears in Heaven? This was her chance to say them out loud and to the person she most anxiously wanted to hear them. But what *would* come out as she opened her mouth to speak?

The thought of having a serious talk with a man she revered and frankly was terribly intimidated by was scary. She bit her lower lip, fretting mutely as Jake's Mustang turned left onto Weber Street, slowly passing house after house, a few now dark with older residents having turned in for the night. Part of her wanted her own house to be completely black with her family already sleeping soundly, but she was sure it was still too early for everyone to be sleeping.

Penny's stomach was in knots as Jake pulled into the driveway and shifted the car into park, turning off the engine. A dim light was shining through the curtains in the living room. No doubt someone was waiting for her to be the last one up the steps to bed before rummaging through closets and other secret hiding places to surround the tree with Santa's bounty. Her family had always opened their gifts Christmas Eve, but Santa showed up Christmas Day, leaving each child unwrapped presents under the tree so they would see them instantly as they walked into the room.

From the time she could remember, Penny rarely slept a wink Christmas Eve. She would lie in bed, a bundle of shivering nerves, so excited to see what would be left for her once Santa had come and gone. She was always the first to rush down the steps when the noises downstairs had ceased and she was sure the coast was clear. Penny would sneak down and survey the treasures under the tree, then dash hurriedly back up the stairs to wake her sisters, letting them know that Santa had brought them exactly what they had asked for – and most of the time, much more than any of them even had imagined. This Christmas Eve Penny would lie awake for a much different reason.

Jake turned to her and said with all the sincerity he could muster, "I love you Penny. Thank you so much for my gift. I hope you know it means a lot to me." He pulled the delicate chain from under his jacket and held up the little key. "I can't think of a better place to put the key to your heart…than right next to mine." He tucked the chain with the dangling silver key back into his shirt and looked directly into her eyes.

She wished she wasn't so distracted, because the sparkle of his azure eyes in the dim light was captivating. Penny was gazing lovingly at them as he reached out to kiss her goodnight. In that moment, she was overcome with love for this sweet, amazing boy. She realized just how much she appreciated everything about him, about his character. How she wished she had been able to see Jake this way when they lived this night the first time. How could she ever have taken him for granted? The way he felt about her was plainly evident as he touched her face. His tenderness silently articulated everything she needed to know about how genuinely he cared for her, how real his love for her had always been.

From those dreamy eyes and strong Cary Grant chin to the shaggy hair sticking out like white straw from under his cap, to his massive hands that could effortlessly throw a football almost the entire length of the field, Jake was undisputedly an incredibly handsome guy on the outside. But on the inside he was even more impressive. Forget Texas, his heart was as big as the state of North Dakota, from Fargo to the Montana border. And she knew now, without question, it belonged to her.

She pulled Jake's class ring from her pocket and slipped it over her thumb holding it up with a chuckle. "Don't worry, I won't lose it," she quipped. "I will figure out a way to wear this one way or another." Jake took her hand in his and looked at her intently. "I meant it, Penny. That ring will always be yours. You're the most amazing girl I have ever met, and it will mean a lot to me to see you wearing it. I want everyone in the school to know that you're my girl."

"Even Dandra Kay Holland?" She teased. He laughed out loud as he emphatically nodded his head up and down, "ESPECIALLY Dandra Kay Holland."

"You better get inside," he said with a sigh, "I heard we're getting more snow tomorrow. Bud said something about taking out the snowmobiles later in the afternoon. I know you are going over to your Aunt's house for Christmas dinner, are you in after that? I know Mom and Dad would love to see you, maybe we could stop by tomorrow evening and say hello. I have a feeling my mother bought you a little something," he said playfully as he leaned over and kissed her one more time.

"I'm definitely in," Penny offered. And she truly was very, very in. She couldn't wait for tomorrow to get there so she could be with Jake again. She hadn't been on a snowmobile in decades, so that experience ought to be interesting!

Penny hopped out of the car and waved a little sadly as Jake backed away. She stood there for a long time watching the red tail lights of the Mustang become faint as he drove down the street, finally disappearing around the corner in a billow of exhaust.

Walking across the yard, Penny tried to gather her wits, preparing for what waited for her on the other side of the cheerful red door. She stopped before reaching the last step and took it all in, looking up and down the quiet street that was her environment for so many years. It looked smaller and more compact somehow, even though as a girl it appeared a much vaster neighborhood.

It was different when she was a child, a simpler time with few worries of kidnappings or terrorism, "stranger danger" or violent crime. In Lisbon it would have been big news for someone to be caught shoplifting or breaking into a home and taking what didn't belong to them. Kids playing pranks or stealing apples from a neighbor's yard was about as bad as the mischief got. Maybe on Halloween a house would wake up to toilet paper strung around the trees and bushes, but certainly nothing that came close to a felony was ever committed as far back as she could remember.

It was a safe place to live, a friendly community that welcomed new families among those who had lived there for generations. Penny marveled at how her own street was incredibly diverse in that several elderly retirees lived next to homes with young families. Those families might be doctors or business executives, but there also were teachers and blue-collar workers. It was a harmonious blend of young and old, and everyone treated each other with kindness and respect regardless of their background, social or financial status. They were just neighbors on Weber Street, looking out for each other. If everyone had grown up in a town like Lisbon, on a street like her own, she imagined it could be a very different world.

Just as Penny was about to go in the house, the front door opened and there stood her father dressed in his winter coat and gray felt cowboy hat, holding a wrapped basket of fruit, nuts and cookies in his hands. She jumped back slightly as his frame filled the doorway. "Gosh Penny, I didn't realize you were there. I'm sorry if I startled you." He said. "Your mom wanted me to run this gift out to the Kinney place. I guess Mrs. Kinney isn't doing well and you know they don't have much. Want to come with me to spread a little holiday cheer?"

All Penny could manage to say was, "sure." Her dad handed her the basket and told her to wait while he backed the car out of the garage. As she stood on the snowy step she saw the big tail end of the Buick backing slowly out of the garage. She took a big gulp of the frigid air, which made her choke a little since her throat was suddenly bone dry.

This was it. It was her chance to talk to her father. The Kinney family lived a few miles west of town on a gravel road out past the old quarry. She knew the roads were slippery and they would be driving slowly. It would give them plenty of time to talk while they made their way to the Kinney's and back. Penny fidgeted with the wrapping paper on her lap as they pulled into the street.

Penny sat there, staring out the window, trying to come up with the words to start the conversation. They crossed the main bridge in town and passed by the little police station where one dim light was shining over the entrance and no car was in sight. "Harold must be on patrol. Sure hope nobody has car trouble tonight," her father said, almost as if to himself.

Seeing that police station brought back the memory of one of the reasons why Penny felt the desperate need to talk to her dad. The main reason, anyway. There were plenty of things in her past that she wanted to apologize for, not the least of which was failing to be the best student she could be and opening her big, fat, sarcastic teenage mouth inappropriately too often. Penny's stubborn nature and quick temper got her into trouble way more than her other siblings, who seemed to breeze through life without much angst. With Penny, on the other hand, everything seemed more of a struggle and she was sure her parents were exasperated with her more often than not. But as far as transgressions go, Penny knew the Gary Falsted debacle was at the top of the list.

Lost or unwanted animals weren't the only things that caught Penny's attention growing up. It was during her freshman and sophomore years of high school, way before Jake Henderson, Penny found herself drawn to one of the boys in class that she would have identified as teetering on the very fringe of accepted high school society; somewhat of an outcast.

Penny had befriended Gary Falsted during one of the English classes they shared. Gary came from a poor family who lived in one of the parts of town Penny had little reason to ever frequent. She felt sorry for Gary, who always walked with his head down and ate his meager lunch out of an old paper bag, alone and off in a secluded corner of the gymnasium that doubled as the lunchroom. It was always the same thing – a bologna sandwich and an apple. Every day. She had driven by his house once and told herself that she needed to make an effort to be nicer to him.

The Falsted house was a tiny ramshackle cabin on the south side of Lisbon, within a block of the lumberyard and across the railroad tracks from the last gas station in town. The front porch sagged dangerously, and there were numerous missing shingles on the roof, which only added to its sad appearance. The clapboard siding showed hints of once being a cheery shade of blue, most of the paint long since chipped off as the years of standing in the harsh North Dakota elements eroded the enamel's protection bit by bit. Dingy paper shades hung at odd angles in the windows, several torn and ragged along the edge.

Penny had heard rumors that Gary's father was a drunk who couldn't hold a job, and had left when Gary and his younger siblings Ray and Goober were just babies. She knew that his mother Ida, who poured drinks and was a waitress at Bueller's Beer Barn, had a certain unflattering reputation for making a few extra dollars on the side at the expense of other women's husbands. Of course, she didn't know any of it to be true for a fact.

Gary himself usually wore the same two or three threadbare oversized flannel shirts and jeans to school every day of the week, and his hair was a mess of black tangles in dire need of some shampoo and a comb. He usually sported a couple of day's growth of stubbly beard and was always in need of a shave. One time Penny felt so bad that he was being teased relentlessly about his appearance that she spent her babysitting money to buy him some shampoo and a comb that was small enough to fit into his back pocket, along with a new razor and extra blades. She had made sure nobody was around when she left the package in his locker after school.

The next day she smiled when she saw a clean-shaven, much more confident Gary walking a little taller down the hall. When they took their seats in Mr. Hamm's Biology class he gave her a quick nod as if to say thanks. Penny had just smiled and told him he looked real nice, making him blush and smile for the first time.

Penny could see him struggling to keep up with the work, and her nurturing instincts had taken over. She offered to tutor him during their morning study hall and he had eagerly accepted. Although Penny could tell Gary had a bit of a crush on her, she kept things strictly tutor/pupil in nature. Even then, she and Jake had been eyeing each other and occasionally he would wave or chat with her before band or choir rehearsal.

What came next would cause heartbreaking consequences for Penny, and created a terrible rift in a home that had for the most part always been fairly harmonious. Her association and relationship with Gary, seen by her parents as someone to avoid, would cause the headstrong Penny to dig in her heels in defiance.

She would allow Gary to walk her home some days after school to the complete and utter disapproval of her mother. "He reeks of cigarette smoke!" she admonished. "This is NOT the kind of boy you should be bringing around here." There were fights and misunderstandings as she tried to defend her relationship, which always was completely platonic. What was wrong with being friends with someone who needed one so badly?

Penny wasn't about to let anyone, least of all her parents, dictate who her friends could be. Penny remained belligerent, even sneaking out at night to meet up with him and the few friends he did have in the park. Gary's friends were the "greasers" and "party boys," the drinkers and smokers. Penny thought they were all decent guys – they just came from circumstances that were far less advantageous than her own.

Over time there were more arguments at home that led to being grounded, privileges taken away, and harsh words spoken in anger. Penny began to sneak out more frequently, sometimes joining Gary and his friends in smoking and once even swiping alcohol from her parent's liquor cabinet. Penny had suspected the boys might be shoplifting and getting into trouble, because she knew none of them had the money for what they were smoking and drinking, but she ignored it.

Her grades suffered, even scoring low marks in the classes she had typically done well. She knew her parents were at their wits' end with her, but she remained insolent and willfully disobeyed. Her father grew quiet whenever she was around and most of the time acted as if Penny wasn't even in the room. That stung her badly, but she knew she deserved every bit of the cold shoulder treatment. She knew she was doing things that made them worry with good cause, but in her stupid teenage brain, she justified everything she was doing and instead hurled insults back at her parents, accusing them of being hypocritical and elitist.

Sandra and Cara were constantly in her face, warning her that the crowd she was hanging out with was tarnishing her reputation at school, and that they were hearing ugly things being said about her. Even then Penny refused to relent. Nobody was going to tell HER whom she could befriend.

Everything came to a head one night when she was in the wrong place at the wrong time, with the wrong people. She had snuck out past midnight and was riding in the backseat of Gary's friend Russell's old Ford when suddenly there were flashing red and blue lights in the rear view mirror. Penny had no idea what was going on, but she was about to learn a very hard lesson.

Harold Williams was the only policeman in Lisbon and evidently had been watching the boys' activity well before Penny had been picked up and began riding in the car with them. Officer Williams asked them to all please exit the vehicle and after some jawboning back and forth trying to act tough, they all piled out of the car and stepped to the side of the road. Flashlight in hand, Harold checked under the front seat, in the glove box and center console, taking his time to turn over every item, check each and every corner. He moved to the backseat repeating his search with the flashlight as the boys kicked the dirt and Penny stood with her arms crossed, convinced they were just being harassed for no reason.

After what seemed like an hour, Harold finally picked up the cushion to the back, which was one long, bench-style seat. To Penny's complete surprise and unqualified distress, the compartment underneath was filled with beer and other bottles of hard liquor. And if that wasn't enough, there were at least a dozen small baggies of what looked like marijuana. Her mouth dropped open and she gasped in fear and dismay. "Oh my God, Gary," was all she could manage to say.

"You're going to need to follow me to the station, kids," Officer Williams said shaking his head. "And you'll need to call your parents." Penny was nauseous the whole way to the police station, which stood on a corner of Main Street just to the east of the one traffic light in town. Everyone who had been driving up and down the boulevard with their dates swung by to gawk at them as they filed into the police station. Nobody said a word as they took their seats and Officer Williams took off his coat, hanging it on a hook behind the door, purposely taking his time to make them sweat.

Penny was shaking uncontrollably and tears were streaming down her face as Officer Williams sat behind his big desk and gave them a very stern look. With all seriousness he said quietly, "You kids are in a lot of trouble. Would you like to tell me where you got all that garbage in your backseat? You know you are all under the legal age as far as the alcohol, and I suspect it goes without saying whatever is in those baggies didn't come from your mother's garden."

When I Get Home

"I want a lawyer!" Gary sneered in an arrogant tone that immediately drew Penny's undivided attention. "I'm not saying another word to you. As far as I'm concerned you can shove those bags where the sun don't shine."

Gary was usually very quiet and unassuming. The venomous way he hissed at Officer Williams shocked her completely. It was as if she was seeing him clearly for the first time. Gary showed no respect for Officer Williams, and the other two boys were equally as insolent and sarcastic. It became crystal clear in an instant that of course, her parents had been right. He truly was someone to avoid. How incredibly naïve and stupid she had been. Sadly, that realization was a classic case of too little, too late.

Her father had warned Penny that if she played with fire, eventually she would get burned. She wasn't just slightly singed; she was in flames. It instantly made her sick with shame and regret. Her parents had wanted to protect her from this very thing. Look at the mess she was in. As she sat there sweating, sick with fear, her only thought was the certainty that they could never forgive her.

"Penny, I've known your folks a long time. Your dad and I went to high school together. I trust if you call him, he'll come to get you. I hope you will learn a valuable lesson here. I know you didn't have anything to do with what the boys have been up to. I saw them loading everything into the car way before they picked you up. But you're going to have to go to court and answer for this, just like they are, because you were with them. It was a bad decision on your part to be involved with these yahoos." With that he picked up the old black phone with the rotary dial and turned it towards Penny. It made an echoing *clank* as it landed in front of her. "Go ahead and make the call."

Penny's fingers were shaking horribly as she dialed the number, 3...4...6...8...9. She felt as if she would vomit as she heard her father's voice on the other end of the phone. Through her tears, she sobbed "Dad, it's Penny."

They rode home in silence, her father firmly gripping each side of the steering wheel; jaw jutted forward, breathing shallow. Penny knew he was trying very hard not to explode at her. She could feel the waves of disappointment and heartache emanating from him. How embarrassing it must have been to have everyone in town watch him retrieve his unruly daughter from, of all places, the **POLICE STATION** for crying out loud! Penny would much rather he yelled at her, hit her, call her every name she was calling herself. The tense atmosphere, the unbearable silent treatment always hurt more than hearing it out loud. "Punish me! PUNISH ME!" she was screaming inside. "I deserve everything you have to say, the worst of the worst."

Unable to stop crying, overwhelmed with guilt and shame, all Penny could say through her choking tears was a feeble, "You were right. I'm so sorry." Her father didn't look at her once on the drive home; never uttered a single word.

Immediately upon arriving home, Penny ran upstairs to her bedroom and flung herself on the bed. Sandra had heard her come up the steps and stood in the doorway of Penny's room, smirking in a way that told Penny she knew what had happened. "Well, I guess you really blew it this time, Goofy. Nice move." She then turned on her heels and left Penny to languish in the agony of the consequences Penny knew she deserved in spades.

For days nobody said anything about what had happened. Penny sat quietly through dinner, tried to do extra chores around the house, tried to be the best possible girl. She came right home after school and did her homework and even did extra credit to try to make up ground in her failing grades. But it was too late.

Nothing she tried would ever repair what she had done. The damage was permanent and hung over her like a black cloud.

Her parents went about their normal routine, and it wasn't long before the incident was old news, but Penny knew it had killed her mother to be the talk of the town, to hear the whispers behind her back. Her parents spoke to her only when necessary, and when the letter came telling her what date she was to show up in court, her father just slid it across the table and said quietly, "I'll go with you." Penny couldn't even look at him; she just bit her lip and ran upstairs so he wouldn't see her cry. She wanted to die rather than to be such a disappointment, such a profound failure. How could she have let her whole family down like this?

Penny tried to stand tall when the magistrate asked her to approach his table at the brief hearing in the courthouse a few weeks later. She could feel her father's eyes on her as she made her way carefully across the creaky wooden floor to take whatever punishment was going to be handed out to her. Would they send her away? Would she be wearing an orange jumpsuit and picking up trash along the highway like she had seen prisoners do before? Her legs were shaking so hard she felt sure the sound was audible in the solemn quiet of the courtroom.

Thankfully, Officer Williams had vouched for the fact he was certain Penny didn't know anything about what was under the seat in the back of Russell's Ford, and a letter to that effect had been given to the judge prior to her appearance.

The humiliation her father felt as he sat behind her viewing the proceeding must have made him so incredibly sad. Here was his beautiful daughter, his little girl with so much promise, so much talent, ruining her own reputation and standing in the community with such foolish, immature behavior.

What was about to happen here could possibly follow her around the rest of her life, and nobody was filled with as much regret for her irresponsible decisions as Penny. The punishment she was giving herself was as bad as anything anybody else could do to her. She was filled with shame and loathing, and in her mind, didn't deserve anything but whatever the law was about to hand down. "Show no mercy," she thought as she stood before the magistrate. "Throw the book at me." Her knees were trembling, but she managed to stand there without fainting.

She didn't remember anything that was said in the courtroom once it was her turn. Her father ended up paying an $85 fine plus $12 in court costs, which promptly was deducted from allowance or reimbursed from babysitting funds. But the aftermath of that awful event couldn't be wiped away by merely paying back a few dollars. It had changed her entire relationship with every member of her family in a negative way – especially her father.

People at school were calling Penny "jailbird" behind her back and she wasn't allowed to try out for cheerleading that fall. Sandra and Cara were teased in school because of her, and took out their displeasure on her by giving her the cold shoulder for a very long time. She wasn't invited to play board games on rainy days and they only reluctantly let her join them to sing around the piano. Friends that used to support Penny turned on her and she felt very abandoned and ostracized from the group of girlfriends she previously had thought counted her as a solid part of their group. For months afterward she was treated like a pariah.

Her parents told her she needed to earn back their trust and she wasn't allowed sleepovers or to stay out past any sanctioned extracurricular event for six months afterwards. Penny never put up a fuss or challenged any of the punishment she received. In her mind she deserved every minute of it, and for years afterwards blamed herself for every ill word uttered, every misfortune that came her way as just reward for her previous heinous deeds. She didn't have much self worth to begin with, but the ordeal with Gary just served to prove she had been right.

Sitting there in the car with her dad, back in 1973, all Penny could think about was her chance to at least try to change things, to give a voice to the amends she had been trying desperately to make over the past year. Just then, the car slipped on ice going around a corner, causing Penny to grab the door handle. Her dad chuckled quietly and said, "We're fine, Penny. Just a little slippery is all."

"Are we, Dad?" Penny finally managed to say something. "It doesn't feel that way to me." He looked over at her for a second before turning his eyes back on the road. "What do you mean, Penny?" Dead silence.

Here it was, her moment of truth, her opportunity. What would come out of her mouth? She said a silent prayer that God would allow her to say everything she had wanted to say to her father in that conversation she had planned to have before he died. This opportunity in and of itself was nothing short of a miracle. Surely the amazing circumstances in which she found herself were the answer to that long-held desire.

Through the years, she had spent countless hours on the couches of counselors talking through her grief, seeking permission to give up her life-long penance. Like a sinner begging for absolution in a confessional, she waited to hear the one meaningful sentence that could wipe it all away. She wanted so badly to be released from this self-imposed prison of regret. But no amount of platitudes or logical thinking could erase her own warped sense of the damage done, which anyone with half a brain could tell her was complete nonsense and a useless waste of valuable time better spent among the living. Penny was so sure her father died believing she would never amount to much.

She had talked to so many people, read article after article about people like her, those who had lost loved ones in an instant living with the ache of regret and longing for closure. It was awful to even admit, but when her friend Doug lost his mother to cancer Penny had actually been envious as he relayed stories about spending time with his mother, resolving their old hurts, healing old wounds from the past, clearing the air.

Doug held his mother's hand as she took her last breath, knowing with certainty that everything that needed to be said, had been. They were able to spend precious moments along the road to their final goodbye. "In the end," Doug had shared, "we were okay. I knew she loved me, and she knew I loved her, and she knew I was thankful she had been my mother. I am blessed with that assurance, and it brings me a much-needed sense of peace. I said and did everything I could; there was nothing left unsaid."

Now it was Penny's turn. She looked over at her father, his handsome face concentrating on the road ahead. She alone knew the sad truth that in just a few short years he would be gone, taken from them in the blink of an eye. The fact she was even here with her father, close enough to touch him should have been enough. Just to see his face one more time, to hear his voice resonating in her ears, to feel the warmth of his hand *should* have been enough. Penny was certain anyone in her shoes would feel grateful simply being in their loved one's presence. For a moment she felt a twinge of guilt in her greed to assuage the sins of her past; it suddenly seemed so selfish.

No doubt across the country on that very day there were thousands of families missing someone they loved around their table. Thousands of families just like hers grieving amidst the holiday celebration.

When I Get Home

Even though it was 17-year-old Penny riding in the car on this snowy Christmas Eve, in reality Penny was 58 years old, completely coherent and blessed with the benefit of hindsight. She was a grown woman who had harbored far too many years of sadness and regret at not being able to undo the shame and disappointment of the past. This had to be her moment, her opportunity; her do-over.

She gulped and closed her eyes, hoping the right words were about to spill out. Hoping it wasn't just some lame comment about the weather, or a half-hearted "thanks for the Christmas presents."

Through the years Penny had thoughtfully considered what she would say to him if she could turn back the clock. Yes, she certainly felt she owed him an epic apology for all the angst and sleepless nights her poor choices and ill-conceived decisions had no doubt caused both of her parents. But as the years ticked by, she realized that what she really wanted to say more than anything, was a very heartfelt and genuine – *thank you.*

Penny felt she owed much of the credit for her gifts and talents to her dad or at least lineage on that side of the family. The Raney family was filled with assorted writers, artists, musicians and creative types. For sure she got her spunk, independent nature and ability to handle whatever happened in life from Grandma M and the Truman bunch; but her ability to write, her sense of humor, her lifelong desire to learn, her sense of adventure – that was all Raney. Penny knew many of the personality traits she considered extra bonuses were a lot like her father's.

Penny recalled after her dad's funeral, one of his good friends who also worked with him shared a story about the wonderful speeches her dad would write, and how he was always a gregarious and sought-after speaker. She knew from first-hand experience that he could definitely be the life of the party and was a lot of fun to be around. Penny was grateful to have inherited his ability to put words together, to make people laugh, to entertain with a certain witty style. She had a great circle of close friends, many of whom would regularly tell her that it wasn't a party if Penny wasn't there.

Like her father, Penny had also been a success in her profession, working her way from Copy Editor to Director of her department with a team of people who reported to her. Penny didn't shy away from responsibility or difficult decisions and had always received excellent performance reviews and her share of professional and industry accolades.

She had come to believe her dad would have been immensely proud of her accomplishments had he lived all of the years he so richly deserved. Penny felt certain he would have been in the front row cheering her on during the amazing victories in life, every bit as much as he would have been in her corner when the inevitable adversities of life threw her a curve ball. He would have been so incredibly proud of each one of his children.

Most of all, Penny wanted to thank him for taking such good care of their family, for being an amazing provider and leader. He was the epitome of a patriarch, devoted to doing what was best for those he cared about. Whatever else happened, Penny never doubted that she was greatly loved. They all knew their entire family was his priority and he would have been fiercely protective of any one of them.

Both of her parents taught them all to be appreciative, to understand and be assured that what their family was blessed to have and to share with each other was something special, something most families would never experience; something never to be taken for granted. Penny knew right now, in this present, that through the coming years none of them ever would. It was the most amazing gift, which couldn't be wrapped and Santa couldn't leave under the tree. It was the gift of their family, and he would never know the powerful bond they had with each other was only made stronger and more resilient by his untimely passing.

Her dad was still looking ahead, keeping his eyes on the road when Penny spoke again. Not at all sure what would come out of her mouth, she took a deep breath. After hesitating for a moment, she blurted, "Dad, I just want you to know that…I love you."

After ruminating endlessly for forty years about how to change the course of history, Penny had instantaneously realized in her heart and mind, those words – those three universally understood words – were really all that ever needed to be said. All the thoughts and feelings of decades were condensed; every apology, each regret, the sum total of a lifetime of "what ifs" was wiped away as she saw the lines on his face soften, the glimmer of a smile emerge.

"I know, Penny. I've always known," he said softly. "And I hope *you* know that no matter what happens, no matter what you could possibly do, nothing…and I mean nothing…would ever change the fact that I love you, too. More than you could ever know." With that he reached over, took her hand and gave it a big squeeze.

Penny wished they weren't driving so she could reach over and hug him with the unbelievable relief and joy that merely hearing those words had released inside of her. Penny was crying real tears. They were dropping one by one like salty raindrops onto the cellophane of the basket meant for the Kinney's. She took a gloved hand and wiped them away, looking out the frosty passenger window as she did.

There was a moment of awkward silence before her father added in a tone Penny knew was an effort to lighten the mood, "You know I really like that young Jake Henderson. He's a good kid, polite, treats you with respect like the beautiful, smart young woman that you are. You deserve someone like that, Penny." Then more seriously, "I just want you to be cautious of investing too much of yourself in a relationship with a guy who is off to college next year. If it were up to me, you'd have the chance to date lots of Jake Hendersons before the right one steals your heart away for good. There is nothing wrong with playing the field a little, you know."

He paused as they turned the final corner and headed west on the street where the Kinney family lived. "I dated quite a few girls before I met your mother. That's how I knew she was head and shoulders above any of the others. I wouldn't have known how special she was if I hadn't met plenty who weren't. Does that make sense?"

Penny nodded, "Thanks Dad. I like Jake a lot. I know this is silly and I'm just 17, but I could see myself ending up with him someday. I mean, when we're done with college and everything." That part completely came out of left field, because what Penny was about to reveal was that she knew Jake would break up with her before he went away to college. Once again, only 1973 Penny was allowed to convey any thoughts.

She was going to tell him not to worry because he would have liked Mark and they had a lot of great years together and reared two amazing children and had made her a grandmother several times over. Those words would never be spoken.

She took off her glove, holding up her hand revealing Jake's ring with the bright blue stone positioned tightly on her left thumb. "He gave me his class ring tonight," Penny blushed a little remembering the passionate kisses they had shared in the aftermath of their gift exchange just an hour earlier. "It means we're going steady," then added with a chuckle, "Dandra Kay Holland is going to lose her mind!" They both laughed out loud.

When I Get Home

"Well," her dad continued slowly, "I'm happy for you. Just remember what I said, okay? And I'm here no matter how it all shakes out. You could certainly do a lot worse." Penny wanted to add, "Oh, don't you worry, I will!" She thought of the boys she dated before she married Mark, some of whom she knew weren't the caliber to receive a resounding two thumbs up. But she didn't comment further, and probably wouldn't have been able to anyway.

They pulled into the Kinney's driveway and her dad got out of the car leaving it running, heat billowing out of the floor vent to keep her cozy as he ran the errand at hand. He came around to where Penny was sitting to get the basket of holiday goodies. Penny handed her dad the basket and watched as he made his way cautiously up the slippery sidewalk, coat collar tucked up around his ears. There were lights on in the house and the door quickly opened after he knocked. Mr. Kinney greeted him with a hearty "Merry Christmas!" before they both disappeared inside.

She looked up at the sky through the windshield. It was still completely devoid of any type of cloud cover. Every star shone brightly and was twinkling as if to form a strand of holiday lights strung across the heavens just for her viewing pleasure. The only word that came to mind was glorious. It had truly been a glorious evening.

Penny thought back to her solo in church, the words of "O Holy Night" reverberating in her ears. How astounding it must have been two thousand years ago as the shepherds saw the angels and traveled by the light of the very same stars to fulfill the ancient prophecy of finding a babe in swaddling clothes lying in a manger.

How much more amazing still that the same God who created the heavens and earth, who gave His only Son to save the world had thought enough of her, of insignificant Penny Tomlin, to bestow upon her a gift more significant and precious than anything her human imagination could have dreamed possible.

She sat for a moment, in complete and utter disbelief that she was experiencing what Jesus Himself had declared to be true – that God knew each of us before we were ever born, knew the number of hairs on our heads, and wants nothing more than to bring light into the hearts of anyone who will invite Him in. Penny had never felt more loved, more cared for and precious than she did sitting in the car on that snowy Christmas Eve. Penny couldn't think of a more flawless ending to a most incredibly perfect evening.

She was still sitting in the stillness of the evening, her fingers subconsciously cradling Jake's ring in her hand when she heard the car door open and her father plopped himself back in the driver's seat. "What nice people," he remarked, as he put the car in reverse and backed out into the main road to head back to town. "They were very happy we remembered them and what they were going through with Mrs. Kinney's illness. Do what you can for others, Penny. It will come back to you a hundred times over." Penny smiled a smile filled with understanding and gratitude, for she knew that to be true more than her father or anyone else in Lisbon, North Dakota in 1973 could ever suspect.

The ride home seemed so much shorter than the drive out to the Kinney place. Before she knew it, they were pulling into the garage of their house on Weber Street. The lights were on in the kitchen and as they walked into the porch and up the steps to the enter through the back door, she could see her mother busily cleaning up the kitchen and organizing food they would take with them to her father's Uncle Barney and Aunt Helen's the next day.

Christmas Day dinners at Uncle Barney's house were always filled with plates of delicious roast turkey and ham, mounds of potatoes with giblet gravy, glazed carrots, fluffy white yeast rolls with plenty of butter and homemade cranberry sauce. As if the main event wasn't enough, there was also a whole table full of pies, cakes, cookies and the most amazing chocolate fudge on the planet. Penny's mouth started watering just thinking about it.

Her Aunt Helen always set such a beautiful holiday table, replete with fresh greenery and flowers. Penny especially loved the little painted china name card holders in various shapes, like angels or snowmen that were set with care around the table so everyone would know exactly where to sit. When they arrived, she would immediately rush to the table to find which porcelain figurine held her name spelled out in elegant gold script. Penny thought it was so formal and fancy, how she imagined rich people were served their meals every day. The extra touches made the celebration particularly special and memorable in her mind.

The table was set with a crisp, white tablecloth accented with red silk placemats upon which rested delicate bone china. Freshly polished silverware sat beside each place setting, which included a dinner plate and smaller plate with individual butter knives just for the dinner roll. There were two crystal glasses to the right of each plate, one for water and one for wine for those old enough to have it.

After everyone was seated, heads would bow as a prayer was offered for the blessing of the meal and for the gift of being able to spend the holiday with family. Uncle Barney made a production of carving the turkey at the table, and soon each plate would be filled to overflowing with the most scrumptious cuisine you could imagine. They all chatted amongst themselves as the delectable dishes slowly disappeared and they couldn't eat a single bite more.

After dinner as the grownups enjoyed coffee and dessert, Uncle Barney would fill his pipe with fragrant tobacco. Penny could still remember how he looked in the pale blue velvet chair, pipe clenched in his teeth, and the oddly sweet smell of it as the smoke swirled around his head. Aunt Helen was forever busy in the kitchen, brewing coffee, cleaning up dishes and making sure everyone felt welcome and completely stuffed.

The kids all gathered in the basement where there was a pool table, or they could play ping-pong and listen to records with their cousins until it was time to go home. The more she thought about those wonderful memories, the more excited she became for Christmas Day to arrive. It was hard to believe it could get any better, but another meal in the presence of her extended family would be yet another highlight of her incredible journey back home.

As they walked into the warm comfort of the family room and shed their coats in the big walk-in closet, Penny began to realize just how exhausted she was from the events of that astonishing day. For the first time since waking up hours earlier, she was actually looking forward to crawling into her bed in the quiet of her old room and relishing the kind of slumber she used to have, deep and sound until the light of day woke her.

"I take it the Kinneys were home?" her mother queried as she put the finishing touches on a plate piled high with cookies and wrapped it in tin foil, setting it off to the side and wiping off the countertop. Her father walked into the kitchen and gave her mother a kiss on the cheek, turning to Penny. "You better get to bed young lady, Santa won't show up until the last light is out, you know!"

Penny stood in the doorway to the kitchen, watching the two people at the center of her 17-year-old world demonstrating the meaning of love with genuine affection. It was something that she never paid much attention to when she was growing up. Oh sure, she was aware that they seemed to enjoy each other and her father was always patting her mother in a teasing way. But here in this moment, watching them through the eyes of a woman who had known that kind of love and affection once, she was thankful for the role models she had been fortunate enough to experience. How could Santa ever come up with anything to compete with the gifts she had already been given?

"I'm completely worn out, so I'm going to head upstairs." Penny walked over to where her parents were standing and gave them an enormous hug, holding them for longer than a typical teenager would ever do. "I love you both, and I want to thank you for everything." She stepped back and looked at them, their faces reflecting both mild surprise mixed with what she thought was a kind of relief. Maybe their Penny wasn't such a lost cause after all.

In thanking them for everything, Penny meant every year, every precious memory, every positive value, every tough love moment of discipline. She absolutely knew beyond a shadow of a doubt that their investment in her upbringing would not be wasted, and she would carry the lessons of her childhood as well as the ability to care, to love, and to pass along those same "golden rules" to her own kids. Never had it been as crystal clear as it had been the past few hours.

Penny was incredibly grateful for whatever wormhole in the universe had allowed her to return as a 17-year-old with the wisdom, history, and hindsight of a woman whose life had been a kaleidoscope of experiences, from devastating tragedies and disappointments to tremendous joy and satisfaction. Ultimately, as the past, present and future collided in one amazing evening, she was left with the resolute serenity that the next venture into her future would all be worth it. Penny knew with certainty what her parents had hoped and dreamed as they watched her grow from a little girl into a blossoming woman…had eventually come true.

Looking at them in the dim light of the kitchen on a Christmas Eve that was quickly fading, Penny realized she had not just traveled back into her past, to her old house and her 1973 family. Most importantly, she had ended up in a good place in her heart and soul, with old wounds soothed, closure granted.

"Good night," she said as she gave them one last, long look and walked slowly past them down the hall, past the glowing lights of the Christmas tree in the corner. Penny was just about to head up to bed when she remembered the pictures she had taken while they were opening presents. She turned and walked back through the living room to the small sideboard sitting against the wall near the kitchen entryway. Penny searched through the pictures until she found the one she was looking for. It was the slightly blurry picture of her father smiling back at her, a look of genuine happiness on his face. She wanted to remember that smile forever. Penny tucked the photograph into her pocket and continued up the steps to her bedroom.

Penny noticed a light emanating from under Sandra's door and she hesitated at first, then knocked softly. "Entre' vous," was the response from the other side. Sandra was sitting on the bed, legs situated tenuously on a footstool, painting her toenails a loud shade of sparkly red. Sandra barely looked up as Penny walked in, her eyes scanning the big room where she and her sisters used to play before it became Sandra's lair. They used to call it "the dirty room" before the bedroom was remodeled. Now it was the picture of 1970s chic with bold avocado green and pink flowered wallpaper, matching green shag carpeting, antiqued wood accents and lots of built-in storage drawers.

Their house was a Cape Cod style with dormer windows, two facing the street and one facing the back yard. The slanted roof created storage spaces along either side of the room. Penny remembered crawling in and out of them as a child, exploring hidden treasures her parents had stored there, including her mother's old hope chest, a large rectangular box stained a light blonde oak color. She recalled opening the hope chest more than once and looking through the items inside. There was a newspaper headline from the day John F. Kennedy was assassinated, and one from the day Neil Armstrong first walked on the moon. It held her father's old pea coat from the Navy and various artifacts from that timeframe, along with photographs from family long dead and gone. There were also a few little baby clothes yellowing with age, and gowns from when each of them had been baptized. It was like opening a time capsule. Penny wondered if that hope chest was still behind the little door in the wall. She vowed to look for it tomorrow.

Penny had been so mad when Sandra got to have her own room, although she supposed it made sense since Sandra was the oldest. Penny thought they all should have had the opportunity by drawing straws like they usually did when there was only one to be had and three in contention. At least then she would have had a one-in-three chance. It would have been way fairer in her opinion. But no, it was unilaterally decided that it would either be the youngest or oldest that would get their own room because good old Penny in the middle could be flexible and room with either. Not so much.

In protest Penny moved herself into the closet in her own room that she shared (save for the wall and louvered door) with Cara. At least it had a real door she could close. Penny always was kind of a loner and her own space in such a crowded house was something she desperately wanted. The rest of the family made good fun of her for the move into the closet, but Penny didn't care.

She was bound and determined to carry out her mission of righteous indignation right up until one night in the dark she felt something crawling on her face. To her horror it was a spider – and a sizable one to boot. From that point all she could think of was what ELSE might be crawling around in the recesses of that modest cubbyhole, so she moved back into her regular room. Given her brooding personality, Penny admitted she probably was still pretty snarky about the whole room thing for far too long.

"Hey, thanks for the lip gloss by the way," Sandra managed, as she put the finishing touches on the last little toe and looked up at her. "I really love it. Those are definitely my colors. By the way, what did Jake give you?" Penny sat down beside Sandra and held up her left thumb showing off the shiny jewel encrusted ring.

"WOW!" said Sandra looking astonished and smiling. "You're going steady? Oh gawd, just wait until Dandra Kay sees THAT." Sandra never thought too much of Dandra Kay either, after she had spread rumors about Sandra and her boyfriend Brett stealing beer from their house during a pool party. Not a word of it was true.

"Yes, I guess it does mean we're going steady," Penny responded, pausing to the point Sandra looked at her with raised eyebrows as if to ask, "Is there more to the story?"

"Sandra, I just want to say I…" In that moment, Penny completely forgot she wasn't going to be able to say anything that 17-year-old Penny wouldn't have said. Instead of a heartfelt, "I'm sorry for all the stupid fights we had growing up and I can't tell you how much I have grown to love and respect both you and Cara and I couldn't have wished for better sisters through the years," all that came out was "I can't wait to see the look on her face!" Penny was surprised and Sandra immediately broke out in a hearty laugh. They both collapsed back on the bed giggling.

Their chortles must have roused Cara, who came in asking what the hubbub was about. Penny held up the ring and showed them the private inscription on the inside. "You are SO lucky, Penny," Cara said as she turned the ring over in her hand before giving it back. "I hope I can find someone like Jake someday." "You will," is what Penny wanted to say. She knew that both Sandra and Cara would find amazing guys and would be married for many years. Not perfect marriages, but solid unions with men who cherished and valued them. Penny loved her brothers-in-law and was happy that two of the people she loved most in the world were well loved and taken care of, even if Penny herself never did find Mr. Right.

As all three of them sat on the bed, Penny listened to her sisters talking back and forth like teenage girls do. All Penny could do was smile, and wish so much she had appreciated special times like this when they had lived them years ago. It had all been far too easy to take for granted. Their immature minds would never have been able to grasp the importance of the life-long bonds they were building back then. It would be years later when they realized just how unique and special their relationship was. Just to be in this room, with the two people who knew her best and always loved and supported her regardless, was invaluable.

As Christmas Eve was drawing to a close, only Penny knew that they would enjoy great times together as they left the nest, went on to college and careers, reared their children and finally became empty nesters and grandmothers. Being able to experience it all again with a greater sense of appreciation would be priceless, and she was ready.

Penny had come to accept the fact she would never be able to share with them (or anyone else for that matter), the unbelievable secret she was living. She understood she would never be able to expose the real truth – she had come back from the future by some fantastic miracle. She acknowledged the fact she could never forewarn the people she loved most about what was yet to come or offer comfort with the knowledge they would survive great loss and somehow move forward together like close families do.

It would be such a blessing to have the ability to provide a glimmer of hope amidst the sorrow and darkness she knew would come too soon. But Penny herself now took comfort in knowing the outcome – that they had all become productive and had enjoyed happiness and success. They had stayed together, laughed together, remembered together. It was exactly what her father would have wanted. Somewhere up in the starry sky on this picture-perfect evening, Penny was more certain than ever, he had probably orchestrated the whole thing.

Looking at her two sisters, gabbing away blissfully unaware, Penny conceded that, in every way, she was prepared to gratefully and happily live every moment of the last forty years all over again.

Cara finally got up and announced she was ready to turn in. Penny followed her out, stopping briefly to look back at Sandra who was still messing with her bright red toes and completely oblivious to Penny's gaze. "Good night," Penny said wistfully as she closed the door behind her.

Cara had already turned her light off, so Penny quietly shut the white louvered door that separated their two sleeping spaces and sat silently on the bed. The faint light from the iridescent green dial of her white clock radio was the only source of illumination. She could barely hear muffled conversation coming from downstairs, no doubt her parents were setting about their annual Santa routine before trying to get a few hours of sleep themselves.

Penny pulled back the window shade to reveal the most beautiful winter scene. The snow-covered rooftops shone brilliantly in the light of the nearly full moon, and wisps of smoke curled lazily into the sky from chimneys all over the neighborhood. A dog barked off in the distance, its long, lonely howl echoing among the barren trees, breaking the stillness of the evening.

Looking out over the frozen landscape below, snippets of fond memories played like a slideshow through her head. As children, they lived for perfect snowfalls the likes of which covered the ground right now. She and the other kids in the neighborhood, Cara, Sandra and Ricky would spend hours climbing up and sliding down the hills across the street, screaming, "BAIL OUT! BAIL OUT!" just seconds before hitting the barbed wire fence at the bottom. Penny smiled remembering squeals of laughter and the taste of snow as she tumbled off of her sled. She decided at 17 she wasn't too old for that kind of juvenile fun. Maybe she would suggest a sledding excursion to Jake. It could be a fun afternoon since they were out of school for the holiday anyway. Maybe tomorrow, she told herself.

Penny walked across the room and switched on the small lamp sitting on top of the desk. She took a moment to look at the Polaroid picture she had carried with her up the steps. Penny was convinced what she saw was happiness and resolute contentment in her father's eyes. In that moment she couldn't believe she had ever doubted he loved her.

She found an empty space on the bulletin board above the desk, and with a little stickpin, fastened it to the cork backing just beneath her Lisbon High School Band certificate of merit. Looking at the picture she touched her fingers to her lips and touched the picture of the man whose eyes she could never, ever forget. "I love you, Dad," she whispered, "Merry Christmas."

Although completely drained emotionally and physically, she allowed herself to be a little bit excited to see what tomorrow held. What did Santa leave for her under the tree in 1973? In a few short hours, she would know! Penny couldn't wait to have Christmas

Dinner at Uncle Barney's house, to spend more precious time with her father. More than anything, she couldn't wait to feel Jake's strong arms around her again, to feel his warm lips on hers, to laugh with him and have the chance to make things turn out so differently between them.

Tonight she was beyond tired and thought for a moment she had better start looking for some pajamas. Penny knew the drawers on her left would hold whatever she needed, but first she just wanted to lie down for a few minutes to let the events of the day sink in, to contemplate what was next. It was all so overwhelming to take in, so unimaginable and magical.

Penny kicked off her boots followed by her stockings. Still otherwise completely dressed, she found the covers on the bed and crawled under them, pulling them up around her chin. She breathed in deeply, her body going limp with the sweet release of finally letting go of the stress and excitement of the day. As she lay there in the stillness, she was certain she smelled a hint of lavender scent as she buried her head into the pillow. It was so relaxing. "I'll just close my eyes for a second," she said to herself dreamily, tightly clutching the ring Jake had given her as she snuggled deeper into the folds of her comfy old bed. She made a solemn vow she would never again take that ring off!

Within seconds of relinquishing conscious thought and giving in to the delicious, warm sensation and comfort of her familiar surroundings, a slumber deep as the ocean and dark as midnight quickly claimed her lucid thoughts as if Morpheus himself had cast a spell upon her. All Penny could see in her mind as she drifted further and further into the chasm was Jake Henderson's smile. In her last willful moments, she struggled to recall the sensation of his body next to hers, the touch of his hand, the sound of his voice whispering her name...

PART THREE
The Celebration

DEEP IN HER silent oblivion, a vivid dream was playing in slow motion through Penny's head like an old black and white movie. She and Jake were back in Sandager Park, chasing each other around the trees. They were dressed in their swimsuits, their bodies slick with suntan oil. The sun was shining down on them, and in her haze Penny could almost feel the intense summer heat of its rays on her face and sweat on her lip. Jake was trying hard to catch her as she ran from tree to tree always just eluding his grasp. She broke free again, sprinting past the swing sets, leapfrogging over a big rock and dashing across the gravel parking lot until she came to the chain link fence that surrounded the swimming pool.

She smiled impishly as she waited for Jake, who caught up with her quickly. He slowly wrapped his arms around her and began softly kissing the back of her neck. "Someone needs to take a swim." He murmured, barely loud enough for her to hear. "Why was he speaking so softly?" Penny wondered. She could scarcely hear him, like he was a mile away. He seemed very far off in the distance although he was right next to her, touching her.

The next thing Penny knew they were inside the fence and Jake was at the top of the high diving board, bouncing up and down waving at her. "Jump in!" he said excitedly as she inched closer to the edge of the pool, dipping her toe in the water. "It's freezing!"

she called back, "you first." Penny could literally see there were chunks of ice floating on top of the water even though there were visible waves of heat radiating upward from the concrete beneath her feet. She wondered how the pool could be so cold in the summer heat.

Squinting into the sun, Penny looked up again, holding her hand over her eyes trying to see him, but the diving board was empty. She looked into the murky water and thought she could make out the shape of someone well below the surface. Sudden panic overtook her as a vision of Jake drowning filled her with terror. She dove headfirst into the arctic fluid, its bone-chilling iciness instantly enveloping her entire body.

Penny floundered, gasping for air. "Jake!" she yelled as she struggled to keep her head above the bitterly cold water. "Help!" there was no answer. She called more urgently this time, "JAKE! Don't leave me, please don't leave me!" she cried, frantically flailing her arms and legs.

"Penny." She heard a soft voice whisper across what seemed like a vast expanse of time and space. "Penny, I'm right here."

"Jake?" she called again. Listening more closely now, she felt calmer just knowing he was near. As she strained to hear her name again, she was comforted by the sensation of a soothing back and forth motion. Were they floating in the water? Through the thinning mist of her slumber she could hear a faint humming sound and the, "click click…click click…click click…of what sounded like a metronome, or a clock echoing around an empty room.

Penny felt herself being pulled gently across the surface of the water, slowly at first, then more quickly as if someone had thrown her a lifeline and was dragging her toward safety. The intonation grew closer and closer the faster she was being pulled. "Penny" the familiar voice said again. "Penny!"

Her eyes opened as she emerged from her foggy slumber with a precipitous jolt, the dream shattered with the startling recognition that someone actually *was* calling her name. It took her a few moments to adjust to her surroundings, to allow the room to come into focus. Who were these people hovering over her? Who was calling her name?

Her mind still muddled, Penny tried hard to concentrate on the gauzy silhouettes gathered at her side. She gradually became conscious that she was in a great deal of pain. Her head was throbbing as if someone had clobbered her with a hammer. She moved her hand to touch the tender spot, her fingers instead coming across an ice-cold compress.

"Penny," she heard again, louder this time. "Penny it's me. It's Jake." Penny was progressively gaining ground, rising out of her subterranean darkness and returning to the here and now. Her mind was struggling to assimilate where she was when she distinctly heard the melodious voice of an elderly woman say, "Oh my Penny, we've been so worried about you." Penny knew that voice. It was Madeline, the lovely woman she had shared a drink and conversation with on the train. The train!

Penny looked up at the people surrounding her, suddenly recalling her trip, the train, the bar car, her plans to be with family for Christmas. She knew exactly where she was and now recognized who was looking down on her, their faces a mixture of grave concern and utter relief.

There were three figures kneeling around the narrow berth she was lying in. Madeline was on the left, James the porter who had helped her when she first arrived was on the right, and there in the middle was the face of the person she was certain she had glimpsed through the crowd as they were stopped at the station in Milwaukee. There before her, smiling his crooked smile and looking at her through a pair of smart black horn-rimmed glasses, was Jake Henderson.

Penny tried to sit up and landed back on her elbows, head still spinning. "Relax Penny, you've had quite a bump on the head," Jake said as he reached out and helped her lie back down, adjusting the icepack that was starting to slide off of her head. "How," she managed, "how did you find me? How did you know I'd been hurt?" Penny suddenly had a million questions pop into her mind. "HOW did I get injured?"

Madeline spoke first. "You had asked me to come and get you as we got close to Fargo so we could travel the rest of the way together. When they announced that we would be in Fargo soon, I came to find you as we had agreed. I knocked and knocked and heard nothing for the longest time. I had written down your compartment number, 121, so I knew I had the right one. I thought maybe you'd just stepped out for a bit or were still sleeping, but as I was walking away I thought I heard you yelling. You actually sounded quite distressed. Thinking you might be having an issue, I quickly found James. He was kind enough to let me in to check on you."

"Yes Ma'am," James piped in. "Lordy, we were terrified when we saw you lying in that bed with a nasty gash in your head. Madeline stayed by your side while I ran to the emergency phone in the hallway and made an announcement asking if there was a doctor on the train."

"That's where I come in," smiled Jake, "Jake Henderson, M.D. at your service."

Penny looked up into his handsome face. Those amazing eyes were as crystal blue as ever, his hair the same stark white it had been all of his life. The only thing that belied the passage of time were the soft crows feet around his eyes and slightly more pronounced smile lines on either side of his grinning lips. He may have a few more lines and wrinkles here and there, but otherwise he hadn't changed a bit. He was still the same attractive, attentive Jake she remembered.

Penny suddenly became incredibly self-conscious about her own appearance. She had to look a complete sight! Jake must have read her thoughts because he added soothingly, "Penny, you look beautiful. And you're a very lucky lady. It looks like that top berth must have fallen on top of your head and left you with quite a serious contusion. That's doctor-speak for big old knot on your noggin!" he chuckled.

For the first time since waking up in this confusion, Penny actually laughed. "I'm beyond happy to see you, Jake but given my druthers, it certainly wouldn't be under these circumstances. You don't know how much I appreciate you coming to my rescue." She reached out and took one of Madeline's hands in hers, then reached out and grasped one of James' as well. "And I can't tell you two how incredibly grateful I am that you decided to come and check on me. I don't know how I could ever properly thank you!"

"I'm just glad you are going to be ok," said James with a reassuring pat to the back of her hand. He stood up, smoothed down his snappy dark blue uniform and straightened his nametag. "Now if you'll excuse me, we're almost to Fargo. I'll be back to help you and Miss Madeline with your bags once we have arrived. It would be my pleasure to make sure you ladies reach your destination and find your family at the station." With that, he disappeared through the door, closing it quietly behind him.

"I need to go back to my own compartment and make sure I have everything packed up," Madeline said coyly. "Something tells me you two could use a little time alone." She winked as she walked toward the door. "I'll be back once we've arrived at the station." Madeline let herself out of the room and Penny's gaze returned to Jake, who was still kneeling beside her.

It suddenly occurred to Penny what a strange coincidence it was that Jake happened to be on the same train. "What are you doing on this train?" Penny's thoughts were becoming much more coherent as the minutes ticked by. Still holding her hand, Jake said, "I am probably here for the same reason you are – no flights available and a day before Christmas. My mom hasn't been well and I really needed to get back to Lisbon to see her," adding softly, "Dad passed away in August and this will be our first Christmas without him. I wanted to be there for her."

"Jake, I'm so sorry," Penny said thoughtfully, appreciating as she always did Jake's sense of responsibility and his caring nature. "I am sure your mother will be so happy to see you and have you home for the holiday. Will you be staying long?"

"Unfortunately, I can only stay for a few days. I will be flying back to Chicago on the 27th. Duty calls. Well, if the airports are open again, that is."

"You live in Chicago?" Penny asked. "I have lived there most of the past forty years. I can't believe we have practically been neighbors! I heard you were a doctor in the Midwest somewhere, but I never did hear exactly where you landed. Are you traveling with family?" Penny hoped it didn't appear too obvious she was inquiring about his marital status. She had already scoped out the ring finger of his left hand and noticed there was no gold band. Could he possibly be unattached? She dared not hope he was unattached AND living in the same city. That would be a stroke of luck akin to winning the lottery.

Jake smiled, "No, actually I'm traveling alone this time. I do have three beautiful daughters and a gaggle of gorgeous grandkids, but they are scattered across the country and have their own families to make plans with for Christmas." He paused and looked absently at the wall beyond Penny's head as if trying to decide what to say next.

"I lost my wife two years ago around the holidays. She fought cancer for a number of years and we honestly thought she had beaten it. When it returned, it took her very quickly." His voice trailed off and he looked down at his hands. "We had a lot of good years together; but truth be told, we were considering a separation when we found out the cancer had come back. You know, same tired story as a million others. Kids grown, drifted apart, sounds a little ridiculous when I say it out loud." He shrugged his shoulders and for the first time since Penny had awakened, Jake seemed to have aged four decades.

Penny, now entirely alert and sitting at complete attention, suffered a pang of regret over having made such a transparent query. Her head was no longer throbbing and she reached out and touched his hand. "You are in the presence of one in those millions," she sighed. "I have been divorced for quite awhile now. Two grown kids, beautiful grandkids and a pretty darn good life, all things considered. I'm very sorry for your loss, Jake. Really I am." She meant it sincerely.

"Thank you, Penny. I guess I've poured myself into my work to the point I have forgotten what it was like to feel much of anything. When I saw that it was you lying there in the bed, it gave me such a start. All I could think about was making sure you were all right. Seeing you so unexpectedly, well, it was like time had stood still and we were kids again. I admit I was excited to have the chance to talk to you, to reconnect."

Jake's smile faded and he became more serious as he continued, "All these years I have regretted the way things ended between us…that they ended at all. You and I had something that was special, indefinable. Even when I was married, even in the good years, I was never as happy as I was when we were together." Jake's steely blue eyes looked into hers with a tenderness that was achingly familiar. Neither of them moved.

The years fell away, the well of emotions flooded to the surface. Penny could sense a lump the size of a golf ball rising in her throat. To hear those kind sentiments from someone she had loved so much and thought of so often was a welcome salve on wounds she realized had never completely healed. Being single for so long, she had forgotten how much she missed the intimacy of being connected with another human being in a way only the two of them shared.

"I know we were just a couple of kids," said Jake as he entwined his fingers with hers, "but I remember what it was like to be with you – to be with someone who understood everything about me without any explanation. I need you to know that what I said to you all those years ago, was exactly how I felt. I have always wanted to apologize for not trying harder to make things work once I went away to college."

Penny wasn't sure how to respond. She wanted so badly to tell him all about what she had just been through; to share with him the strange and incomprehensible tale of their reunion on some other plain, in some other universe. It was still so incredibly real to her. It didn't seem like decades since their last conversation, their last encounter, but rather mere minutes. And yet it was too fantastical to be anything but an extreme hallucination brought on by the accidental bump on her head.

"I'm Chief of Cardiology at Northwestern Hospital, one of the most prestigious institutions of healing in the world. I'm a dedicated physician devoted to matters of the heart…who admittedly hasn't managed his own very well. Pretty ironic, no?" he chuckled, taking her hand and kissing the back of it tenderly. "I have always wondered what happened to you." Looking deep into her eyes, "It is impossible to forget your first love, you know."

Penny's own heart was racing like a runaway train. She answered with a barely audible, "I know." They held hands for a long time, neither of them knowing what to say next, both of them stunned at the unbelievable turn of events that had brought them to this moment.

"NEXT STOP...FARGO!" The announcement crackled through the loudspeaker, breaking the silence of the awkward moment. The train was slowing, and Jake moved across the room lifting the heavy shade covering the window. Bright morning sun flooded the tiny compartment with light. "We need a little light in here!" Jake said as he bent down to look through the window. "Thank goodness the snow has stopped!"

"I must look a fright." Penny laughed as she slowly stood up, turning around so he could get the full 360-degree view of one very rumpled passenger. She looked in the small mirror on the back of the door and touched the butterfly bandage that Jake had apparently used to close the wound on the top of her forehead. "Expert job, Dr. Henderson, I'm impressed!"

"You have no idea how happy I was to be your attending. You are one unforgettable patient." He grinned removing his glasses. Then more softly, "I should let you get your things together. Is someone coming to get you at the station?"

"Yes, my mother is supposed to be picking me up. And I've offered to drop Madeline at her destination in Moorhead. We're heading to Minnesota to spend some time with Sandra and her family over Christmas." She hesitated for a few seconds before adding, "It is so funny, Jake, here I hadn't been home for the holidays in at least a decade and who do I run into but the only other person in North Dakota besides my own family that would have made it all worth the trip." She shook her head still unable to grasp the bizarre kismet of it all.

Jake smiled as if he understood exactly what Penny was saying. "Before I forget, do you mind if I ask where you work? Perhaps we could get together sometime when we're both back in the city. When are you heading back?" Jake acted almost a little nervous about asking her, which made Penny smile. As if she would respond with anything other than an enthusiastic yes!

"I'd enjoy catching up with you, Jake, very much. I work at the *Chicago City News*. You can't miss us....big building with a black glass façade right on the corner of Michigan Avenue and Monroe Street. I work on the fourth floor, Chief Editor." Penny hoped she didn't sound like she had expectations. "I'm not going back until December 31st. I was able to get a fabulous deal on the ticket because nobody else in their right mind would think to travel on New Year's Eve! I will probably be ringing in 2015 with the bartender and maybe two or three other passengers long about the time we pass through Milwaukee."

"Well," Jake said as he walked past her and opened the door. "I hope you and your family have a wonderful holiday. Please tell them I said hello, and Merry Christmas!" He stood for a moment, like he was trying to memorize every detail about her. "I can't tell you how good it is to see you, Penny. I mean that."

"Please greet your mother for me and have a lovely time yourself. And thank you again so much for coming to my rescue." Penny said. "Really, Jake, I couldn't have asked for a more dashing hero." She touched his arm as he turned and walked through the open door.

"The pleasure was entirely mine." He said as he hugged her tightly and planted a soft kiss on her cheek. Penny took in the scent of him, an amalgam of earthy men's cologne and Juicy Fruit gum. In that moment the details of what had caused them to drift apart seemed irrelevant, the passage of time immaterial. And as usual, the nearness of him left her a little breathless.

The thought of seeing Jake again when they returned to Chicago (even if it was just to catch up on the past few decades over dinner and a glass of wine or two) left Penny grinning ear to ear. They parted with one final smile after which, Jake Henderson long lost love of her life, quickly disappeared down the hallway.

"We have arrived at the station! We have arrived at the station!" a digital voice repeated with authority through the intercom system. "Fargo, North Dakota. Please disembark to your left, and check with gate agents if you have questions regarding connections. Happy Holidays, and thank you for choosing Amtrak."

Penny gathered her things together, being careful to avoid a repeat clash with the top berth again. She was still trying hard to recollect exactly what had happened the night before. The last thing she remembered was trying to get the top berth unhinged so she could store her bag off of the floor. Looking at the broken leather tie that secured the berth to the wall she could only surmise that Jake had been right, it must have broken. Given the size of the unsightly variegated bruise now prominently gracing her forehead, the impact must have been significant. It had, after all, knocked her clear back to 1973!

Penny sat for a moment in the chair by the window, looking out over the frozen scenery, and watched the flurry of activity as waves of passengers engaged in the process of beginning, continuing or ending their journeys. Of course it had all been a dream, hadn't it? But it was so incredibly vivid!

Most dreams quickly fade into obscurity with only the slightest of detail lingering upon waking. Even in her slightly traumatized state Penny could remember every moment of what she had just lived. From waking up in her old bedroom to the Christmas Eve lasagna she swore she could still taste; from the solo at church to the amazing time with Jake in the park and the profound experience with her father afterwards, Penny remembered every… single…second.

As with most intense experiences she had gone through over the years, Penny's first instinct was to write it all down. She didn't want the details to diminish, the powerful emotions to dissipate. Penny didn't want to gamble on forgetting a solitary one of the compelling and heartfelt words that were spoken, nor risk having them vanish with time. No, this was far too important, and she made a mental note to capture as much as she could recall and commit it to her journal just as soon as she had a free moment.

Right now it was time to get off the train and find her mother. Penny grabbed her computer and placed it carefully into the carrying case. She set her bag by the door and gave herself a fresh coat of lipstick and brush of face powder, a little "paint on the barn," as her sister Cara would say.

Just as she had finished her touchup, there was a soft knock at the door. Penny opened it to find a smiling Madeline with an equally ebullient James behind her, a cart for their bags in tow. "Let me get those bags for you Miss Penny," James offered as he swiftly added her bags to the cart and gestured for them to take the lead, "Ladies first!"

Down the narrow passageway they walked, breathing in the fresh invigorating air filling the hallway as they neared the exit. "Brrrr," said Madeline. "It is easy to forget how cold it is in these parts after living in Florida." She drew the collar of her winter coat up around her cheeks as James helped her from the train onto the platform. Next he took Penny's hand and escorted them both into the station that was teeming with people, like a beehive on honey harvest day.

It took Penny several minutes to spot her mother standing near the baggage claim. Penny's most recent experience was with the Betsy of 1973 and she suddenly realized she had been looking for the much younger version. Betsy was smartly dressed in a trendy dark green wool coat with a rhinestone broach on the lapel Penny recognized as one her grandmother had worn many years ago.

"Mom!" Penny called and waved across the room. Betsy nodded and smiled in recognition gesturing back. Penny and Madeline made their way through the crowd over to where she was standing. James was right behind them with the cart full of bags.

"Mom," Penny said grabbing her in a hug so enthusiastic it almost landed them both on the floor. "It is so good to see you." She held her mother snugly in her grasp for longer than she was certain she had ever done before. Suddenly flooded with unexpected emotion, Penny could feel her eyes filling with tears. "Well," she sniffled slightly as they parted, laughing at the surprising display, "I guess its official. I have missed you…and I have missed being home for the holidays."

"Penny! What on earth happened to your head?" The puzzled look on Betsy's face as they parted was one of obvious concern. Penny had been so caught up in the joy of their reunion she completely forgot her mother wouldn't know about her fight with the upper berth and her subsequent need for a bandage the size of a man's wallet. "Are you all right?"

"It's a long story, Mom," said Penny, wondering how she would ever explain just how long of a story it really was; how she could ever convey her amazing account in a way that would make sense. "A very long story, but I'm going to be just fine. We can talk on the way to the lake."

Penny turned to Madeline and James, "Mom, these are my two guardian angels, Madeline and James. I met them on the train, and without them I might never have made it this far. Madeline needs a ride over to Moorhead and I told her we insist on helping her get to where she is staying. I knew you wouldn't mind, it is right on our way out of town."

"Of course not," Betsy replied. "It is the very least we can do. I'll go bring the car around so we can get the bags in the back. It is so nice to meet you both, and I can't thank you enough for helping Penny." Betsy reached over and shook Madeline's hand and nodded and smiled at James, whose hands were full of baggage.

Standing in the middle of the busy depot Penny was finally able to take a deep breath knowing she was where she wanted to be. Getting on that train had been the right decision, despite the bump on her head. She still needed some time to process everything that had happened to her. The amazing experience of being in Lisbon again was so surreal. Even now she had to consciously remember that she wasn't 17 anymore and it wasn't 1973. Penny could tell her equilibrium was still a little off kilter.

"It is good to have you here, Penny. I know Sandra is so excited to have you home, too. It will be a grand time. Shall we get going?" Betsy said leading the way out the front door.

The parking lot at the Fargo Amtrak Depot was just across the street so it took Penny's mother only a minute or two to bring the Buick sedan around to where James could easily fit their bags into the trunk. Penny made sure Madeline was tucked into the front seat before turning to James who had just carefully inserted the last suitcase before closing the lid. She subtly handed him a $100 bill folded to the point he wouldn't know the denomination until he looked at it later. It was the very least she could do.

When I Get Home

"Thank you so much for taking such good care of me, James. I'm not sure what would have happened had you and Madeline not been worried about me. I could have missed the stop in Fargo and ended up in Spokane!" Penny laughed and gave him a congenial hug.

James, slightly embarrassed by her show of affection, smoothed his uniform and straightened his hat as he grabbed the cart and steered it clear of the car. "I hope you come back and travel with us again, Miss Penny," he stammered as he discreetly inserted the folded greenback into his trouser pocket. "I promise we will get that berth fixed. Now, you and yours have a very Merry Christmas!"

She wished him the same, as James opened the back door and made sure she was buckled in before closing it. He smiled sunnily and waved a cheerful goodbye as the car pulled away from the curb. Penny waved back at him through the rear window as they drove away.

Penny slumped back and allowed the soft cushion to embrace her. Against all odds and through the snowstorm, she had made it to Fargo! With a satisfied sigh she smiled as she settled in for the ride. In less than two hours they would be with Sandra and her family, drinking wine and singing carols around the piano and waiting for the lasagna to finish baking. The celebration would officially be underway.

They made a right turn out of the parking lot and down 4th Street making their way over to Broadway. Penny couldn't believe how much had changed in the past couple of decades. The city had evolved from a lazy town cradled by the banks of the great Red River of the North, to a bustling metropolis almost twice the size of the Fargo of her childhood.

A downtown that had fallen into vacant disrepair in the '80s and '90s was now a thriving destination filled with toney restaurants and chic high-end boutiques. The renewal of the once-forgotten heart of town was now a center of commerce and entertainment that rivaled that of any other major city in the tri-state area. It was gratifying to see the arts community was alive and well.

They drove by the Fargo Theater, still prominently displaying the original art-deco marquis that had graced its exterior since first opening in 1926. These days the theater was a hot venue for concerts, plays and other live events, drawing attendees from a wide area and contributing significantly to the rebirth of the area. Penny recalled seeing *Saturday Night Fever* at the theater years ago, marveling even then at the stunningly ornate décor of the majestic landmark.

It must have been the exhaustion from the trip or residual effects of the slight concussion she had suffered on the train, but Penny could feel the quiet conversation coming from the front seat lulling her to sleep again. She fought the urge to close her eyes, trying to concentrate on the polite chitchat Madeline and her mother were engaged in. She didn't want to miss a moment of the trip from here on out. It felt wonderful to relax and enjoy the bright sunshine while their journey took them down streets piled high on each side with freshly plowed snow. Even though much of the scenery now seemed foreign to Penny, she had to admit, it was good to be home.

As the Buick continued over the bridge on Highway 10 into Moorhead, Penny enjoyed the view from the back seat, still in awe of just how much the city had flourished since her last visit. She heard Madeline giving directions as her mother laughed and continued with whatever story she had been sharing. They turned left into a neighborhood that was built around The Meadows Golf Course and soon had pulled into the driveway of a lovely white two-story home with a red brick portico sporting a festive silver wreath on the door.

As soon as they had stopped, the front door opened and someone Penny assumed was Madeline's brother-in-law Tom came out to greet them, all smiles and open arms. Penny exited the back seat to open the car door and make sure Madeline was able to gain her footing on the slippery driveway. They didn't need two accidents the day before Christmas.

Tom enveloped Madeline in a reunion bear hug that Penny could tell was both joyous and yet tinged with bittersweet grief. Madeline had, after all, come home to bury her beloved Walter. As they stood in the driveway embracing with tears flowing freely, Penny retrieved Madeline's bags from the trunk and proceeded to carry them to the front door. "Here, here," said Tom, "let me get those for you."

Tom took over the baggage duties while Penny took an unsteady Madeline's arm and walked them both cautiously up the steps that led to the porch. A woman Penny surmised must have been Tom's wife was standing in the doorway, a blue sweater wrapped around her shoulders. "Please come in, all of you!" she called, making sure Betsy could hear and motioning her to join them inside.

Penny politely declined the kind offer, indicating they had their own celebration waiting for them at the lake. She warmly embraced Madeline for a long moment thanking her again and wishing her a lovely visit despite the sad circumstances. It gave her an opportunity to once again breathe in the unmistakable scent of Shalimar.

Penny closed her eyes and for a moment allowed herself to be enveloped in the warm Grandma Mary hug being offered by another sweet woman with the very same initial, the very same perfume; just a few more seconds to relish the memory before she had to leave.

Penny could tell Madeline was in wonderful hands as she carefully made her way back to the car and waved her final goodbyes, sing-songing a hearty Merry Christmas to the trio standing in the doorway.

Settled back in the warm car, they proceeded out of the development and back onto Highway 10. "Such a lovely woman," Penny's mother remarked as they once again headed east, "so sad to be planning a funeral during the season of celebration. I think we'll try I-94 instead of going the back way," her mother said. "I think the roads will be better."

"You're the boss," Penny responded. "I'm going where you're going."

The roads were definitely clearer on I-94 but Betsy was still cautiously driving well under the posted speed limit. Although Penny was anxious to get to the lake, she was fine with making sure they made it in one piece. Penny continued to look out the window at the beautiful frozen scene, still unspoiled after the most recent snowfall, save for the pathways cut down the highway by the snowplows.

As they drove past the Barnesville exit, Penny was daydreaming, wondering if everything she had packed for her mom, Sandra and the grandchildren had made the journey unscathed. She had purchased a pair of pajamas and slippers for her mother, gold earrings for Sandra and games for the kids. She had bought a bottle of Todd's favorite wine and tucked that in her bag at the last minute as well. It wouldn't be long until they would be turning left onto Highway 108 towards Pelican Rapids. The home on West McDonald Lake was getting closer by the mile.

When I Get Home

While her mother concentrated on the road ahead, Penny's thoughts once again returned to her "trip" back to Lisbon and the clear memories she had of that experience. It was so incredibly real to her, making it nearly impossible for her to believe it had only been a dream. But it had to be, didn't it?

What seemed most implausible was that Penny had been fully *aware* she had merely been a visitor in that space and time. She remained fully conscious as the 58-year-old Penny the entire time she was living those few hours in the body of her teenage self. The images and feelings which remained were disquieting, leaving her mind grappling to make sense of the flashes of past mingled with present that lingered even now.

She closed her eyes and could smell Jake's cologne as if he were standing right next to her, could feel the warmth of his lips as they kissed her tenderly. It felt like it had only been a few brief hours since they had been together as the two kids in love they had been. Penny longed to go back, to fall asleep again and wake up in her cozy bed on the second floor of their house on Weber Street. She wanted Jake to pick her up to go sledding tomorrow. She wanted to wear his ring, to never let him go again.

She knew that she had left behind Jake's class ring and the picture of her father hanging on the bulletin board in her bedroom on Weber Street. She wished they could drive to Lisbon and walk into the front door of their old house so she could rush up the steps to retrieve them, never to let those precious gifts out of her reach again.

Penny closed her eyes and recalled the sensation of hugging her father, of saying (and hearing) "I love you," of seeing the smile on his face. She wanted it to be burned into her memory, able to recall the sounds of his voice whenever she felt lonely or afraid.

She wanted it to stay with her forever, and part of her was afraid it would disappear again all too soon.

All Penny knew was that she had been given an unbelievable gift most people only dream about. She had been given the chance to go back and tell the ones most dear to her that she loved them and how important they would always be in her life, and to gain a priceless sense of reconciliation with her past; a past that had left an anxious and uneasy place in her soul for so many years.

With the clarity and perspective of time, Penny had instantly understood how precious their relationships were and continued to be, and appreciated from a totally new perspective how quickly life can be disrupted. Only by going back to experience herself at a young age could Penny possibly recognize the value of how their early years together had cemented those ties; how undeniably their love for one another as a family had sustained them all these years.

Penny opened her eyes shaking her head slightly as if the motion could unscramble the tangle of thoughts she was desperately struggling to unravel.

"You're awfully quiet, Penny. Are you sure you're all right? You did take quite a bump on the head. I know Jake told you it was just a slight concussion and you'd be fine, but let me know if you need to stop." Penny could hear the concern in her mother's voice. She wanted to talk to her mother about everything she had been through. But how could her mother ever comprehend what had happened on the journey to Fargo if Penny couldn't even rationalize it herself?

"Yes, it has been quite a trip so far, Mom; more than you could ever imagine." Penny hesitated, gathering her thoughts together before speaking again. "I know I haven't said this to you nearly enough over the years, but you've been a great mom. I know even when I was at my worst, when I was giving you and Dad fits, you always loved me," Penny could see her mother's eyes begin to fill with tears as Betsy stared ahead at the road. "Trust me...I know I wasn't an easy kid. I've made so many decisions through the years that I've lived to regret and you were always there to support me. You had more faith in me than I had in myself."

Penny looked out the window and continued. "We were all so lucky to grow up when and where we did with parents who were dedicated to making sure we were raised properly. I am grateful that we always had everything we needed and much of what we wanted. You and Dad raised us to have high standards, to care for others, to behave with integrity and to value the treasure that is our family above anything else. I don't know why we aren't given that insight when we're young and foolish."

"Oh, Penny, I..." her mother started to speak but Penny interrupted, needing to finish her thoughts. "I love you, Mom; and I know beyond any shadow of a doubt that Dad knew I loved him, too. We didn't have nearly enough years together, but I know how much you and Dad loved me, loved all of us."

Betsy cleared her throat. "Penny, of course your dad and I loved you and all of you kids. I'm not sure why or if you ever did doubt that, but please don't. We all say and do things as children we'll most likely regret as adults. And blessedly, we do get that invaluable 20/20 hindsight as the years go by–most of us, anyway." They both laughed.

"That's why they call it *growing up*. If everyone knew what life was all about and what was important when they were children, well, I think it would probably be a much less interesting world. I always knew you'd turn out to be the amazing woman you are. I hope you know how proud I am of you, and how incredibly proud I am positive your father would have been."

Penny wished she could give her mother the biggest hug ever but that would have to wait. For now, she would have to be content in the knowledge that whatever had happened to her on that train to Fargo, something had clicked inside of her heart and mind. She felt decidedly changed for the better. It was time to stop questioning why.

"Only a few more miles," her mother offered. "I am so excited to see the little ones. Christmas is always so much more fun through the eyes of a child." Penny couldn't agree more.

They drove through the little hamlet of Pelican Rapids, still sleepy and slow moving with the fresh inches of white fluff that had accumulated over night. Penny and her mother chatted about the holiday plans as they continued on for a few more miles, winding slowly along the snow-covered highway, passing frozen lakes and ponds until they came to the familiar crossroad at the crest of the hill. They turned left down Engstrom Beach Road to "Hankey's Hideaway," the name Sandra and Todd had christened their beautiful log home on the lake.

As they made their way down the last few blocks to their destination, Penny was filled with an overwhelming sense of gratitude. This had already been the most amazing trip, one that she would never forget. And in just a few minutes they would all be together, celebrating Christmas around the tree, singing and enjoying each other's company. She was beyond excited to start the festivities.

Rounding the last corner, Penny could see Sandra and Todd's lake home just up on the right. The big evergreen tree in the front yard was covered in a layer of heavy white snow, but she could see the green and red lights peeking out from beneath it. There was a big snowman on the front lawn, carrot nose and black charcoal eyes and all; no doubt the work of Sandra's grandchildren.

When I Get Home

"Boy, there sure are a lot of cars parked up and down the street by their place. I would imagine their neighbors also have family visiting for the holidays. It is nice people were able to get out and about despite the weather," Penny remarked to her mother as they pulled into the driveway and honked the horn.

A smiling Todd appeared in the doorway and immediately put on his coat and hat to come help with bags. Sandra waved from the screened-in porch, clutching her sweater around her neck in the cold. Penny couldn't wait to get out of the car and into the warm cabin. She could see smoke curling skyward from the chimney, which meant Todd had already started a nice, cozy fire.

Todd grabbed one bag under each arm and offered his elbow to Betsy, helping her up the front steps. Penny took her smaller bag and computer case and carefully made her way behind them. While Todd helped their mother into the house, Penny dropped her bags in the porch and embraced Sandra in a very long hug. "You have no idea what I've been through to get here!" Penny exclaimed with a mixture of excitement and complete exhaustion.

Sandra looked fabulous as always, much younger than her sixty years, and beaming ear to ear. "Come on, let's get you settled so we can start the party. I can't wait to hear all about your trip. Good grief, what on earth did you do to your head?" Sandra queried finally noticing the big white bandage on her forehead. I have you in the guest room downstairs where it is nice and dark and quiet, just the way you like it."

Sandra took one of the bags as they walked into the living room. Penny could see the tree had mountains of presents underneath it. "Wow, are those kids going to be spoiled," Penny thought to herself as they made their way to the door leading to the finished lower level. There must have been over a hundred gaily wrapped gifts.

The stairs leading to the basement were dark. "Is there a light switch down there?" asked Penny, half afraid she would trip and tumble the rest of the way down.

"I'll turn it on in just a second," said Sandra.

Just as their feet reached the bottom step, Penny could hear Sandra fumbling for the lights. Before she could flip the switch, she heard a familiar little voice yell, "SURPRISE!!!!!!"

Sandra flipped the switch and there, gathered in all their illuminated glory was the entire family – including Penny's own two children with her grandchildren, excitedly beaming. Todd stood with Penny's mother in the front row along with Cara and Judd and their kids and grandchildren. Ricky and Renee and their children were directly behind them. Finally Penny's gaping mouth and unbelievably surprised gaze turned to Meredith and Jamey, Susie and Jason and her own adorable fidgety, squirmy grandchildren who were purposely hidden behind the others to save as one last marvelous bombshell.

"Were you surprised, Nana?" cried her grandson Stephen, literally jumping up and down with sheer delight at catching her so off guard.

"Oh my goodness," Penny finally managed as the tears came streaming down her cheeks. "Oh my goodness I had no idea. How did you...? When did you...what the?" She was truly and utterly speechless. Not only was she not going to be alone this Christmas, she was going to be spending it with her entire family. It was the first-ever Raney family reunion at the holidays. She was beyond stunned, way past surprised. Penny was nothing short of completely flabbergasted!

Everyone suddenly and very animatedly started talking at once, a big happy room filled with every person in life that she held dear. All Penny could do was laugh and cry, hug and joke, trying to take it all in. The lively group continued to gab and chatter as the kids ran upstairs to shake Christmas packages and break out some board games. "Last one up is a rotten egg," squealed Trevor, Cara's oldest grandson as he raced ahead of the pack.

Their enthusiasm reminded Penny of years ago when her own cousins would come for a visit at the holidays from faraway states. They played for hours entertaining each other, dressing their Barbie Dolls or putting on musical shows and little plays. The youngest Raney generation was a nice mixture of boys and girls, where Penny's cousins had been all girls. Ricky was the only male in her entire generation of cousins. Things had nicely evened out over the years.

"If we don't get the lasagna in the oven we're never going to eat on time," Sandra finally said. "Todd, why don't you get the champagne opened and be sure the fire is still going. That wind is starting to pick up again and I don't want the little ones to catch a chill. This is going to be such a special night."

Everyone followed Sandra up the steps and filled the kitchen and great room with laughter and conversation while Todd opened several bottles of champagne with a "pop" and poured them into plastic champagne glasses. Cara made sure the kids had sparkling grape juice so everyone would feel a part of this extraordinary holiday celebration.

Reunited again, the three sisters who were closer in heart than in distance these days, went to work layering the delicious pans of lasagna with meat sauce, cheese and noodles. They hugged and laughed out loud and chatted about the train trip, her bump on the head and what a unique coincidence it was that Jake Henderson would be the doctor on board to come to her rescue.

"I don't believe in coincidences," said Cara. "What if you ran into him again because you always were meant to be together?"

Cara sighed deeply at the romantic notion of it all. "That would be so incredible. Do you think you'll see him again? You really should look him up when you get home. Jake Henderson is one fine man, that's for sure."

"I hope so, but you know how people are these days. You enjoy catching up but life is so busy, everyone so fixated on their own schedules – especially at our age when kids are grown and there are grandchildren in the picture. Always some kind of event here or there and frankly, it is easy to get complacent and a little stuck in our ways. I know I have been guilty, guilty, *guilty* of that myself," Penny remarked as she finished assembling her pan of lasagna.

Sandra tucked the final noodle in place on the pan she had been working on and spooned the remaining fragrant, meaty tomato sauce over top. She sprinkled the entire surface of the casserole with a generous helping of mozzarella and parmesan cheese and sealed each pan with tin foil. "There," she said resting her hands on her hips for a moment. "Let's get these in the oven and then we can enjoy our champagne for a bit before we have to make the salad and garlic bread."

Just then Ricky walked into the kitchen. "Mmmmm, something smells amazing!" he remarked.

There they were, all four kids in the same room most having traveled hours to get to the lake, to spend time with each other, to savor the holiday with the only people who mattered. They stopped for a moment, looking at each other with a mixture of happiness and appreciation. Without saying a word, the four siblings gathered close, their champagne glasses clinking together as if to say "I can't believe we're all here." Tears flowed until they started laughing at themselves for being so overwhelmed with emotion. "Good times, good times!" Cara said through the waterworks.

When I Get Home

Penny could tell her kids were having a great time talking with their cousins, as she overheard bits and pieces of conversation about the children, jobs, travel. Champagne and laughter flowing particularly freely among that generation, she could tell it might be one of those nights when nobody would get much sleep. Penny didn't care. She was home!

It seemed so surreal to have everyone in the same room. How they managed to pull it all off without her suspecting a thing was nothing short of miraculous. Betsy was notorious for spilling the beans and Cara couldn't keep a secret to save her life. But here they all were, enjoying each other's company in the glow of the fireplace and in the shadow of the most magnificent Christmas tree. Gratitude was radiating around the room in a way that was unmistakable and tangible. How lucky they all were to be part of this amazing, loving, warm and funny bunch of people.

That they had gone to the trouble by springing this surprise at all was heartwarming. Had she really come off as being that blue? Had she been sounding like Wendy Whiner in her conversations with Sandra and Cara about always being the 5th wheel and feeling the odd man out for being the only one without a successful relationship, without someone special to care for and to care for her? Had they all felt sorry for her?

Whatever the reason for this exceptional gathering she decided to stop giving it so much thought and enjoy another glass of that fabulous champagne Todd was pouring at the end of the kitchen counter. Maybe it was just the wonderful setting or the fact she was surrounded by so much love, but even the champagne tasted distinctive and singularly delicious.

For the next couple of hours the house was humming with conversation, people busy getting the table set and making final preparations for their holiday feast. When dinner was about thirty minutes from being ready to serve, Sandra gathered everyone together in the living room. She gave each grandchild one of the pieces from the manger scene and gave them instructions on what to do.

As has been the custom for years when they were all together, Sandra had scripted out a brief Christmas Eve service complete with reading the story of Jesus' birth from the Bible and the singing of a few beloved carols. Cara's husband Judd and her son Jarrod played guitars as even the smallest children joined in to sing "Away in a Manger."

Candles were lit and pieces of the manger scene put in place in order of importance by each of the grandchildren, as the Bible verses were read by each of the adults. First the cattle and camel, the angel, the Wise Men, Mary and Joseph and finally, the oldest grandchild carefully placed the baby Jesus in the manger.

After a quiet moment of reflection, Penny offered a prayer of thanksgiving for each and every one who had made the trip to share this holiday. She asked God to watch over them for safe passage home, for the blessing of family, and in remembrance of those in Heaven who would be reunited with them all again someday; gone, but never forgotten. "Amen" rang the chorus around the room when she was done.

The quiet of the poignant service was broken by little 5-year-old Allison chiming in, "Let's eat. I'm starving!" Everyone laughed and, in a flurry of activity, quickly took their places around the big table. Plates were passed, piled high with rich lasagna, and salad and baskets of warm garlic bread made their way around the table enough times where everyone was more than satisfied.

It may have taken hours to prepare for the feast, but it seemed the lasagna was devoured, the plates cleared and dishes done in no time flat. Good thing, because the children were antsy to get on with opening the presents.

They gathered as best they all could in the great room and watched what started out as a fairly civil "one at a time" gift opening quickly dissolve into an "every man for himself" extravaganza. Paper was flying, kids were enthusiastically scampering around showing off their treasures and Penny just sat back taking it all in, marveling at how incredibly fortunate she felt to be here, to be among the people she loved most in the world. This could not have been a more perfect holiday celebration. She would take another train trip and suffer another bump on the head any time if this was waiting for her at the other end of the line.

Presents opened, paper cleared from the floor, everyone helped get the house back in some semblance of order while the children played contently with their new toys. People were busy talking and enjoying the charged atmosphere of the post-gift excitement as Sandra quietly walked up to the second floor loft overlooking the main level. She took a seat at the grand piano that occupied the space and softly began to play a song, the words to which Penny knew by heart, and that captured the moment in a way no single verbal expression ever could.

Penny heard the familiar melody come floating over the railing. She caught Cara's eyes and they both took their glasses of champagne and headed up stairs.

"Up in the attic, down on my knees, lifetime of boxes timeless to me," Sandra was singing. Before they even got to the top of the steps Penny and Cara had joined in.

"Letters and photographs, yellowed with years, some bringing laughter, some bringing tears. Time never changes, the memories, the faces of loved ones, who bring to me..." By the time Sandra began to play the chorus, the entire next generation of girls – Penny's daughter Meredith, Cara's three daughters Kendra, Nicole and Kaitlin and Sandra's Justine were up the stairs and gathered around the piano joining in perfect harmony, the sound filling the house with the most lovely chorus of voices. The room below had become silent and still, as all eyes and ears, down to the littlest grandbaby, tuned in to the message being delivered with such genuine emotion.

"All that I come from and all that I live for and all that I'm going to be, my precious family is more than an heirloom to me."

Penny had sung those words to the song Amy Grant so beautifully stylized numerous times before, always with a little lump in her throat at the sentiment so powerfully rendered in each verse. Tonight more than ever before as they sang together, eyes moist and arms wrapped around one another, the meaning was never more crystal clear in her heart and mind.

Nothing matters from beginning to end but the people you love and the people who love you back; everyone that meant anything to her – all of her precious heirlooms – were in this house, this place they were continually drawn to and cherished beyond what any mere words on a page could ever describe.

"Time never changes, the memory, the moment His love first pierced through me…telling all that I come from and all that I live for and all that I'm going to be. My precious Savior is more than an heirloom to me. My precious Jesus is more than an heirloom to me."

Sandra played the last bars of the music and sat quietly with her hands on the keys for the longest time. Not even the baby was making a peep. It was as if the grandchildren, maybe for the first time ever, understood they were part of something much richer, deeper and far more meaningful than just a chance to play with their cousins. It wasn't about presents and Santa; it wasn't just about this holiday.

All around the room Penny could detect their recognition was suddenly profound. Light bulbs were flickering in fledgling minds, the moment sealed in their young memories forever. She knew they were keenly aware that these people, these fabulous, incredible people, would be there for them always, and they were part of something much more significant than any one holiday celebration.

They were more than siblings, cousins, aunts and uncles, grandparents and great grandparents. They truly were past, present and future, charged with passing on a legacy and heritage of love and family that was rare and priceless.

There wasn't a dry eye among the grown ups as they choked back the tears, the words of faith and family resonating with them long after the singing had stopped and the reverberating piano strings were silent.

It was Todd who finally had the wherewithal to clear the major lump in his throat, wipe a tear from his eye, and compose himself enough to speak. Raising his glass high, he said emotionally, "I would like to propose a toast, that in the mad dash for the dinner table, we somehow forgot. I think it is even more appropriate right now. I have often told Sandra that she brought beautiful music into my life the day I met her. I can tell everyone in the room feels the way I do. We're all blessed to have each other and to know beyond any doubt, these times together are what make life worth living. Thank you all for coming and for adding exactly who you are to this spectacular bunch." He paused briefly to compose himself before continuing. "And now, in the wise words of Rob Raney, the man who started the tradition and remains at the heart of it all – may we never have it any worse!"

Glasses raised and clinked around the room and hugs abounded as the words "may we never have it any worse" were repeated enthusiastically and yet reverently over and over by young and old alike. Penny knew without question as she looked down at the room filled with her family, her heirlooms, as long as they had each other they never…ever…would.

PART FOUR
Going Home

THE DAY PENNY left to go back to Chicago was bright and sunny, with a biting wind that whipped fallen snow crystals into ice pellets assaulting the car windows like tiny bullets, as they drove back to the train station in Fargo. She and Sandra rode in relative silence, having talked themselves clean out of things to say over the past week. Christmas was a blur of activity from the time she arrived until the time she squeezed Cara and Ricky goodbye, and each of the children left with their families, one by one.

Penny was able to spend quiet evenings lingering by the fire, glass of cabernet in hand, engaged in those long, meaningful "sister" conversations. It was so much more special with the added bonus of Cara, whose laughter and sense of humor was always so contagious. Hugging her as she left was always difficult, as they never knew when they would see each other the next time.

Real life was about to take over everyone's lives again but the mission to reconnect and ground herself, refresh and relax had been a resounding success. As much as she had enjoyed herself, though, it was time to go back to Chicago.

Her holiday vacation drawing to a close, Penny surveyed the barren landscape, as they made their way north along I-94. They passed mile after mile of desolate wind-swept drifts that resembled a vast ocean of frozen waves lapping against the barbed wire fences. An errant corn stalk here and there poked through the snow as a reminder that this flat grassland was fertile and had allowed generations of farm families to make their homes and their livings in this beautiful, often desolate place. It was only sleeping for now.

Spring would come again soon enough, bringing with it fields of bright sunflowers, golden wheat and fragrant alfalfa, the colors and smells of her childhood. The big steel grain elevators gracing the outskirts of every little prairie town would be full with another harvest in a few months, and the cycle of seasons and of life would continue.

The skyline of Fargo came into view and Sandra finally spoke. "It isn't a big city, but I look forward to seeing it every time I'm away for a while. I have such great memories of visiting the grandmas when we were kids, shopping trips, King Leo Drive In for hamburgers on the way home." She chuckled at the memory. "We may travel and roam all over this planet, but North Dakota will always be more than just a place. It really is who we are in our souls, don't you think?"

"Yes," Penny agreed. "I love Chicago and the life I have made for myself there. I don't think I could ever come back here to live. But I wouldn't trade being from here, growing up here, for anything." Sandra nodded and smiled.

All too soon they were at the station and saying their goodbyes. Penny stood with her bags as Sandra came around the car and gave her one last hug. "Please let me know you made it home safely, okay? No more bumps on the head!" They both laughed to keep from crying.

"Well, I guess I better be getting back to the lake," said Sandra fumbling in her purse for a tissue. "Todd made reservations at our favorite restaurant in Detroit Lakes for New Year's Eve dinner."

When I Get Home

"I almost forgot it was New Year's Eve tonight. I bet it will be an empty train, good chance to catch up on my reading," Penny said as Sandra pulled her gloves on and got back into the car.

Penny waved as Sandra's vehicle merged with others dropping off their treasured cargo. She stood for a long time watching until it disappeared around the corner.

"Looks like you could use some help with those bags, Ma'am," a familiar voice called from behind her.

Turning around she caught sight of a crisp navy blue uniform and a grin she would know anywhere. "James!"

"Welcome back, Miss Penny." James said, flashing the whitest smile and tipping his hat. "We have your accommodations all ready for you. Right this way." He motioned for her to follow him as he took her bags and tucked them under his arms. Like so many other experiences of late, she couldn't help but think his opportune arrival to assist hadn't been happenstance.

They made their way through a terminal much less crowded than when she had arrived. Apparently she had been right – not many people had chosen to travel on New Year's Eve. At least she would most likely have her choice of seats in the bar car. She was actually looking forward to a nice, quiet trip home.

James in the lead, Penny followed him through the terminal and out to the platform where only a few passengers were boarding the train at various entrances. "We're down this way." James put down the bags and helped her up the steps and into one of the cars. "Almost there," he said as they made their way down the narrow corridor and stopped in front of a door that had a brass plate affixed to it. The fancy script lettering identified it as "***Suite 500.***"

"Oh James," Penny said as he slipped the key into the door, "there must be some mistake. I don't have a suite."

James opened the door and stepped aside so she could enter the room. It was easily five times as large as the little compartment she had occupied on the way to Fargo. "There must be some mistake," she said, still confused.

"No, Miss Penny, this is your compartment for the trip back to Chicago, with our compliments," he said. And then quietly out of the corner of his mouth, covering it as if someone walking by might hear a secret meant only for her. "I believe they wanted to make sure there wasn't another rogue berth incident."

"Oh my goodness, please convey my thanks to the management!" said Penny, as she went over and sat down on the full-sized bed. It was a four-poster affair covered with a luxurious down comforter in a deep blue paisley print. At least half a dozen big, fluffy pillows were neatly placed along the ornately carved headboard.

A gorgeous bouquet of multi-colored roses sat in a crystal vase on the nightstand. They filled the entire room with the most heavenly fragrance.

Across from the bed was a small door that was open to what she could see was her very own bathroom. "So this is how the other half travels," she thought to herself as James arranged her bags in the closet. As he moved to open the shades to let in the mid-morning light, Penny noticed a bottle of champagne on ice, along with the most fabulous platter of fruit and cheeses.

"James, this really is so lovely. I can't thank you enough. I am going to absolutely love my trip back to Chicago. I may not want to get off the train!" Penny laughed, still reeling at the surprise of such royal treatment. It stood to reason in this litigious society, that the best defense is a good offense. Penny wasn't going to argue, just thanked her lucky stars.

"We'll be getting under way soon, Miss Penny. I'll leave you to get settled. If there is anything I can help you with, anything at all, just dial "0" on the phone right here." With that he pointed to a receiver attached to the wall by the bathroom. James then quietly walked out the door, closing it behind him.

Penny moved over to the table by the window, plopping herself down in the comfy chair. She took a deep breath and closed her eyes, listening to the sounds outside the train as remaining passengers hurriedly climbed aboard.

What an experience the entire trip had been – from almost missing the holidays with her family, to having the most unbelievable journey, in more ways than one. For the first time since arriving a week ago, Penny allowed herself to reflect upon what she had come to refer to as her "passage."

As inexplicable as it seemed, as ethereal and otherworldly, Penny believed without question what she had experienced as she apparently lay unconscious in the berth the night she first boarded the train…had been real. By some mystical twist of fate she had managed to pierce the veil of time to experience what others only dream about. She had returned to her life in 1973, completely coherent and fully aware of what was happening, with absolute clarity and comprehension.

Penny was convinced she had somehow been transported back in time, but not as some sort of wake-up call. Penny was no Jacob Marley, and her journey through the past was no fantastical Christmas tale revisiting the sins of bygone years in order to change her future.

No, the more she thought about it and relived each moment again and again, Penny was certain it was quite simply the most astonishing proof that prayers, no matter how unfathomable, can be and are answered. Isaiah 55:8 says, "For My thoughts are not your thoughts, nor are your ways My ways, declares the Lord. For as the heavens are higher than the earth, so are My ways higher than your ways and My thoughts than your thoughts..."

Penny had decided not to question how it happened or even that her passage had happened at all, for she knew it had. When she woke and realized she was no longer in her bed in Lisbon in 1973, part of her had been incredibly relieved. The burden of what choices to make, which decisions to change and how that would have transformed what she had considered a pretty good run at life was lifted the moment she opened her eyes.

An even bigger part of her was sad that what had, just a few hours before, seemed like the opportunity to relive her life starting at a critical juncture was snatched back in a way that seemed almost cruel. She had been able to spend time with two people she had loved and lost – her father and Jake; that in and of itself was such a miracle, such a blessing and worth any amount of angst and regret in the aftermath.

Old wounds had been assuaged, and her heart reawakened to the thought that maybe love was still within the realm of possibility, even at her age. Those were gifts of immeasurable value in her mind, and she did feel changed in a myriad of ways impossible to quantify, much less describe with any degree of accuracy.

The train shuddered slightly and began slowly inching away from the station platform. Penny looked out the window as speed continued to climb and the buildings in downtown Fargo began to appear smaller as the distance grew between them and the open tracks ahead.

Soon they were rolling through the countryside, passing farms and small towns. The gentle swaying and click click...click click...click click...was comforting to Penny as she sat by the window watching the sunlight fade with each passing mile. The sunset reflecting off of the glistening snow was like a billion sparkling prisms. She was leaving the land she loved, but also excited to return to her own place, her own bed, her own life.

Penny read her book at the table by the window until after they had traveled through Minneapolis. A note by the fruit and cheese platter had indicated she could order anything she liked from room service, all-inclusive. She decided to take advantage of their generosity by ordering dinner, which consisted of a perfectly medium rare filet mignon with roasted root vegetables and a salad. A decadent chocolate mousse had been a nice unexpected surprise addition when the tray was delivered. Happy New Year, indeed!

After dinner and a few more hours of reading, Penny still wasn't feeling tired. She supposed it had been the anticipation of going home that had her overly excited and unable to shut down. She decided to venture to the bar car. It was after 11:00 and maybe there were a few people with whom to ring in the New Year.

Penny couldn't remember the last time she actually was awake at midnight as one year ended and another began. She hadn't had any significant relationships to speak of since her marriage to Mark had ended. Maybe it was time to start a new tradition.

She took a quick shower, letting the warm water run down her back, taking with it all the stress of the past few weeks. It felt so good to be heading back to a place she loved. After the shower she ran a brush through her hair and put on some fresh makeup. From her suitcase she found the black cashmere sweater she had packed for the occasion and put it on, along with the one pair of black pants she thought actually made her look thin. Slipping on her favorite suede boots, Penny took one last look in the mirror. "Not bad for an old broad," she said, smiling at the reflection to make sure she didn't have lipstick on her teeth.

As she suspected, there were only a few patrons in the bar car. One rather disheveled man in a coat and tie that was now hanging loosely around his neck was sitting at the end of the bar nursing a Budweiser. There was a young couple at a table by the window holding hands and talking softly, oblivious to their surroundings and obviously in love. Directly in the booth behind them was another couple who looked to be in their seventies. They were mindlessly staring out the window in silence, each cradling a glass of wine in their hands, seemingly bored with the situation and apparently each other. Not exactly a raucous crowd.

Penny took a seat at the far end of the bar and decided to order vodka with club soda and wedge of lime in a tall glass. It was New Year's Eve, after all. She thought a cocktail would be appropriate for the occasion. The bartender silently placed it in front of her, returning to whatever he had been doing before she arrived. Penny took a long sip of the refreshing beverage, feeling the alcohol burning slightly as it went down her throat, the warmth of it hitting her stomach. Before long, she was feeling a bit of a glow.

Without Penny asking, the bartender brought her a fresh drink when he saw the first one was nearly empty. "On me," he said. "It is only a few minutes until midnight. I'll be proposing a toast to anyone who cares to join me," he said with a smile before turning to walk away again. "Thanks," said Penny as she finished the first with a last long sip. "I think I will."

"Mind if I join you?" came a deep voice from behind her.

"Oh great," Penny thought to herself. "All I need is some goofball trying to pick me up." She was about to dismiss the gentleman by suggesting she was waiting for someone when she happened to look up. There in the reflection of the mirror behind the bar stood none other than Jake Henderson.

Penny whirled around still completely in shock. Jake was right in front of her with his crooked smile, black horn-rimmed glasses slightly askew. He was wearing a stylish tuxedo complete with bowtie and bright red cummerbund, a matching silk scarf draped around his neck. He looked incredibly debonair, a white-haired amalgamation of Clark Gable, Cary Grant and George Clooney. The sight of him took her breath away.

After a long moment of being too surprised to say anything she finally managed, "What on earth are you doing here? How did you know I would be on this train?" She looked at him still utterly bewildered; wide-eyed, hands shaking, heart pounding.

Jake took her hands in his and offered, "Penny my dear, I was valedictorian of my senior class in high school, I graduated magna cum laude from the most prestigious medical school in the country; I was an Eagle Scout, for crying out loud. I think I can manage to find one girl named Penny on the only train heading from Fargo to Chicago through Milwaukee on New Year's Eve." His laugh was the most amazing music to her ears.

Penny grinned and shook her head, laughing with him at the absurdity of it all. "Bartender," she said over her shoulder, not taking her eyes off of Jake, "I think we're going to need one more of these." Jake slipped his arm around her waist and they held each other for a long moment. She could feel the heat of him through her sweater, the scent of him made her close her eyes. "You are more beautiful than ever." He whispered in her ear.

The bartender obliged and set the drink in front of Jake, who had taken the stool next to Penny. As he put the beverage down, the bartender raised a glass of his own and said loudly, "Raise your glasses everyone, it will be 2015 in 10…9…8…7…6…5…4…3…2…1…HAPPY NEW YEAR!!!!!!!" The strains of the familiar tune set to the words of famous Scottish poet Robert Burns began playing through the loudspeaker, and the few people in the bar including Penny and Jake, sang along.

"Should auld acquaintance be forgot, and never brought to mind? Should auld acquaintance be forgot in days of auld lang syne. For auld lang syne my dear, for auld lang syne. We'll take a cup of kindness yet, for auld lang syne!"

Looking deeply into Penny's eyes as he drew her closer again, Jake said in his best albeit feeble, attempt at a Scottish accent, "This auld acquaintance never ever was, and never, ever could be...forgot." With that he leaned down and brushed the hair away from her face, smiling all the while. "Hey hey, Babydoll. I have something for you." He said softly kissing her on the cheek.

"You do?" Penny stepped back looking at him quizzically. "What is it?" Her mind was going a hundred miles an hour trying to figure out what he could possibly be talking about.

Jake reached into his pocket and pulled out a little silver heart-shaped box. Penny gasped in recognition. "Oh my gosh, Jake. I can't believe you kept it all of these years."

Penny watched as Jake carefully pulled from his other pocket a thin chain with a tiny key attached to it, no bigger than a paper clip. He put the key into the lock in the middle of the heart and turned it. The lid to the silver box popped open.

Penny's eyes welled with tears as she looked into the red velvet lined box and saw what was sitting inside, beneath the picture of a young Penny and Jake, giddy teenagers so much in love. It was Jake's class ring with the shiny blue sapphire stone, the band underneath still wrapped with faded pink yarn.

"I told you a long time ago that only one person would ever wear this ring, Penny. I always mean what I say." He removed the ring from the box, took Penny's hand in his and slid the ring on her finger. Even though four decades and two dozen pounds had passed since the last time she wore it, the ring fit perfectly.

Penny looked up at Jake, still unable to speak. They were both overcome with years of emotion mingled with just the right amount of vodka. "It is far too rare that second chances come around," continued Jake. "I don't know what I did right in the world to deserve to run into you again. I still shake my head at the fantastic serendipity of it all, but I am not going to question the insight of a universe wise enough to make it happen. I just know that I'm not going to let you go again." He pulled her close and kissed her, this time on the lips, deep and warm and with the passion she had missed for so long. They stood there in the empty bar, wrapped in each other's arms for what seemed like an hour.

"I think we need to have a toast, don't you?" she finally was able to speak. The closeness of him had nearly brought her to her knees. Jake Henderson, love of her life, was right here and the future seemed as wide open with possibilities as the train tracks that lay before them. They both held their glasses in the air. As Jake put his arm around her waist, they toasted to 2015, to finding each other, and lastly, to second chances.

Penny could feel forty years of time and distance evaporating as they laughed and talked and kissed into the wee hours of the morning, until the skyline of Chicago was visible through the breaking dawn. Every fiber of her soul rejoiced in the fact that they were together, here in *this* time, in *this* place. Penny knew in her heart she was finally where she was meant to be. Her miraculous night in Lisbon and finding Jake again were the last long-lost pieces of the puzzle finally put into place. Everything fit, everything made sense.

Penny realized she was at peace for the first time in her life, holding the man she had always loved. As they approached Union Station, Penny knew she was where she belonged in every sense of the word. She was truly and forever, "home."

Epilogue

Penny could see the sun barely beginning to peak its golden head an inch at a time above the still-dark horizon as she raised the shade of her airplane window to greet the new day. The moon was becoming a mere sliver amid an endless expanse of stars that were fading quickly with every second in the emerging light.

Beside her, Jake remained sleeping soundly in his first class compartment, headphones still attached to his head, soft snoring barely perceptible above the din of the jet engines behind them. Penny looked down at him and smiled.

A perky flight attendant with the prettiest shade of red hair brought her a cup of steaming hot coffee, silently mouthing "cream or sugar?" so as not to wake him. Penny shook her head no, took the cup from her and tentatively blew over the dark auburn brew to cool it as her gaze returned out the window. Barely a cloud was in the sky to obscure the amazing view.

Before long she could feel Jake stirring next to her, gradually bringing himself to a seated position, his mop of white hair sticking up in classic "bedhead" fashion. He yawned deeply then reached over and kissed her softly on the lips.

The plane banked fairly steeply to the left and Penny could see miles of calm blue water beneath them, smooth as glass and getting closer as they neared their destination.

"Good morning, Mrs. Henderson," he winked as she handed him her cup of coffee to share. They held hands as the plane fluidly turned a slight right, then left. "Almost there," he said into her ear. She squeezed his hand. Her smile was so wide she was afraid her lips would crack.

Outside the window Penny could see a small island appear off in the distance, barely visible as they continued to descend through the morning mist. It was a tiny green dot at first. As they flew closer, she could make out two large mountains rising out of the tropical foliage, surrounded by the most gorgeous turquoise water Penny had ever seen in her entire life. As they rounded the island she could see an endless sugar-white beach and rows and rows of palm trees gleaming in the bright sunshine. Paradise!

Penny felt the slight jolt of the landing gear being lowered, the plane decelerating significantly as the flaps came down to slow their speed even more. "Ladies and Gentlemen, in preparation for our final approach please return your seatbacks and tray tables to their full upright and locked position," a sweet female voice with slight accent announced over the intercom. "We should be on the ground shortly. Once again, thank you for flying Air Tahiti Nui, we hope you enjoy your stay and come back to see us very soon. And as we say here on the island, MAEVA! Welcome to Bora Bora."

The wheels touched down and the jets reversed, slowing the airplane to taxiing speed as they made their way to the small airport and waited for the jet way to connect so they could finally stretch their legs. They had made it.

"Honeymoon, here we come!" beamed Penny as they gathered their belongings and joined the line of passengers every bit as anxious as they were to be off the plane and to drink in the sultry air. They retrieved their luggage from the carousel on the lower level and walked outside to the curb, where a pleasant native gentleman in khaki shorts and a brightly flowered shirt stood holding a sign that said, "Henderson."

"That's us," said Jake as he motioned for Penny to follow him. They both slid into the back of the big black car and for the first time in almost two days of traveling, they both sucked in a deep breath and let it out. "My God this place is heavenly," said Jake. "You could smell the flowers as soon as we got off of the plane!" Penny nodded enthusiastically, because it was true.

As they left the gates of the little airport, the humid air filled their senses with the fragrance of the exotic orange, red, pink and yellow blooms that lined each side of the roadway. The perfume truly was amazing, heavy with sweet underlying notes of lily and gardenia.

There was a bottle of champagne on ice and two glasses with "Mr. and Mrs." etched into the base of each flute. "It's five o'clock somewhere, Mrs. Henderson," Jake said as he popped the cork and poured a generous amount into Penny's glass and then his own. "Indeed, Dr. Henderson," laughed Penny as she took a sip and let the fizz tickle her nose as it trickled down her throat.

They sat as close as close could be the entire way down the winding roads, past colorful little villages, past people riding bicycles carrying wares on their backs and in baskets, past deeply suntanned old men with bare feet and fishing poles, their strings of boldly colored fish swinging beside them. Penny smiled the entire way, chatting and pointing out the interesting sites as they bumped along the dusty road.

After about an hour in the car, they turned down a road lined with magnolia trees whose bright white blooms were the size of pie plates. They finally pulled into the long circular driveway of what she could tell was their resort hotel. It had a tall thatched roof and white shutters open to the outdoors. The pristine grounds and landscaping were immaculately manicured, with amazing multi-colored flowers everywhere.

Penny could see there were large ceiling fans with paddles made to resemble banana leaves twirling lazily in the breeze, and the floors were a lovely shade of pale gold terrazzo tile. There were men in the same khaki shorts and shirts scurrying about helping guests with luggage and escorting them inside. Glamorous native women in short dresses in the same floral pattern as the men's shirts greeted each new arrival, "MAEVA!" they said enthusiastically. "Welcome."

As Penny and Jake walked up the steps, one of the women rushed over and put a garland around Penny's neck, made from the most exceptional flowers she had ever seen. The lei was an explosion of miniature pink hibiscus, purple orchids, orange birds of paradise, all with the overwhelming aromatic scents of jasmine and lavender. On Jake's head they put a simple crown of tiny white orchids. "MAEVA!"

While Jake checked in at the front desk, Penny wandered through the lobby and out onto the back patio. She could feel her eyes watering as much from the emotion as the gleaming sunshine. She spotted the little thatched huts on stilts scattered out over the most remarkably clear crystal blue water. The sound of the waves calmly lapping the white sand, and the gentle calling of seagulls soaring overhead brought with them an overwhelming sense of peace. Several men dressed only in baggy shorts paddled by in a wooden dugout canoe, humming some type of ancient native tune; a quiet chant, a whispered prayer. The haunting melody hung on the breeze long after they had drifted by.

Penny could only stand there, still barely able to grasp the fact she was in a place she had only dreamed about as the little girl in

When I Get Home

North Dakota; the girl who had dared to hope one day she would see an enchanted setting like this.

As Penny surveyed the breathtaking scenery and felt the balmy tropical sun washing over her, all of the events throughout the years bringing her to this incredible spot on the globe, this unbelievable paradise ran through her head. The thought occurred to her in an instant that she was where she was destined to be, not just with Jake, not only in this place, but in every sense of the word.

Penny smiled with self assurance that everything she had been through on her life journey was exactly as it was meant to be. If she had made other choices and decisions along the path to where she stood at this very moment, she might not be standing here at all. If she hadn't grown up where and when she did, if her father hadn't tragically been lost at such an early and impressionable age, where would she be? If she hadn't struggled and suffered and learned; if she hadn't based each move in her life on history, on experience, on sheer gut instinct, she might have ended up somewhere completely different.

Where she was right now in her life, at this age and in this time, was better than she ever could have dreamed possible. Penny knew beyond any shadow of a doubt she had made all the right decisions and choices along the way. She smiled, brimming with confidence and certainty as if she was aware for the first time; she wouldn't have changed a single, solitary thing.

Just then Jake walked up behind her, wrapping his arms around her waist and pulling her close. "Welcome to paradise, my lovely bride," he whispered into her ear. She closed her eyes and stood there feeling the warmth of him, the scent of the man she had loved her entire life, her husband of three days. It was all so incredibly perfect.

Jake spotted a waiter walking through the lobby holding a tray of what looked like delectable, fruity drinks, each sporting a small paper umbrella. "We'll take two of those," he called as the server rushed over to oblige. Soon, each of them was sipping the most scrumptious tropical beverage through a long curly straw.

As she moved in to kiss Jake's handsome face, one of the beautiful native women in a floral dress approached them with a camera. "Do you want me to capture this moment to take home with you? Just $5," she smiled widely and motioned for them to stand closely next to each other.

"Yes," said Jake and Penny in unison, laughing, as they stood happily surrounded by flowers, holding each other tightly and grinning from ear to ear. The camera clicked away as they lifted their glasses toasting to the moment, their honeymoon, to the rest of their lives. Then looking intently and purposefully into each others eyes in a steadfast, tender gaze they both recognized as the most genuine and heartfelt forever kind of love there is, Penny softly whispered…"We do!"

THE END

Acknowledgements

I WOULD LIKE to express my heartfelt gratitude to the extraordinary people who saw me through the process of writing and bringing this labor of love to the point of being able to hold it in your hands. To all those who provided feedback, encouragement, talked things over, read, offered comments, and allowed me the privilege of including their remarks or suggestions, I thank you.

To my loyal, dedicated friend and eagle-eyed editor Lisa "Bible Camp" Bible, my amazing sister Dr. Sara "Sandra" Hagen, and wonderful friends Linda Smith and Stephen P. Simms, I can't tell you how much your time and attention to detail meant to me as I worked to craft a story that even those outside of my own family could identify with and hopefully enjoy.

Above all I need to thank my incredibly talented niece, Nataly Anderson Levi, for taking this story and creating the beautiful cover which makes this book so much more special. I stand in awe of your amazing ability and am so proud to count you among my precious heirlooms.

Last but certainly not least, I want to thank all of my friends at VeraVia Health and Fitness Resort in Carlsbad, California, for starting me on this journey. With your unwavering support and encouragement, I reached for something I never would have been able to accomplish. You taught me to believe in myself and that inside each of us is the ability to achieve great things. Love to you all!

Time In A Bottle
Words and Music by Jim Croce
Copyright © 1971 (Renewed 1999) Time In A Bottle Publishing and Croce Publishing
All Rights Administered by BMG Rights Management (US) LLC
All Rights Reserved   Used By Permission
Reprinted by Permission of Hal Leonard Corporation

HEIRLOOMS
Amy Grant/Brown Bannister/Bob Farrell
© 1983 Word Music, LLC,
Bases Loaded Music, New Spring Publishing, Inc.
All Rights Reserved. Used By Permission

About the Author

PAULA JEAN RANES was born and raised in the small town of Lisbon, North Dakota. She attended the University of North Dakota, and comes from a family of talented writers, artists, and musicians. Paula loosely bases many of the people and places in her stories on her own personal experiences.

Ranes is a single parent of two adult children and has three beautiful grandchildren. She looks forward to someday spending her retirement writing more books. She currently splits her time between her homes in Westerville, Ohio, and Ft. Myers, Florida.

Paula can be contacted at pjranes@mail.com.

Made in the USA
Lexington, KY
11 December 2015